Worse Than Strangers

Also by Kyleigh Leddy

The Perfect Other: A Memoir of My Sister

Worse Than Strangers

— A Novel —

Kyleigh Leddy

GALLERY BOOKS
New York Amsterdam/Antwerp London
Toronto Sydney/Melbourne New Delhi

Gallery Books
An Imprint of Simon & Schuster, LLC
1230 Avenue of the Americas
New York, NY 10020

Interior design by Jaime Putorti

Manufactured in the United States of America

ISBN 978-1-6680-9251-4

Whether you love a mother, lost a mother, are a mother, or never got the mother you deserve, this book is for you.

Thank you for letting me share my Rose with you.

And, most of all, to Mom, who is better than fiction.

Now they were as strangers; nay, worse than strangers, for they could never become acquainted.

—Jane Austen, *Persuasion*

Worse Than Strangers

Chapter One

Lottie

October 11, 1998—Nantucket Island

Regret isn't passive. It's not something you can stuff away, suppress deeper and deeper. The less you tend to it, the more it grows.

I know a thing or two about regret. Life has been as good to me as it could bear to be—better than most fared, surely—but I still have had my fair share of disappointments and mistakes, secret hopes dashed before they could get running.

None of that compares to what I feel right now.

The letter arrived this afternoon. The return address marked as from California, the postage stamp featuring the Golden Gate Bridge against a sparkling navy sky. The words are wobbly at times, as if the writer was rushed or emotional, but the message is clear as a bullet.

It's too late.

"I appreciate your reaching out," it begins. "And I deeply regret disappointing you."

I thought that maybe if I contacted him now—if I confessed I was to blame for everything—there would still be a chance to make it all right side up again. I was wrong.

I read the letter again, three times, hoping the content will magically change. I can hear my husband stirring in the bedroom. It's October and our small beach town—thirty miles out to sea—is in hibernation. Only the locals pocket the streets, occasionally bumping into the phantoms of summertime. I once read that paranormal activity increases around the coast. Something about the fog and the dense ocean air making energy linger.

I'm not sure I believe in any of that, but the past does feel ever present on this island, like multiple timelines are existing at once. We're constantly stumbling into long-gone versions of ourselves.

"Are you coming to bed?" calls my husband, Charlie, from the other room.

He can't know about this. "In a moment!" I strain to sound cheery.

I read the letter once more. I could tell Rose, but what good would that do now? Telling her would only appease my own guilt. She and her baby girl, Lily . . . only a year old. They are going through enough already. She doesn't need this, too.

No, this secret is mine alone to carry.

"Lottie?" Charlie calls again.

The old, warped floorboards creak. I see my husband rounding the corner. I'm standing by our fireplace: The floor-to-ceiling bookcases he built for me years ago are to my left. In a rush of instinct, I take the letter and tuck it into a small, hidden compartment behind the shelf.

"What are you doing, honey?" my husband asks moments later, placing a hand on my shoulder.

"Nothing." I smile. "Just picking out a novel before bed."

"Okay, dear," he says, kissing my cheek. "Choose wisely."

I wait until Charlie heads back to the bedroom before I settle down on an old armchair. Oh, Charlie. What would he think if he knew what I'd done?

The fire crackles. I look back at the bookshelf. I know the letter is tucked in there, but right now, it blends in like it never existed at all. Maybe that's for the best. What's done is done. All that's left to do is live with the weight of my guilt and hope it doesn't grow.

But then again, it's easier to rationalize a regret when it's not your life you ruined.

Chapter Two

Lily

May 28, 2022—Nantucket Island
Twenty-Four Years Later

Regret is a strange emotion to feel in the ice cream aisle of the largest grocery store on Nantucket Island, but there it is anyway, nestled between the lemon sherbet and the peanut butter swirl.

It's Memorial Day weekend. I just returned to the island yesterday morning for the summer. I'm twenty-five years old, and my life feels like one long, bad turn.

The grocery store is unreasonably cold, and I shiver in my thin yellow sweatshirt, bending to read the labels. A group of young girls walk by, laughing in hushed voices. I can tell they're likely under twenty-one by their outfits: They're wearing tank tops and jean shorts despite the temperature outside. I can also guess what they're doing here: waiting out the line at the Chicken Box across the street, still the biggest and most popular dive bar on island.

On a typical summer weekend, the line winds all the way to the Stop & Shop parking lot. There's a chance they'll get in, but more likely than not, they'll be turned away and have to go to one of the notoriously underage spots downtown. Luckily, the Box rarely confiscates fake ID's, and half the fun is trying to sneak in anyway.

"Lily," my mom says, appearing behind me. "Are you ready?"

"I'm still deciding," I tell her.

"It's ice cream. There are no wrong choices."

Easy for you to say, I think. Perfect Rose Gardner, who has never made a wrong choice in her life, except maybe the one that led to my birth. Dating my father was, by all accounts, a mistake, but even that one feels slightly like my fault.

An older woman shuffles by, leaning on her cart as if it's a substitute walker. She's wearing a red shawl that looks almost like a cape. Long, mismatched turquoise necklaces hang from her neck, knotting together like roots of a tree. She winks at me as she scoots down the aisle, stopping to buy a bag of frozen cherries three doors down.

I freeze, panicked. Does this strange woman somehow know me, or is she in the habit of winking at strangers? Regardless, I look away. The last thing I need is to run into someone I know. The only people I want to see tonight are Ben & Jerry, and even them, only in passing.

I grab a mint chocolate chip container from the freezer and absentmindedly scratch lines into the frost on the lid with my thumbnail, a nervous habit.

"Okay," I say, letting out a breath. "Ready. Let's get out of here. Quick."

"You're being so dramatic," says Mom, but she's smiling. She puts an arm over my shoulders, and the weight is comforting. Even still, she is taller than me.

"Don't be worried if I suddenly sprint away. It's just because I've seen someone I know," I warn her as we walk toward checkout.

"You would really sprint out of here?"

"Absolutely. I'll set a world record."

Mom laughs. "You ran a fifteen-minute mile in your high school gym class. Sweetie, I love you, but you're not exactly an athlete."

"Well, that was before I had the motivation of avoiding further public humiliation."

Mom rolls her eyes but I know she's amused. She's used to my dramatics, but this time, I'm serious.

In a town as small as Nantucket, the likelihood of bumping into someone familiar is high, and I cannot afford those odds right now. If I see someone I know, they'll ask how I am, which will lead into one of two outcomes: me either lying or crying. I can imagine the conversation now.

How are you? "Oh, fine, I just decided to abandon my lease and crash with my mom all summer because my life is an absolute and total disaster!"

I lost my job in New York City two weeks ago. When I saw the email, I fainted on the subway. It was a real dramatic faint, too—cinematic even. I almost wish there was security footage. When I first moved to the city, I thought, like all young people think, that I was going to be something—make something of myself, become the "artist" I always dreamed of—but instead, there I was, passed out on the ground of the 4 train, my unconscious lips kissing the dirty ground.

I think about that moment now as we make our way to the front of the store. I've already recounted the story several times, smoothed it into a polished comedic bit.

"And that's how I discovered rock bottom tastes exactly like the floor of the subway!" I said to Rose's friends the night I arrived on island.

We were grabbing drinks at Cru, an upscale waterfront bar right on the docks downtown. The chilled white wine created a pleasant condensation on the glass. Everyone roared with laughter and I laughed, too. A light wind was blowing off the harbor, and I could hear the honking of yachts pulling into place. It was hard to feel the full impact of failure in a setting like that, with the breeze cooling my forehead, the wine warming my chest.

This is a skill my Great-Aunt Lottie taught me: "People can't laugh at you if you beat them to it. The line between humor and tragedy is narrow, so for as long as you can, you might as well choose the funny story."

However, today, it's harder to find the humorous angle. Maybe that's because Lottie isn't here to remind me of it. The thought of her dislodges something heavy in my chest. We lost her a year ago, and yet sometimes it still doesn't feel real. This is our first summer without her. She fought the cancer for six years. Still, it wasn't enough.

Rose squeezes my shoulder, as if she can sense my train of thought. "I'm going to grab some detergent quick," she says, starting to walk away. "I think we're running low."

"No!" I whisper-shout. "Mom, let's get out of here."

She turns to face me, already searching for the aisle. "You took ten minutes to pick out an ice cream flavor and I can't stop to grab some basic household necessities?"

She's right, of course. Rose is always right, but it's hard to rationalize the panic radiating in my body. We planned to stop here briefly on my way to drop off Mom downtown to meet up with her friend. Despite her invitation to join them, I've decided to stay home and chauffeur her there and back instead. We only have one car and the cost of taxis is outrageous—sometimes up to fifty dollars for a fifteen-minute, seven-mile drive. My reward for my services is to buy myself a pint of ice cream with the leftover gas money. The grocery store is closing in ten minutes. Hence, this brief pit stop.

My eyes dart across the mostly empty aisles as I follow Rose. Whenever I have friends visit, they always marvel at how ordinary the grocery store is, as if something this common, this commercial, couldn't possibly exist on an island thirty miles out to sea, amidst the sand dunes and pink flowers and manicured hedges. Chains were banned in 2006, so most of the other stores and boutiques on Nantucket are now independently owned.

Real tourism doesn't start until July when kids get off from school and families swarm the island. The only reason there's activity at all is that it's Figawi weekend, a sailing race that begins in the Cape at Hyannis Yacht Club and loops its way to Nantucket and Martha's Vineyard. Legend has it the regatta got its name in 1971 when a couple of friends had an impromptu race across the Nantucket Sound, and upon seeing the rainy, chilly, and notoriously foggy weather conditions, shouted, "Where the fuck are we?" which, with the winds and the accents, sounded a little like "Where the Figawi?"

Every other year, I would be participating in the festivities, but that was before I ruined my life.

I catch up to Rose in the cleaning aisle. She's inspecting the shelf, looking for the fragrance-free brand she likes.

I spot a bag of pods on the lower shelf and grab them. "Here! Now let's go."

"It was your idea to stop at the store, Lily. And you know I don't like the pods. The liquid detergent is better."

"Mom, look at me." I gesture to my outfit: old leggings, oversized sweatshirt, fluffy pink slippers. "Do I look like I'm fit to be seen in public?"

To make matters worse, my hair is pulled half back in a clip, and the curtain bangs I spontaneously asked for in the midst of my quarter-life crisis keep escaping from it, blocking my vision.

"I'm going through a personal transformation," I told my hairdresser, pausing for dramatic effect. "I want my new hair to reflect that."

"Okay," she said, and then proceeded to ruin my life.

She wielded her scissors as if they were garden shears until all that was left was the ugliest topiary imaginable. And it was on my head. I thought the bangs would make me feel better, but of course they only made everything worse.

"Lily." Rose's "mom voice" makes a reappearance—calm but authoritarian—the same tone she used to take when I was a toddler having a meltdown. "It's not my fault you left the house in your pajamas."

Right now, Rose is wearing flared white jeans, raffia wedges, and a chunky tan-and-white sweater. For not the first time, I'm struck by her simple elegance. When I was a kid, Rose's beauty was a popular point of teasing. "Lily's mom is HOT!" I remember hearing as early as sixth grade from Stephen Levinson, the very boy I had a crush on. Once, when I was fifteen, I tried to be clever and rebutted with "I have her genes. You should date me now and consider it a long-term investment." But even I doubted the statement as soon as I said it.

With Rose's sleek red hair, long legs, and high cheekbones, no one with eyes and half a brain could disagree. I always hoped I would grow up to look like her, but it seems the only feature I managed to inherit is her red hair. Although, hers is straight and smooth while mine is curly and unwieldy. On my mom, the color looks powerful and singular. On me, it looks like my head is on fire.

"There it is!" says Rose now, pointing to a top shelf. She frowns. "It's so high up, we might need to ask someone to help us."

She looks around, searching for an available employee, but I've already devised a plan.

"I've got this," I say, beginning to climb. I step on the lower shelf and stretch my hand up. The metal groans but stays put.

"Lily!" Mom shouts. "This is ridiculous. You're going to get hurt."

The detergent is just within reach. I can almost grab it. "Give me a boost," I say.

"Lily, get down."

This has always been our dynamic. When I was growing up, Mom used to call me her "wild little thing," because she was always off chasing after me.

I climb another shelf and . . . there it is! I wrap my fingers around the handle and jut it out into the air like it's a trophy.

"Woo-hoo!" I yelp. "And you said I wasn't athletic. Look at me now!"

Rose is laughing but she also looks nervous. "Okay, okay. You're right. You're the most athletic person in the world. You would absolutely set a world record, no problem. Now, please, just get down."

"Thank you," I say, beginning my descent. "That's all I wanted to hear."

I'm almost back on the ground when I hear someone call out my name.

"Lily Gardner?"

I turn around slowly, a heroine in a horror movie. In the harsh fluorescent light of Stop & Shop, I find myself for the first time in a year face-to-face with Henry Wright: my ex-boyfriend, the former love of my life, and the very last person I want to see.

He looks the same but also somehow more himself. His back straighter and his shoulders broader. His face filled in. His hair is shorter, cropped like a helmet, his jacket is less baggy, and his shoes are the kind of purposefully roughed-up, pre-scuffed sneakers that cost upward of five hundred bucks. We used to make fun of that kind of thing.

I drink him in for several seconds, excruciatingly aware of my own disheveled appearance, before I can process the full image. He's holding hands with a girl. She has neat, short blond hair, no ill-conceived bangs in sight, a small smile, and an even smaller nose. She wears a white eyelet sundress, and the combined effect makes her look like an angel or a ghost, depending on your point of view. Right now, for me, it's a bit of both. Even more terrifying, a beautiful ghost.

The girl smiles wistfully at Henry, the way people in love always smile: as if they know the secret of the universe, which of course they do. I recognize the expression, because not too long ago I used to look at Henry the same way.

Something on the girl's hand catches the light, attracting my attention downward. On her fourth finger is the unmistakable glint of a diamond ring.

At that precise moment, my footing loses traction, my hands slip, and everything in the world comes crashing down.

Chapter Three

Lily

Later, in the privacy of our car, I permit myself a single scream.

"Jeez, Lily!" says Mom, startled. "You're going to scare the whole island!"

"The therapist you made me see in the city told me about a technique she calls 'scheduling your grief.' I'm just following orders."

According to said therapist, you're supposed to allow yourself to feel by setting aside specific times of day to cry. Rose is a clinician on the island and because of her, I'm perhaps the most therapized twenty-five-year-old in the state. Somehow, it hasn't made me any less of a disaster.

"Isn't that for crying, not screaming?" Rose points out.

"It's all the same."

I lean my head against the steering wheel, and the horn lets out a loud squawk. A figure looks up from a shopping cart, alarmed. It's the same red-shawled woman who passed us in the ice cream aisle a few minutes earlier. Her hair is such a brilliant shade of white it looks almost blue in the light of our high beams. It's the detail, the vague resemblance to Aunt Lottie, that does me in.

It is a ridiculous idea to "schedule your grief," I decide. A capitalistic scam, another inhumane effort to reach optimal productivity. Feelings are not supposed to follow a schedule. Some messes cannot be contained.

"Are you okay?" There's real concern in Rose's voice now. "I thought that went fine! All things considered."

I look up from the steering wheel to raise my eyebrows. "All things considered?"

"Yeah! You were cordial, sweet . . . polite."

"I fell off a shelf in the grocery store and was covered in bottles of detergent. Which hurt, by the way." My body is tender, riddled with soon-to-be bruises.

Mom touches a welt on my forehead. I wince. "Well, that part could have gone better."

I groan and hit my head against the wheel again. "I'm an idiot."

"You're not an idiot."

"I gave him a handshake." Once I had removed the detergent containers from my body, the two of them approached, and in a brilliant flash of idiocy, I reached out and shook both of their hands.

"Yes, well, I suppose that part could have gone better, too, but like I said, at least you were polite," says Rose.

I can still feel my heart hammering in my chest and my stomach churning. Before today, the last time I saw Henry was at Lottie's funeral last Memorial Day weekend. He looked as innocent and clean as summer rain in that pressed black suit.

Henry and I broke up a little over two years ago, right before the pandemic, but we never stopped speaking. The world shut down; we left the city and returned to our respective families for quarantine. Me, here. Him, home in Connecticut and then, later, Boston. We would talk late into the night, text all day, send each other funny videos on social media to break up the fear and despair. We said we would stop if one of us met someone, but neither of us did. I was more preoccupied with the world potentially ending, and Lottie's increasingly defeating treatments, to even think about romance. I assumed he would eventually come back to New York and leave Boston. I assumed that someday, maybe, we would give it a try again.

There was a part of me, however small or suppressed, that even dared to hope he would be here this summer—both of us single—and we would meet again, but this time, it would be right. It would stick.

Then, three months ago, he told me he met someone. He said they had been seeing each other for a while, all throughout the pandemic, but it recently became "serious."

Now I realize that by "serious," he meant he is engaged. Quite the understatement.

"How is this possible?" I say aloud, mostly to myself.

We dated for five years, have been in each other's lives for seven. How long could he even have known this girl? Less than two years, max?

Mom reaches out and smooths my hair, tucks back the stupid bangs. "You must've known he was going to move on eventually?"

"Of course," I say, but it's not the truth.

Our breakup never felt solid. I never mourned; I didn't even cry once. Not talking to him the last three months was a stark change, and sure, it was difficult to resist dialing his number. My fingers naturally gravitated to his name in my phone. Still, it didn't feel over.

An engagement?

Rose must detect the truth in my face, because she sighs. "Oh, Lily-pad," she says, her nickname for me.

I notice the clock on the dashboard. It's almost eight p.m., time for Rose to meet up with her friend. I realize how selfish I'm being, keeping everyone waiting over my melodramatics.

"It's okay," I say. "Enough about me. Let's get you downtown."

I take a deep breath. I'm backing out of the parking spot when I hear a loud honk. There's a red Land Rover pulling out at the same time. Our bumpers almost hit but don't: a near miss.

My heart picks up speed. I'm driving Lottie's old Jeep, and beyond being the only car we have, it holds extra sentimental value. The good luck charm Lottie placed underneath the rearview mirror—a gold evil eye pendant hanging from a string of colorful beads—still dangles exactly as it did the day she left. Evidence of my great-aunt's life is everywhere: the worn leather seats, the sand in the plastic mats, the "lucky pennies" she kept in the center console. The interior even smells like her, if that's possible. Or maybe Lottie just smelled like the island, sweet honeysuckle and salt air and warm sand and freshly mowed grass.

If I had totaled the car—one of the last places we can still feel Lottie's presence—I'd never forgive myself.

"Lily," says Mom in a serious voice. "Are you sure you're okay to drive? I can drive. Or, I can skip tonight altogether. We can go home and watch a movie instead."

"No, I don't want to ruin your night. It's okay. I can do this. I'm an adult."

If Mom disagrees, she doesn't argue. We're quiet as I drive the familiar route to town, passing the long line for the Chicken Box. I wonder if the girls from the store have made their way in by now or if they were rejected by the bouncer. I wonder if their lives are going to fundamentally alter tonight like mine did the night I met Henry seven years ago.

"Remember how scrawny Henry was when we first met?" I say.

Rose shifts in her seat. "He was a sweet kid."

We were eighteen, about to head off to college. It was Memorial Day weekend, just like it is right now, and I started working at a sweatshirt shop downtown. The job was boring and repetitive, folding T-shirts and various other Nantucket merchandise for hours on end. I'm wearing one of their products: a souvenir from the summer that changed everything. One of the other employees invited me to a house party on Cliff Road after work, and it was there that I met Henry.

I remember spotting him by the pool. It was still cold out, and none of us wanted to jump in, but he was trying to start a movement. He dared me to go first, and I did, because why not? He followed shortly after. We spent the rest of the night huddled in pool towels, shivering in our wet clothes, talking in the corner. Later, one of his friends drove a bunch of us home in the back of his pickup truck. We sat side by side, towels flapping in the wind, watching the clapboard houses in town grow smaller. The truck bumped over the cobblestones, Henry wrapped an arm around me for stability, and it felt like the beginning of something—like my life was finally starting. The cold air dried our towels, and when it was my stop, he asked me out before I could hop out of the truck: my very first date.

Everything was simpler back then.

"Remember our first date to the movies?" I say to Rose. "Remember how nervous he was?"

"Is this reminiscing really helpful?"

We were shier than when we first met, because we no longer had the fever of the party and the beer to encourage us. When he approached, he left at least three feet between us and said, "Hi," with an awkward wave, and I said, "Hi," back and forced my body into motion to give him a side hug that was all arms and elbows. I remember how he said, "Shall we?" formally, and I giggled and said, "We shall." He opened the door for me and I imitated a curtsy, and he asked, "Did you really just curtsy?" And I admitted, "I think I did."

I had only ever been on "group hangs" in middle school and high school, where the large numbers provided a sort of protective buoyancy. When we took our seats, my palms were clammy, and I kept them stiffly at my sides, which Henry misinterpreted as a signal that I didn't want to hold hands.

The air smelled like Sour Patch gummies and buttered popcorn.

Afterward, he suggested we go for a walk on the docks. I had dressed up for the occasion: a nice dress and wedges that were far too fancy for a movie date. As we walked, I remember thinking it was the first time in my life conversation flowed effortlessly with someone who wasn't Rose or Lottie. Talking to him felt like one of the satisfying tennis rallies Lottie was always watching on television. Every ground stroke I hit, he returned with equal force. It was beautiful, almost holy. The conversation was so mesmerizing I didn't even notice that the straps of my shoes had begun to dig into my ankles, making my skin slick with blood.

The blisters turned into scars: thin, raised white lines like the rings of a tree. I showed them to Henry weeks later.

He said, "I guess you'll never forget me then."

I said, "I guess not," and the idea wasn't sad yet.

"He can't be engaged," I say now. The idea makes me sick, physically nauseated. I think about the scars on my ankles—the ones I still have to this day.

"I know," Rose sighs. "It's hard to believe, but he is. And you have to move on, honey. I know it's hard, but it's the only way."

"Is that what you did?" I ask. "I mean, how did you get over him?"

Sometimes, I have a hard time saying the word "dad." Even "father" unsettles me. The words seem to imply a certain intimacy my father doesn't deserve. They connote a role in my life he has never played.

Rose has been single ever since she left him when I was only a year old. She went on a few dates here and there, but never anything lasting. I think she wanted to protect me, keep me from getting attached to anyone who could hurt us like my father did. Sometimes I feel responsible for her singleness. She always put me first, even to her own detriment.

Mom looks surprised. "What do you mean? How did I get over who?"

"My father, obviously," I say, confused. "Who else would I mean?"

Her cheeks look pinkish and warm to the touch. "No one. I mean, of course you meant your father."

It's a strange reaction. She sounds almost . . . guilty. "So, how did you get over him?"

"Oh, I don't know. It was never . . . Well, it was never really anything to get over."

"You had a baby," I say, taking one hand off the wheel to gesture to my person.

"Of course. I just mean, I don't know. I loved your father, but he disappointed me pretty early on in the relationship. I guess my expectations were never that high." I feel her eyes looking over at me. "I'm sorry, is this awful to hear?"

I don't speak to my father. He was cheating before I was teething. Gone by the time I could walk, and married to his mistress by my third birthday. For the next couple of years, my father was more shadow than presence. He flitted in and out of our life like bad weather.

Although he occasionally came around on holidays, and to my chagrin, Rose always let him stay even when he arrived with no warning. She claims it's "healthy to forgive," which strikes me as odd for a therapist, who should set better boundaries. But he was a caricature to me. Whenever I thought of him, I thought first of the back of his head, that thick, dark hair. When I pictured him in my mind's eye, I saw him leaving.

"So, you were never in love?" I ask.

Rose met my father, James, when she was my age, twenty-five. He was a friend of the family. His last name is Gardner, and she always jokes she liked the pun of it all. She was a Rose and soon she would marry a gardener. When I was born a year later, she continued the bit by naming me Lily Gardner. Two girls, two flowers. Despite calling off the engagement, I suspect she still legally changed her name because she was both tired of being an Elliot and committed to the wordplay.

"I loved him," she says. "But it was a quieter kind of love. Not the all-consuming, 'can't sleep, can't eat' kind of thing."

Henry and I were like that, too. The love snuck up on us over the course of that first summer. We didn't know yet that Lottie was sick. I was worried about going away for college in September, leaving Rose all alone, but Lottie convinced her to stay throughout the fall. That helped quiet some of my concerns. At least they would have each other. We spent June, July, and August all together like that: Rose, Lottie, me, and eventually Henry, too. It was perfect. It was bliss.

It feels like a lifetime ago.

Outside the car window is the dark harbor; the masses of boats are specks in the water. I can barely make them out in the dim light. They look like toothpicks at a distance. A few years ago, there was a town debate about a little red rowboat named *007*. It had been in the harbor for decades, and when the owners decided to change its name to advertise their business, there was an actual petition passed around to force them to change it back.

I thought the whole scandal was silly at the time, but now I get it. Good things should be preserved. Tradition means something.

My heart hurts.

Cobblestones rattle the frame of the car as we enter Main Street. It took me a while to get used to the bulky vehicle with its high beach tires. Turning the wheel takes more force than I was accustomed to. Lottie taught me to drive on the sandy back roads by the airport, the interminable place between beach and road. The way the tires slid against the loose sand unnerved me at first, but I got my bearings eventually.

I pull over into a free spot by the brick crosswalk, turning off the engine.

Mary: That's the new girlfriend's—correction, fiancée's—name. She reminds me of Mary Had a Little Lamb. The girl looked like she could be a part of a fable or a fairy tale. She looked like the kind of girl you marry, which, clearly, she is.

The physical pain is shocking. My chest is sore, as if I've been punched in the sternum. I felt this way when the end of that first summer came around, I left for college, and Lottie confessed she was sick—the grief so violent, I could vomit. It was seasickness with nowhere to land: an unmooring.

I recall what my mom said about all-consuming, "can't eat, can't sleep" kind of love.

"Wait, so if you didn't feel that way with my father, then who did you love that way?"

Rose opens her mouth to answer but a knock on the window startles us both.

"Ladies!" a voice shouts. "Open up!"

I see my mom's best friend, Josie, in the window.

Josie is a jewelry designer with her own shop on Water Street. She makes the most beautiful freshwater pearl bracelets. Rose met her at the domestic abuse hotline where they both volunteer. She is also a real estate empress. She comes from a long line of brokers, and her family owns the most successful agency on island. They helped

Rose design and ultimately rent out part of the cottage after Lottie passed. Josie has become one of my mom's dearest, most loyal friends and, as such, a close friend of mine, too.

"Gardners!" Josie taps the window again. "OPEN UP!"

She enunciates every other syllable like she's singing a melody. She's clearly tipsy, and while she's not yet slurring her words, it's evident that she's one or, at best, two drinks away from it. She must have gotten a head start with other friends. I roll down the window.

"Lily! Come out for just one drink, pleeeease!" she says, jutting her bottom lip out in a cartoonish pout.

"I can't. I have a hot date with some ice cream." Although, I recall that in my anxiety over seeing Henry, we ditched the ice cream in the detergent aisle and beelined out of the store.

"Come on!" persists Josie. "I'm more fun than some boring ice cream."

"Are you sure you don't want to join us?" asks Rose. She looks worried again, still sitting in her seat belt, making no moves to get out of the car. "I don't want to leave you alone like this."

"I'm fine," I promise. "Besides, remember my outfit?" I point toward the pink slippers even though Rose can't see them from this angle.

Mom looks at me, lips curling into a smile. "We can fix that!"

"How?" I frown, skeptical.

"We'll switch clothes."

"You're going to wear this out in public?"

"Sure," says Rose. "Who cares? I'm an old broad anyway."

"That's right, Lil," Josie chimes in from the window. "We're getting gray waiting for you."

The sentiments are especially ironic considering how young they both look and how miserable I feel. I'm not capable of showing anyone a good time right now.

"It'll be fun." Rose smiles. "I promise."

Part of me wants to join, only so I don't have to go back home and be alone with my thoughts, but I also don't want to bring the mood down.

"Mom, I can't. I don't feel like running into anyone else tonight." I think about Henry again and feel something sharp poke my chest like a loose wire. "Besides, you're a therapist in this town. What are you going to say if you run into any clients and you're wearing slippers?"

"I'll tell them exactly what I'm telling you right now."

"What's that?"

She shakes my shoulders playfully. "To loosen up!"

Chapter Four

Lily

Eight minutes later, we're standing in the public bathrooms on Old South Wharf, typically reserved for boaters. There are clean white public showers and three toilets. Like everything else on Nantucket, even the public bathrooms are aesthetically pleasing.

"Can you throw me your bra?" I shout over the stall divider.

"You didn't wear a bra?"

"I thought I was just going to the store for ice cream and dropping you off!"

"Still," my mom chides. "You never know if you'll get pulled over or something. Every time I leave the house, I think to myself, 'Is this the outfit I want to get into a car crash wearing?' If I'd be embarrassed to be seen in the emergency room in it, then I shouldn't be wearing it out of the house."

"That's a little morbid," I say. "Also, I sincerely hope your first thought in a car crash wouldn't be vanity."

Rose laughs and the bathroom stall creaks open. I finish pulling the sweater over my head and open my own door. She's standing by the sink, arms crossed, wearing my same outfit from earlier, but on her it looks fun, whimsical even. It's wacky, sure, but Rose can pull off anything.

In the warped mirror on the wall, I catch sight of my own appearance. What made my mom look like an advertisement for coastal living doesn't have the same effect on me.

When I was a little girl, I used to go to sleep at night and wish I could wake up looking like Rose. These days, I'm not terribly preoccupied with my looks. I know that I'm attractive enough that sometimes baristas flirt with me, and yet not so good-looking that they would ever give me the coffee for free.

Rose's beauty is different—it's a magnet.

"How are you feeling, Lily-pad?" asks Mom now.

My face is hot the way it always is when I'm about to cry. My ears feel stuffed and there's a faint buzzing sound from the pressure. It's the look in her kind brown eyes. Around my mom, it's impossible to pretend that anything is okay.

"I'm okay," I say, but the sentiment is lost to tears.

"Oh, honey. It's going to be okay." Mom wraps her arms around me. "Let's go home. Josie will understand."

Growing up without any siblings or cousins, I relied on Mom to play the familial roles of an entire clan: protector, nurturer, friend, sister. Rose knows me better than anyone, and I know that when she says we can go home right now, she means it—she would drop everything at a moment's notice, turn around, go back to the cottage, and let me wallow.

But I refuse to ruin her night.

"I appreciate it, Mom, I really do. But I'll be okay." I grab some tissue paper and dab at my face. My reflection in the mirror is splotchy.

"Are you sure you're okay, though? You're not having one of your panic attacks again, are you?"

I watch my expression in the mirror wince. The attacks began with my job three years ago. At first, I thought it was vertigo. The world would tilt; the ground slithered. It was different from dizziness. Dizziness is the unbalanced, woozy feeling you experience when dehydrated or lightheaded. Vertigo is something else entirely: a dislocation of self, a physical movement. One shakes you while the other disembodies you.

When I finally went to the doctor, thinking I had some rare neurological disorder or a brain tumor, I was told it was "only a panic attack." I remember how my ears burned with shame. "Only a panic attack," the doctor said, as if it were a small allergy.

Rose scans my face now, wearing the clinical guard I've seen on her face whenever a client calls with an emergency: a careful, evaluative scrutiny.

"I promise, I'm fine." I don't want to be another worry for her. Besides, the tears have subsided. I take a rattling breath.

"Fine, you're the boss." Rose claps once, moving her arms as if to physically shake off the seriousness. "Now, let's go have some fun."

We stand in line for the drinks at the Gazebo, the open-air bar on the opposite wharf. It's a circular pavilion with wrapped around wooden benches. It is also the only spot on the island with a strict twenty-five-and-up policy, an effort to curb underage drinking. One-dollar bills are stapled to the peaked ceilings. A pirate's flag hangs above.

I've always liked how there are really only a few bars you can go to at night, so if you're hoping to run into a certain someone, it's all but guaranteed, creating the kind of narrative tidiness of a Shakespearean play in which all major events occur on one set.

I shift from foot to foot, trying to get the bartender's attention. The bar is right by the docks in the middle of town, and tonight it is swarmed with sailors. Someone bumps into me, almost knocking a cranberry drink onto my mom's white jeans. Correction: It is swarmed with very drunk sailors.

My fingers move instinctually to my phone to text my best friend, Jade, about seeing Henry, but I pause. Ever since I bailed on the lease for our apartment in NYC and left her stuck with a subletter, we haven't been speaking. Even before that, we were getting into petty arguments about cleaning and whose turn it was to call the landlord about the latest problem. The truth is, ever since Jade got a boyfriend, she's been spending all of her time with him. Somehow, during the pandemic, all of my friends found partners and hunkered down. It feels like everyone else is moving on, growing up, and I've been stuck alone, wishing I still had Henry.

No one warned me that my twenties would be this lonely.

If I reached out now, maybe Jade would answer, but I don't want to disturb her. Currently, my life feels like a ticking time bomb, and it's all I can do to shield everyone else from the inevitable mess of its explosion.

Finally, I get the attention of the bartender. He looks barely seventeen, skinny, and tan even though the summer has just begun. He has bright blue eyes and sand-colored hair. Is he old enough to serve liquor or is my perception of age worsening? Everyone looks like babies to me these days: beautiful, stupid babies. Just like Henry and I were when we first met.

"Can I have three mudslides, please?"

The bartender nods and takes my card. I try not to think about the bill. I have savings, but my former assistant job at a magazine didn't exactly pay well to begin with. Now, without the income, I only have so much runway.

"Nice order." A man appears behind me. "I like your style."

He's not so much unattractive as unsettling. The stranger has blond hair, a crooked smile, and a smooth, shiny forehead that suggests his nightly skin-care routine is longer than mine. He's wearing a striped blue-and-white sweater over his shoulders.

I press my lips into what I hope is a dismissive smile and turn away.

"How long are you on island for?" he says to my back.

With an exhale of impatience, I spin back around. "I'm here all summer. My mom lives on island year-round."

What I don't say is that I have nowhere to return to. My apartment in New York has already been packed up, all of my belongings either sold to the subletter or put into storage. Many of my friends are still in the city, but they're preoccupied with their own lives—careers and partners and futures to tend to, a problem I don't share.

"Oh, nice, I'm just here for the race. My buddy is the captain of the boat *Liquid Assets*. But I'm coming back in August for a wedding. My sister is getting cuffed."

He holds his wrists together like they're in invisible shackles. When locals say they hate summer people, this man is exactly who they mean.

"Very cool," I say, turning back to the bar again. To my left, I can hear the blender churning: a mix of vodka, coffee liqueur, Bailey's, and chocolate drizzle waiting for me.

"So, should I get your number or what?" The man appears to my left, leaning against the bar so we're now at eye level. His breath smells sour.

"Um, actually . . ." I search for an excuse. "I have a boyfriend."

"I don't believe that."

Shock makes me stupid. "Oh, uh, thanks?"

An older man walks into the Gazebo and approaches him. He looks like an age progression of the younger guy: sleek, gray hair, Nantucket-red pants, an almost identical sweater tied around his own neck. I'm convinced that the worn-down "Nantucket reds" are just an excuse for insecure heterosexual men to wear pink without saying it's pink.

The two embrace in that weird, masculine ritual I've never understood: half hug, half push.

"Wait." I tap the younger man's shoulder before the two can walk away together. They are already in the midst of a conversation, gossiping about someone named Chuck cheating on his girlfriend last night at the bar Straight Wharf. "Why would you say that about me?"

"Uh, what?" The man exchanges a look with the newcomer—are they father and son? Boss and employee? Captain and first mate? He's smirking as if to say, This chick is nuts. It's an expression I'm familiar with these days. "What are you talking about? I don't even know you."

"Why would you say that you don't believe I have a boyfriend?" It's as if *loser* is written across my forehead, as if he can smell the reek of fresh heartbreak.

"I don't know, dude. You just give off a single vibe."

"Well, I'm not," I say, raising my chin stiffly. "In fact, I'm engaged. We've been dating since we were eighteen." Why am I still talking?

"Okay?" The man laughs. "Whatever you say."

The bartender appears with the mudslides, saving me from further humiliation. My ears ring as the men continue to laugh.

"I'll come back with your check in a second," the bartender says, but I can still hear the cackling. I can't wait. I have to get out of here. I balance the drinks—one in each hand, another resting against my chest—and hurry back to the wobbly round table Josie and Rose are sitting at.

When I return, they're in the middle of a conversation about our family.

"How long are they staying for?" asks Josie, leaning against the table.

Mom sighs. "I think only for two or three weeks in July, but it's long enough."

They're talking about my grandfather and Aunt Elizabeth. Or, as I like to call them, the gruesome twosome. My grandfather has three great loves: his cat, Aunt Elizabeth, and any decent mirror capable of reflecting his own personhood back to him. He is the single most vain, pompous person I have ever met, and Elizabeth is a chip off the old block.

"Are they staying with you?" Josie asks.

"No, thankfully. I had already rented out the other half of our cottage before I knew they wanted to come visit," says Rose. "I need to find them a place still, but it's hard in their budget."

"I'll help," says Josie immediately. "Don't worry about it. I'll have my brother find them something off market."

"You don't have to do that—"

"I insist," says Josie.

Our cottage is technically two small houses attached at the front by a breezeway. It's single story with a peaked roof, small living room, kitchen, and two bedrooms on one side, and a guest bedroom and attached bathroom, kitchenette, and outdoor shower on the other. Rose has been renting out the smaller of the halves for the last two years.

I love our home. Everything about it reminds me of the best parts of the island. The force of the wind sometimes causes the house to creak, gets into the nooks and crannies and whistles a tune. Everything about it reminds me of Lottie.

"Who are you renting to this year? My brother didn't mention."

"I'm not sure. Some woman named Rachel rented it for the entire summer, but she said her brother might come for a few weeks of the lease."

"Is he single?" There's mischief in Josie's eyes.

Rose laughs. "I have no idea. I doubt it, but I didn't exactly inquire if my tenant was single. That must be in violation of some sort of housing law."

"Well, if he is, send him my way!" says Josie. "This island is getting stale."

I decide now is a good time to interrupt. "Um, Mom." I place the mudslides down on the wooden surface. "Would you mind signing the check for me?"

I can't face the man at the bar again. I'm such an idiot. How many times in one night can a single person humiliate herself? Surely, I'm on track to set a record.

"Of course, honey." Rose gets out of her chair. I'm thankful she doesn't ask questions.

While she's gone, Josie and I chat about her summer plans, the nephews and nieces who will soon come to visit in June. As she talks, I take a long pull of the mudslide, scraping the chocolate sauce off the sides of the cup, mixing it in until the liquid changes color.

I look around the bar. The boats in the harbor are bobbing up and down under the moonlight. The island is beautiful at night, even when it's cold. It's the very same dock Henry and I walked on our first date, and I have the strange urge to draw it.

The impulse is odd only because it's been dormant. I used to love to draw. Painting is my preferred medium, but whenever I left the house, I used to bring a sketch pad with me in case inspiration struck. I would only show my work to Mom, Lottie, a few teachers at school, and eventually Henry.

"That's, like, really good," I remember him saying the first time I showed him something I created. "Like, really, really good."

My plan after college was to work at a magazine, learn the ropes, and eventually become an art director. I knew making it as an artist is near impossible, but this way, I could at least be around art, and maybe that was enough. The plan was to work on my own projects on the side.

I applied to internships at every major publication and studio in New York City. I got the standard mass rejection emails—hundreds of them—but one offered me an interview. It was for a position as executive assistant to Clive Bozeman, an art director at a prestigious fashion magazine. His name sounded almost too pretentious to be real, but the role was a once-in-a-lifetime opportunity.

I borrowed business clothes from Rose, took the ferry to the Cape, and then rented a car to drive to New York. I came with pitches, ideas for more content, a list of my favorite covers going back ten years.

When Clive called to say that I had the job, I felt the world spinning, as though for the first time everything, absolutely everything, was moving for me. The whole world conspiring for my success. My dreams within reach.

The delusion lasted for a while—a few months maybe, if that—but then it faded away to reveal the truth, the way all lies we tell ourselves eventually fall flat.

"Who's that man your mom is talking to?" Josie points toward the bar, where Rose is standing suspiciously close to the older guy from earlier, the one in the Nantucket reds who was with the blond jerk.

The man is leaning in closer and closer. Mom is smiling, but it's hard to tell if the attention is wanted or not. Like I said, she's a magnet, even in slippers.

The man's younger, smarmier counterpart is leering at me, a smirk teasing his lips.

"Oh no."

When Rose returns, her cheeks are flushed.

"Who was that?" I ask. "Did he ask you out?"

"Who?" says Rose, playing dumb.

I roll my eyes. "The man at the bar who was obviously hitting on you."

"Oh." Her blush deepens. "Yes, I suppose he did."

"Are you going to go?" Josie's glee is apparent. She claps her hands together in excitement. "He was handsome!"

Josie thinks everyone is handsome.

"Maybe," says Rose, suddenly shy. "I don't know."

I often wonder why she doesn't date more. I know she wanted to protect me when I was younger, but I always assumed—and hoped—that when I went off to college, she would find someone. Now, with Lottie gone, too, I worry about her future loneliness. Nantucket is a beautiful place, but at the end of the day, it's an isolated one, too. I don't want my mom to become an island of her own.

"You should go," I encourage, even though the man isn't exactly my cup of tea. I want my mom to know she has my blessing. "You should give it a try."

"You think?" Rose scrunches up her nose, considering. "Maybe."

We're silent for a moment as she seems to contemplate the idea, but I've moved on to something else that is still bothering me. "Hey, Mom?"

"Yeah?"

"When we were talking earlier about the 'can't eat, can't sleep' kind of love, you said it wasn't like that for you and my father, but it seemed like you had someone else in mind. Who was it?"

Her blush is now maroon. "Oh, never mind all that."

"Wait, this sounds juicy! Tell me more!" chimes in Josie. I'm surprised she doesn't know either. Rose has always been reticent, quietly stoic and self-sacrificing, but surely she must have told someone about this mystery man?

"It's in the past," says Rose, waving dismissively. "Ancient history."

"Come on, tell us!" insists Josie.

Rose squirms in her seat. I don't think I've ever seen my mom squirm before. She's usually preternaturally composed.

"Oh, look!" she says, changing the subject. "It's Lottie's favorite song. We have to dance." Over the speaker system, "You're So Vain" by Carly Simon is playing.

"But no one's dancing!" Josie laughs. She's right. The bar is packed but everyone is either sitting at tables or standing in their own small clusters.

"Well, then we have to be the trendsetters," Rose declares. "You know, in some countries it's illegal to sit down during a Carly Simon song."

Josie shrugs and gets up, and without another thought, the two of them begin twirling each other around, circling the bar. A few sailors nod appreciatively as they dance through the crowd.

"Come on, Lily. Join us!" Mom does an elaborate moonwalk in my direction. I can't help but laugh at how ridiculous they look.

"Fine, fine," I give in, joining them.

We spin together in a practiced move we've had down since I was a little girl: the pretzel. My mom would build a fort in the living room and pretend we were camping outside with lanterns. She hung glow-in-the-dark stars from the ceiling. At eight o'clock, there would be s'mores melted over oven burners until they were blackened. At ten o'clock, we would watch *Dancing with the Stars* and imitate the contestants.

The weight in my chest from the Henry sighting momentarily lightens, and my heart unclenches as we sing along to the song.

"Hey, how about I step in and give you a proper dancing partner?" A man appears behind us, tapping Rose on the shoulder.

It's the guy from the bar, the younger one who laughed at me. He makes a disgusting winking motion, the left side of his mouth pulled upward like an invisible fishhook is attached to it. He boxes me out, grabbing my mom by the waist and stepping on her slipper.

Rose jolts back a step. "Oh, that's sweet but I'm old enough to be your mother." She wiggles out of his grasp, trying to disentangle herself without being rude.

This is Rose's fatal flaw; she's always so worried about hurting someone else, she makes herself uncomfortable.

"I assure you, you do not look like my mother."

From behind him, the sound of his cronies laughing. The older man, the one who asked out Rose, is nowhere to be seen. Maybe he went off to the bathroom or to another bar on the wharf. I wonder if he would disapprove, step in.

Rose gingerly removes the guy's hand from her hip like she is removing a leech. "I'm dancing with my daughter tonight."

She pinches my cheeks and wraps an arm around my shoulders, and we turn to spin away from him.

I'm still heartbroken, still a mess, and I can tell the bruises from my fall at the grocery store are already beginning to form—another physical reminder of Henry—but in this moment, I feel blessed. I'm lucky, I think. I'm lucky, and life cannot be so bad if I am so lucky as to still be here, dancing with my mom.

The man looks from me to Rose and back again as we twirl away, beyond his reach.

Chapter Five

Rose

May 29

The birds beat me to the punch the next morning. I can hear their chirping as the morning light trickles in.

There must be a robin's nest outside. Lottie used to keep a bird-watching book on the living room coffee table. She would draw the birds she noticed in the garden, chronicling their colors and feathers, and including a list of interesting facts about the species in the margins. Lily and I used to love scrolling through the book every now and again, marveling at Lottie's talent, those bright shades and sharp, clean lines.

Lottie said that after my mother's death, she appeared to her as a blue jay, which always struck me as odd seeing as how I both couldn't imagine my mother as a bird for obvious reasons and have also heard that blue jays have a sort of negative reputation for being aggressive.

But Lottie believed in stuff like that—past lives, reincarnation, marriage—the more outrageous, the better.

"People are so quick to limit themselves," she would say. "It is easier to shrink the world than it is to expand your mind to wonder."

Lottie said profound statements like that in complete, eloquent sentences, and then a minute later, as if a spell had been broken, she would laugh at herself and shrug.

"Well, what do I know!" she would say, surrendering her philosophy to a small smile.

Lily and I called these moments of profound wisdom "Lottie-isms." They became our guiding principles.

I often wonder if the bird-watching book is what first sparked Lily's love for art: all those hours watching, mesmerized as Lottie created something out of nothing, as if by magic. Drawing was never Lottie's main passion—she had wanted to be a writer when she was a girl—but she had an eye for it nonetheless.

It's seven a.m., and I'm sure Lily is still asleep. She never wakes up before ten on the weekends. I'm the opposite. The early morning is when I feel most at peace. Before the rest of the island awakens, Nantucket is mine and mine alone.

We left the car downtown overnight so no one had to be the designated driver. Now, it's my responsibility to take the local bus, the Wave, back to where we left it. Otherwise, it will surely get towed. The new renters will be here at noon and everything has to be perfect for their arrival. I stretch and rise out of bed, beginning to get ready.

I stop by Lily's room, peering through the door she left ajar. There she is: unconscious, peaceful. Her curly red hair splayed across the pillow, tangled anew.

My baby.

"She's not a baby anymore," said Josie last night when Lily was at the bar buying drinks. I was telling her about the Henry run-in, warning her not to mention the subject.

"You can't protect her from everything," she said.

It was like telling me to let Lily tumble over a cliff. Abandon her to the wolves. Of course, I know Lily isn't a baby anymore. I trust her. I trust the woman she's becoming, but every time I look at her face, it's as if I'm seeing all the versions she's ever been lined up at once, like some sort of matryoshka doll. I blink and there she is at fifteen, seven, and five. Her cheekbones less angular, her eyes wider, but her mirth as wicked as ever.

A text pops up on my phone, letting out a beep. It's the man from last night, William.

I was charmed to meet you, it reads. *Dinner soon?*

I suppress a shudder at the word *charmed.* It's so formal, over the top. When I met William, he brought the back of my hand to his mouth and gave it a quick kiss. It was like watching a cheesy adaptation of a Regency novel, one of Lottie's favorites.

I spare another glance at Lily, content in her dreams, before continuing to get dressed for the day. I hate that she's going through a rough time, but I also cherish having her here, safe and cozy in her bedroom, where she belongs. I grab a Post-it and write her a note in case she wakes up before I'm back.

Out the door, I begin to walk to the bus and mull over the idea of saying yes to William.

When I found out Lily was returning home, there was a part of me that was thrilled. Raising her alone was hard, but more often than not, we were partners in it. She was my companion, my buddy. I often wished I had someone to share the lows of parenthood with and shoulder the challenges, but I also had the joys all to myself. We created a life together, a life we were proud of, and we still had Lottie.

When Lily left for college, I dropped her off, unpacked the car, and then sat in the university parking lot for a few minutes, catatonic. Her absence was a physical presence, a shift in the atmosphere. The air whistled with the sound. For the first time in my life—in all my loneliness—I felt truly alone.

Then Lottie told us she was sick. I packed up our small house in New Haven and came back to the island. I haven't left since. Nantucket has been a lifeline. With Lottie's help, I built another life for myself here: a community, friends, a career, purpose. I made myself whole again. I didn't let Lily see my devastation over her absence. I didn't let her know about my loneliness.

Having her momentarily back brings me joy, another bonus summer for us where we'll be together all season. And yet, I also know she is going to leave. It's inevitable: It's what's natural and right. During the pandemic, we got used to living together again, but kids are supposed to leave their parents. Parents are supposed to be okay with that. However, now Lottie is gone, too.

Where does that leave me?

The streets are narrow around here with no sidewalks, and cars keep passing, forcing me into neighbors' yards. Lottie's cottage—now my cottage, I suppose, although it's difficult to think of it that way—is situated one block away from the start of the famous bluff walk, a long trail that curves between the edge of the cliff and through the flower-lined yards of residents to the beach.

A flagpole stands in the center of the cobblestone-lined rotary. Beyond it, the tiny town that constitutes Siasconset, affectionately referred to as 'Sconset village by the islanders. Compared to downtown, it's nothing, but this area of the island will always have my heart. It feels as if you're stepping into another era, where neighbors chat over morning coffee and the mail carrier knows your name.

There's a market that sells milk, eggs, pantry items, pastries, fresh vegetables, and homemade ice cream. There's the post office, and a sandwich shop called Claudette's with a reliably long line. There's a liquor store, a restaurant, and a clothing shop smaller than a walk-in closet.

That's it, but as a preteen, I thought it was the whole world. I loved the autonomy of being able to walk into the village to buy my own ice cream or run an errand for my aunt. It made me feel like an adult, back when it was still thrilling to feel like an adult.

Maybe I also love this area because it's the place I first met him.

Of course, that didn't last. It's been over thirty years since we've laid eyes on each other. But here, with the island frozen in time, I can still imagine him strolling by, solid as fog.

"Hi, Rose!" one of my neighbors calls out to me, waving. She's tending to the flowers in her yard. I wave back.

It was a close call with Lily last night. I'm not even sure why I don't want her to know about it, except that talking about him makes it all feel more real somehow, ever present. Lily has never shown such an interest in my past before. Maybe it's the reappearance of Henry, or the loss of her job, or the fact that she's now the same age I was when I had her, but the questions threw me for a loop. Every time she asked me about my past relationships, my heart jolted and shrank. It's pathetic, really, that he's still the first person I think of when someone asks me about love. After all these years, I can't shake him loose.

I look at my phone again.

Charmed. William was "charmed" to meet me.

There are parts of William that remind me of James, Lily's father: his clothing, the polished, overpruned manner in which he spoke. But William was also nice. There was a degree of uncertainty, awkwardness, that warmed me.

"Can I buy you a refreshment?" William asked last night, almost bowing.

"A refreshment?" I repeated, amused. "That's a little formal for a place like this."

All of the Gazebo's drinks are served in plastic cups. The most complicated item on their menu is a mix of cranberry, Red Bull, and vodka.

William looked down at the creaky floor. "Can I buy you a drink?" he corrected.

I felt bad then. Lottie used to joke that I can see the good in anyone, even a murderer. She also told me, "Just because you can see the best in someone doesn't mean they deserve your empathy." Still, it was challenging not to find William's deference, his desire to please, well . . . charming.

Besides, as Josie pointed out, he's not exactly bad looking either. And it has been a very, very long time since I've been on a date.

The gray shingled cottages are close enough together that it's impossible to avoid glimpses of their residents through the open windows: a middle-aged couple washing dishes at the sink, a young girl reading a book on the wicker couch of a screened-in veranda. Life everywhere.

An older woman in a crisp button-down is painting on her front porch balcony, capturing the light bouncing against the water in the distance. The sight makes my chest expand and then constrict. Why does everyone look so like Lottie these days?

I pause on the side of the street to read the text again. I have several notifications from clients of mine asking to reschedule or venting about a relationship of their own. I love my work. I'm not like Lily or Lottie. Where they receive inspiration from turning inward, I receive mine by looking out at others in my practice as a therapist. When I see something click with a client for the first time, that's when I feel most aligned in my purpose.

Still, there are days like this—days when I feel my personal resolve tempered—when I wish there was someone besides Lily I could lean on, too.

Maybe "charmed" isn't such a bad word. There are loads of worse ones. Yes, William's silver hair was a little too overgelled, but hey! At least he has hair.

There were men I dated when Lily was younger, but I was always careful to keep our lives separate unless it became serious, which it never did. No one was ever significant enough to introduce her to. Or maybe I just never let it get that far.

Even though she seemed okay with the idea last night, Lily doesn't need to know yet about this either: I don't want to worry her until it's solid. Josie said she's not a baby anymore, but I've always done my best to protect her.

When Lily was born, I remember the first emotion being incomprehensible joy. Here was this tiny miracle in my arms, red and squealing. And then the next emotion immediately tumbled along: pure terror. Before Lily, I had fears, and worries, and hopes, but there was an elasticity to my life. If something bad should happen to me, the world would keep spinning. My dad didn't need me; neither did my sister. And my mother was gone. But now I had Lily, and Lily needed me, and everything, absolutely everything, took on a newfound precariousness. I suddenly understood those stories of mothers lifting up cars, pumped with adrenaline, to save their children trapped beneath.

It was like before motherhood, I had been floating, swept every which way, and now I had this anchor tethering me to earth. To be a mother is to be in constant fear. Did I do enough? Did I mess her up? Will she be okay?

The panic attacks Lily has been having worry me. Even though they've been occurring less frequently since she left that awful job, I still worry that any sudden movement—any change—could set them off again. How is it that I can help my clients with their problems, but I can't seem to reach my own kid?

The bus arrives, letting out a puff of steam.

Dinner on Wednesday? I type to William.

My thumb hovers over the message for a moment before I press send.

What's one more secret, after all?

Chapter Six

Lily

I have officially outgrown the bed Lottie got me when I was a kid. When I wake up, my feet are almost dangling over the edge. I stretch, feeling the bruises from the grocery store incident.

I have a vague sense of embarrassment, and as I try to remember yesterday's events, images flash by all at once: Henry's face in the aisle, the bottles of detergent, the man at the bar, Mary's diamond ring.

I groan audibly, burying my face in the flower-printed pillowcase. Next door, I can hear what sounds like the hum of a hair dryer, which means Rose is already awake. No surprise there. She's probably lived a whole life today, while I'm still in bed.

I grab my phone from the nightstand, open up Instagram, and search Henry's name. It's a reflex, like biting your nails, like forgetting to put on a seat belt, like sticking a fork in a toaster. I had him blocked this past year, so I wouldn't be tempted to check his profile. Now I let myself see everything I've missed.

Here, the girl is everywhere.

There are vacation photos taken in Greece, yellow flowers for Valentine's Day with the city skyline behind it, and even, I notice with a sinking sensation in my chest, images of them in Nantucket at Queequeg's, my favorite restaurant. Mary is shorter than I am, and in the photos, she's cuddled up into Henry's arm, smiling sweetly for the camera. She fits better there, in the crook of his shoulder, than I ever did. She looks like she belongs, like she could make it a home.

And then, the final blow. Henry on one knee in Boston Common at the golden hour. Behind them, the Public Garden. The bridge perched above the scene like a witness from God.

In all of the photos—the story of their romance—I check the date and can pinpoint the times we were still texting or catching up on the phone.

Just four months ago, we stayed up for hours on Christmas Eve talking. We did this frequently since the breakup. Our only rule was to never talk about our romantic lives, but we could discuss everything else: our families, jobs, mutual friends, movies, the past.

Had he been engaged then? His voice sounded the same, familiar and warm. Was it all an act? Was Mary in the other room, wrapping presents?

Something in the pit of my stomach pinches and loosens, and then I am running to the bathroom. The door sticks with humidity, so I bang my body against it, hitting the wooden frame with my hips until it budges open. I lean over the porcelain toilet seat, vomiting until I'm certain there's nothing left in my body.

I'm not sure if it's the hangover, the heartbreak, or both.

Sometimes the edge of a panic attack will sneak up on me like a villain in a horror movie. It will lurk behind the shower curtain, waiting for the opportune moment to strike. It's like I can feel the edge of it, threatening me in the periphery. Other times, it rolls in unannounced. Those are the worst ones, relentless and vicious as weather.

Right now, I can feel the burgeoning signs: the perspiration above my lip, tingling in my hands, dizziness, dark clouds infringing on my vision. I take slow, deep breaths like Rose taught me until it begins to dissipate.

I stay like that for several minutes, waiting for a second wave of puke, but it doesn't come. Still, I let myself slump there an extra few minutes, alternating between staring at my phone and the white ceiling fan, until Mom appears in the doorway.

"Lily-pad," she says cheerfully, not commenting on my current state. "You have to get up, the renters are arriving soon."

Rose is wearing a crisp white dress. Her hair is curled and shiny, her makeup fresh and dewy. She looks like the sun, and when she sees me, practically hugging the toilet, she just laughs. "Well, you've looked better."

"I've felt better," I groan back.

Something about my tone must alarm her, because her expression shifts. "Are you okay?"

I try to get up, still dizzy, and force a smile. "I'll be fine," I assure her, just like I did last night. I don't want her to worry.

Rose looks contemplative. "I know you're in rough shape, but are you still able to help me deliver the renters' welcome baskets?"

"Sure," I say. "Of course, but why do you need me for that, again? I'm happy to help, but I'm not sure I'm the best welcoming party."

"It's cuter this way," Rose says. "It's part of our charm as a mother-daughter duo. Much cuter than an old lady like me showing up alone. And, since I'm letting you stay here all summer rent-free, I get to parade you around town. It's only fair."

I roll my eyes at the "old woman" comment. Rose is only fifty and looks more like forty.

"Fine, fine. Anything for my dear mother . . . Also, how are you not hungover?"

"Years of experience." Rose winks.

Twenty minutes later, we're standing outside in the garden waiting. I've managed to make myself presentable by slicking my hair back into a low bun and throwing on a simple blue dress I borrowed from Rose. I always jokingly refer to her closet as the "Nantucket mall," because of how often I go shopping in there.

It's warmer than yesterday but the air still has a bite to it. Mom has a bouquet of white lilies and roses in one hand and a set of keys on a shell key chain in the other. I'm holding a wicker basket filled with a sampling of treats from all over the island: chocolate-covered cranberries from Aunt Leah's, Triple Eight blueberry vodka from Cisco Brewers, a fresh loaf of herb bread from Something Natural, sugar-covered donuts from Downyflake, and a cozy beach towel that reads "Nantucket Beach Permit" across it.

The garden is Lottie's masterpiece. The rose-covered arches and lush garden have practically become a fixture of the island's tourism. Right now, only a few early buds have begun, but by the middle of summer, pink roses climb up a trellis on the street side, engulfing the roof. In the front are flowers of all kinds: white hydrangea bushes, perennials with funny names like Vision in White astilbe, buddleia, daylilies, foxgloves, and peonies. A rose of Sharon hedge and honeysuckle bush provide a leafy wall of privacy from the street.

In Lottie's absence, Rose has maintained it on her behalf. It's all she can do to keep away the deer that circle the place like burglars, considering it their own private dining room. She has also made several significant renovations to both of the cottages, preparing the smaller one as a rental.

Rose painted the old warped cabinets in the rental unit a cheery light yellow. The countertops have been replaced with marble. A fleur-de-lis tile backsplash in French blue sits in front of the new white stovetop.

It is designed like an art exhibit, the colors carrying you from one room to the next. The blue continues into the living room, a harmony of light and dark juxtapositions with painted plates hung on the wall. It's like the garden is inside the house. It's the antithesis, the antidote, to the trend of minimalism, the plain cookie-cutter beach houses that have become the norm.

The extra rental income has been essential, allowing Rose to save up for when she eventually opens her own private practice.

In the corner of our living room, Rose designed a nook into the wall so Lottie could take her coffee and read by the window when she got too sick to go on her daily walks on the beach. A wood-burning stove sits beside it. Everything about the place sings warmth.

To finish it off, I painted a mural in Lottie's former bedroom: a sprawling, decadent image of the flowers outside in full bloom. I included a small image of Lottie bending over in the garden, tending to her peonies in the corner. When Lottie first saw it, she wept, which made me cry, too.

The only missing touch is its name. On Nantucket, it's a maritime tradition to name your house. The oldest accounts start in the late 1600s, but the practice became especially popular after the War of 1812 when privateers, enlisted to help fight the British, became pirates. To curb the problem, a maritime law was passed requiring all US vessels to be named. When the rocky shoals of the island led to shipwrecks, these quarterboards washed ashore, and people would grab them from the beach and use them as decoration for their homes.

Today, carved names hang above the entrances of almost every house in 'Sconset. Lottie never got around to naming the cottage, although the three of us played around with various ideas for years, each one more ridiculous than the last. With Lottie gone, neither of us has had the heart to revisit the conversation. For now, it remains nameless, which feels oddly poetic, since after Lottie's passing, the two of us have been lost ourselves, ships without a name or a destination.

A taxi appears on the road, and out walks a handsome man in his early fifties. He has fluffy black hair with subtle streaks of silver running through it. He has stubble on his chin and looks tan and active. In his arms are two canvas and leather duffels.

What happens next is too confusing for my brain to process. When this man, the renter, sees my mom, he drops his bags immediately to the ground.

"Rose?"

I look at my mom, but her face is strangely empty. All of the usual, subtle micro-expressions wiped clean and replaced by the singular emotion of shock.

"What are you doing here?" Rose's voice is strained, choked sounding.

"I'm—I'm here." He clears his throat, and the resulting voice is deep and commanding. It's the kind of voice that could quiet an entire room. "I'm renting for the summer."

Despite his confident demeanor, a flush of color spreads up his neck to his cheeks. It looks out of place on his otherwise masculine features, betraying him. When Rose says nothing, he continues, taking a few hesitant strides toward the house through the wooden arbor and onto the lush green grass.

I remain transfixed, frozen, incapacitated.

"My sister rented it for me," he explains. His voice isn't nervous but there's an uncertain tilt to it, like he's afraid of Rose's reaction. "It was a Christmas gift."

"Your sister? The name on the contract was Rachel Simmons, not Rachel Wentworth. I know your sister, I would've—I just mean—I would've recognized her."

"She got married," he says simply, still rooted in the same spot on the lawn.

"Oh," Rose says. "Well, yes, of course she did. I suppose."

I look between the two of them, trying to configure a cohesive narrative.

"As did you, I see," says the man, nodding in Rose's direction. "I mean, I didn't recognize your name either. No longer an Elliot."

I wait for a response from Mom, expecting her to perhaps tell the story behind the name change. I wish I could pull her aside behind the honeysuckle bush and force her to explain. It's a rare sight to see Rose Gardner speechless. There is a long stretch of silence punctuated only by the sounds of the robins cawing by the rosebush behind us.

"We hope you enjoy your stay?" I say hesitantly, taking a cautious step forward.

My eyes dart back and forth between the renter and my mom, still trying to figure out the connection. I cross the short patch of lawn to hand over the basket. The renter looks at me with a little too much intensity as I approach. He's doing his own calculation.

"Um." I put the basket in his hands. "Here you go!"

I back away to rejoin my mom. What the hell is going on here?

Rose stays silent, staring blankly. The man takes a step forward. His hands are stretched toward her and he looks genuinely panicked.

"If I had known it was you, Rosie," he says with a sudden urgency, the intensity lowering his speech, "I wouldn't have come. I'm not trying to pull anything funny, I swear."

He holds his hands up as a physical display of surrender. There's another moment of profound silence.

"You still have all of your hair, I see," Rose says with an ache in her voice, and then, as if shocked by her own words, she snaps back into focus. "I mean, it's fine. The door is right here."

She gestures to her left and hands him the bouquet she's been holding. There's an instant when their hands almost touch, and it seems to disproportionally embarrass them both.

"You can drop your bags off there. On the entranceway table, there's a list of restaurant recommendations, instructions on how to work all of the appliances, a password for the Wi-Fi, and some suggested activities." Her sudden businesslike tone startles both me and this strange man. We look at her, our faces full of question marks.

Rose turns and heads back to the house. She pauses with her hand on the doorknob before seeming to realize that she's still holding the shell key chain. Without another glance, she throws the keys over her shoulder. They land on the grass in front of the renter's feet.

I'm astonished by her rudeness, and for a few beats, I keep standing there. The renter stares at the keys on the ground, not bothering to pick them up. He looks like someone has grabbed him and physically shaken him. I fight the urge to turn and run: Emotions are Rose's domain, not mine.

I've seen Rose Gardner lose her cool exactly two times in my twenty-five years on this planet. First was the day we lost Lottie. Today is the second.

"Um, do you want me to help you get settled?" I ask half-heartedly.

"No." He bends over to grab the keys. "It's okay, thank you though, dear. I'll be okay." He picks up his bags and heads to the screen door of the cottage with his head hung low.

Before he goes inside, the man pauses, turns around, and clears his throat. "Apologies, my manners have escaped me. It was really nice to meet you. Please thank your mother for me, too. I promise to stay out of both of your ways."

He has the diction and practiced speech of someone raised with exceptional politeness, and in an odd way, he reminds me of Rose, who is usually so sure of herself in every social encounter.

The renter gives me a tight smile and disappears behind the screen door, leaving me in the garden all alone.

Chapter Seven

Lily

The Summer House is a boutique hotel and restaurant only a fifteen-minute walk from our home.

On the property is a series of small suites in the style of cozy cottages. As a child, I thought the ivy-covered structures looked like houses for fairies. A beachside bistro under a peaked white tent and swimming pool are located down the cliff side, nestled into the sand dunes. It's Rose's favorite spot on the island, and we always come here for special occasions: birthdays or celebrations or after the end of a particularly challenging day.

A few hours after the mysterious renter's arrival, we walk up to the restaurant. There's a squat white building with green trim and a candle-lit porch. Guests are stretched out on the lawn chairs. A little girl in a pink dress is blowing bubbles out of a plastic tube. Everything is bathed in a soft orange light.

Rose was uncharacteristically quiet on our walk over. We haven't talked about the strange situation with the new renter yet.

"How was your meeting today?" I ask once we are seated at the old wooden bar. "It was a session with a client?" After the renter appeared, she immediately left. I want to ask her what the deal is with him, but this seems a safer question for now.

Around us are empty white-clothed tables, but we always prefer to eat here, right by the grand piano. The musician is playing an acoustic version of "Tiny Dancer," and a bartender who looks about my age is mixing cocktails a few feet away. I watch the silver cylinder shake as he tosses it over his shoulder.

"No," Mom responds, refolding the napkin on her lap. "It was with the real estate office downtown."

"The real estate office?" I'm confused.

"Yes." Rose clears her throat, brushing stray strands of hair behind her ears. "It was about an opening on Federal Street. There's a small upstairs office space available for rent above a boutique."

"What?"

"You know I've always talked about opening my own private practice, and I've been thinking now could be a good time."

"Oh my gosh, MOM," I screech, slapping my palms against the table. A fork clatters next to me. "Mom, this is amazing. This is so exciting. How was the place? I want to see it. Have you told your office yet? When are you thinking of starting? What would the rent look like?"

"Lily-pad." Rose smiles. "Slow down! I haven't made a decision yet. I'm just exploring options. But yes, I'm thinking it would be great to have the practice up and running by September."

The idea fills me with a sort of ecstatic glee.

This has been a long time coming. Rose has worked as a therapist my entire life, but I know she's wanted more autonomy and control. She was thinking of starting her own practice before Lottie got sick again, but then with the caretaking and renovations to the cottage, it became unfeasible. I take this to be a sign of her healing process, a way to finally move forward.

"And how about you?" Rose asks. "How's the job search going?"

Like that, my revelry extinguishes. "The job search will begin tomorrow. Officially."

My plan this weekend is to print out flyers and offer my photography services across the island: weddings, graduation photos, engagement shoots, whatever. I'll be there. Maybe I'll even try to start a new art project again.

And if all else fails, I can always ask for my college summer job at the sweatshirt store back.

"Wow, congratulations," I repeat, forcing the last thought away. "This is really amazing." I hold up my water glass to cheers her.

"Now," I continue. "When are we going to talk about what happened with the renter?"

"Do we have to?" Rose hides her face in her hands.

"Yes."

"Okay," she sighs. "That was Tommy—I mean, Thomas—Wentworth. He's an old friend of mine."

"Just a friend?"

"Well, no. I suppose he was more than a friend."

"He certainly seemed like more than a friend."

"Okay, yes."

I raise my eyebrow to signal for her to keep talking.

Rose sighs. "I met him here, on island, the summer I turned eighteen. We fell in love, but I was going off to college and my father didn't approve. Tommy was a few years older than me and had already been accepted to the Coast Guard Academy. He was staying here at the station by Brant Point. I knew he was going back to the academy in the fall, and then he had five years of service after. It would be incredibly difficult for us to stay together."

"So, what happened? You broke up when the summer ended?"

"We tried to stay together, but I was persuaded to break it off. I thought I was saving us both from a long-distance engagement. I thought . . . well, I guess I didn't realize how rare it was, you know?"

This surprises me. The Rose I know is quiet and self-sacrificing, but she certainly isn't weak. I've never known her to care what anyone thinks. I feel an overpowering emotion I can't quite place. "Who told you to break it off?"

"My dad," she sighs. "He wrote me a letter demanding I end it. He said we were too young and that I would be destroying my life. He said it was silly to attach myself to someone who was going to be away for so many years." She pauses, rolling her eyes. "And also, that he didn't come from 'the right sort of family.'"

Another thought crosses my mind. "Wait, did you say 'engagement'?"

"Yes, we were engaged for a few weeks."

"A FEW WEEKS?"

A sophisticated-looking woman glances up from her table with a scowl pulling down her wrinkled lips. She's wearing a black dress with a matching black sweater, making her look vaguely like a nun.

"Sorry, sorry," I say in a quieter voice. "What happened?"

"He knew I was nervous about being separated for so many years, so in September, he asked me to marry him. He wanted me to know he was serious."

It's then that I recognize the emotion I'm feeling. It's betrayal. I can't believe I've never heard this story before. We cut a deal early on to be honest with each other. Growing up I told Rose everything, and I thought she told me everything in turn. My hopes were her hopes.

Her heartbreak was my hometown. We were a team. We made decisions together.

I guess I never grew out of that feeling. It seemed that mysterious, invisible line that separates one person from another didn't exist for us. Now I realize I was wrong about that. I can't help but wonder what else she's been hiding.

"So, you broke up that summer and never spoke again?" I ask.

Mom shrugs noncommittally. "It wasn't like that." She takes a deep inhale. "Anyway, a few years later, I met your father, and the rest is history."

"Wow."

"Yeah."

We linger in the silence for a moment, both lost in our own thoughts. After a beat, I dare to ask another question. "So, what did it feel like to see him again today after all those years?"

Sometimes, after a long day of my mom seeing clients, I like to imagine I'm a therapist for her, the one person to whom she can complain, let go of the clinician's practiced neutrality.

"Horrible." Rose lets out a choked little laugh. "I don't know. I just can't figure out how this is possible. How did he not remember Lottie's address? And I mean, what's going to happen the rest of the summer? He'll bring his wife, his kids, to our house? The cottages aren't exactly far apart."

Actually, I think but don't say, they're attached.

"What makes you think he's still married?"

"He had a ring on his finger," says Rose. "You'll notice those kinds of details once your friends start getting engaged."

I give her a look. "Start to get engaged?"

Rose leans in, cupping her chin in her right hand. "I'm sorry. How are you feeling about Henry?"

"Horrible," I repeat. We both laugh, but the sound is false, hollow, like canned laughter on a sitcom track. "I don't know. It doesn't feel real."

"Neither does this." Rose puffs air out of her cheeks. "Well!" She claps her hands together. "We're a fun bunch, and we haven't even ordered dinner yet." She starts to stand, wringing her fingers around the napkin before smoothing it out, placing it carefully folded on the wood of the bar. "I'm going to the bathroom, and when I get back, we can talk about happier stuff. How does that sound?"

"Sounds like a plan," I agree, but the truth is that I have more questions, many more questions.

While she's gone, I try to imagine a younger version of Rose and the renter I met today. I picture them falling in love, Nantucket like a character actor setting up the scene: all blue and purple hydrangeas, dappled sunlight through old oak trees, swollen brick sidewalks, hot sand dunes, tall seagrass, shingled houses with white trim and crawling flowers. Families riding by on matching beach cruisers. Doorframes expanding in summer heat. Everywhere you turn looking like an advertisement for a better life in a higher tax bracket.

I can see it. I can see Rose younger, happier, and there's a part of me that's guilty. She's always insisted she doesn't regret anything, but it couldn't have been easy raising me alone. I wonder how her life would have turned out if she had married this Thomas Wentworth. Would they have kids? A family of four, perhaps?

It sounds strange, but I want that for her. I want her to have the life she planned for, even if it were to mean a life where I did not exist.

I'm so lost in my thoughts, I don't notice the bartender approaching.

"Excuse me," he says. "I don't mean to be rude, but I couldn't help but overhear that you're looking for a job."

When he smiles, I notice a row of white teeth. The two front ones are slightly longer than the others. It's goofy but not in an unattractive way. He has curly, deep brown hair and strikingly blue eyes, the kind that are almost navy around the irises but Gatorade blue at the center. They're shadowed by thick, bushy eyebrows.

I nod, taken aback. "Yes, I am."

"We're not hiring here anymore, unfortunately," he says. "But I have another day job where I give tennis lessons at Great Harbor Yacht Club a few days a week. I know we're in desperate need of a check-in person at the front desk. The pay is decent, better than retail, and the staff is fun. If you're interested, I can put in a good word."

There's an appealing quality to him, a combination of confidence and sheepishness. He looks trustworthy, his fingernails nervously tapping against the counter. His nose is slightly too big for his face, and there's a compelling asymmetry to his features. Beauty can be bland, so perfect your eyes practically skip right over it, but the flaws, the crooked imbalance, always make me want to linger. It is beauty you can hang your hat on. For the second time this trip, I wish I had my camera or something to sketch on.

"That's amazing, thank you. That's so generous of you, really. Um, sure, that would be great."

"Awesome." His face splits into a full grin. The expression reveals two deep-set dimples in either cheek. "Can I have your number then? And I'll text you what my boss says."

He hands over his phone. It's thick and boxy, and there's a large crack in the middle of the screen, which has begun to chip off in small parts. To my mortification, just as I'm entering my number, Mom returns from the bathroom. The stool scrapes loudly against the ground as Rose takes a seat, leaning over to look at the phone.

"What's this?" she asks, humor in her voice. "Did you make a little friend while I was gone?" Rose winks at the bartender who, to his credit, smiles confidently back, unfazed by the teasing.

"This is . . ." I hand the phone back to him. "I'm sorry, this is so rude of me. I didn't catch your name."

"You can call me Theo. All my friends do, and apparently, we're little friends now."

He addresses me when he's speaking but, at the end of the sentence, turns to wink at Rose, who immediately throws her head back laughing.

"You're funny," she says. "I like you."

"Thank you," says Theo. "I like you, too, but I think I might be a little too young for you. Do you happen to have a daughter who looks remarkably similar to you?"

Rose roars with laughter again, slapping her knee and almost spilling her water in the process.

"Okay, enough," I say.

Theo and Rose share a wry look, both giggling like little kids conspiring together in class behind the teacher's back.

As they laugh, I can't help thinking again about this mysterious Thomas Wentworth character again. I've never known my mom to be anything but steadfast, collected and disciplined and selfless. Today, talking about Thomas, she seemed different. She seemed . . . vulnerable.

What are the odds this man from her past would return like this—living directly next to us for the entire summer?

Henry's face appears in my mind, floating up to the surface and blocking everything else out almost like it was summoned.

My past may be doomed, but that doesn't mean it's too late for Rose. And unlike Rose, I know it's never really over.

Chapter Eight

Lily

May 30

Once again, Mom is gone before I wake. There's a sticky note on the back of the door and a silk dress hanging from the frame.

"At work," the note reads in Rose's flowery script. "I got this for you for Friday's event. 7pm at Bartlett's Farm, don't forget. Won't be back until after dinner."

It's Memorial Day, but leave it to Rose to work on a bank holiday.

I walk to the full-length mirror on the back of the door and hold the dress against my body. The green fabric is near identical to the color of my eyes. So thoughtful, I think. Rose has always been the best at giving gifts. As a kid, I thought she could read my mind.

The dress is for the event on Friday, in four days. I assumed I would just pull something together from Rose's closet, but knowing she thought of me ahead of time like this warms my heart.

Every summer since Rose first became involved in the island's mental health community, we have volunteered at several charity events. It's the busiest time of the year for fundraising, and many of the local nonprofits rely on one summer party to sustain their programming for the entirety of the year. This is the benefit of the summer people. Usually, we will run the auctions or help set up decorations.

At the end of July, Rose is being honored at the Dragonfly fundraiser as the Clinician of the Year. The event raises money for the National Alliance on Mental Illness (NAMI) and the local therapy office, Fairwinds. Rose is expected to give a speech, which she has been working on for the last month. I can hear her sometimes, practicing in the shower, but I can never quite distinguish the words.

I take a quick shower and get ready for the day, determined to make the most of it. If Rose is busy, I might as well make myself busy, too.

First up: flyers. I sit in Lottie's nook and bring out my sketch pad from beneath a pile of books on the shelf. Through the wavy glass of the window, I can feel the morning sun. Outside is Lottie's beloved garden, still in the process of blooming.

I start out small, sketching some of the flowers outside: the rosebuds crawling up the trellis, the daisies poking their heads out hesitantly. The more I draw, the more I begin to lose myself in the process. It's like being submerged underwater. I lose track of time, watching as the sun progresses a shadow across the page. Eventually, I bring out my watercolor kit and fill in the image.

I never have a plan before I sit down to paint. It's like the image tells me what needs to happen next, and all I can do is hurry my hand along before I miss the directions. I've always loved the peace in the utter immersion of it. The fury of invention and then the finished project—knowing I created something from nothing.

The first time I admitted I wanted to be an artist, I said it like it was a curse. Rose was driving me to a friend's sixth-grade birthday party. I remember my heart was pounding against the seat belt. She pulled us into a parking spot and said, "Okay, honey. Have fun! I'll be back in a few hours."

But I didn't leave. I just kept sitting there, my hands slick against the leather seat.

"Are you okay?" Mom asked.

"I have to tell you something," I said in a grave voice.

I'm not sure why I chose that particular day, except that I couldn't keep it in any longer. The car was where the majority of our revelations and deep conversations took place—the front seat was like a confessional booth for us, almost holy.

I must have alarmed her, but to her credit, she remained calm.

"What's wrong, Lily-pad?"

I took a deep breath in. "I want to . . . I want to be an artist when I'm older. Like for real."

Inexplicably, there were tears in my eyes. I had loved drawing since I was a kid, and friends and teachers frequently told me I had talent, but this was my first time admitting out loud that I wanted to pursue it seriously. Art was not some fun, absent-minded hobby for me. It was not the activity of a girl trying to kill time. I needed it. I needed to do it constantly. I wanted to be taken seriously.

"Well, that's great!" Mom laughed, relieved. "Now, you better get inside before you're late. I'll see you later, honey. Have fun!"

That was the end of it, but it was like I had walked through a hailstorm and emerged miraculously untouched. From that day on, Rose supported my dream, but I always felt some hesitancy from her. I know she wants the best for me, but for her, that means stability. It means a reliable income and health insurance.

Lottie was the one who truly saw my vision. When I was seventeen and applying to colleges, thinking about majoring in something practical like marketing so I could at least fall back on a corporate job while still retaining some creativity, she said to me, "There is nothing more irresponsible than ignoring a dream. It will eat away at you if you don't pursue it. And that is the real tragedy."

It was Lottie who encouraged me to keep painting when I had self-doubts, Lottie who told me to take art classes in college, even if everyone else said it was a waste of tuition. It was Lottie who told me I could be anything. She was married to a good man, Charlie, my great-uncle. But he passed when I was only eight. All I remember of him is his love of the constellations. He would take me on the deck at night and point out the stars.

After he was gone, Lottie was heartbroken, but she remained resolute in her grief. She worked more on her craft, started writing the book she always wanted to write. She held up Rose and me, despite her own suffering. She was the strongest woman I ever met.

I notice a ladybug making steady progress on the windowsill, its tiny legs marching forward. I try to count the dots on its shell but can only see one side of its small body.

Good luck, I think with a smile. Lottie used to always say that ladybugs are good luck. I hope she was right about that one. I hope she was right to believe in me, too.

When I'm done with the drawing, I hold the paper against the sunlight. To give myself credit, I think I did a decent job capturing the garden in its full splendor. There are a few lines I'd like to clean up, but for the most part, it looks okay. In the middle I write my advertisement: "Photography services available for weddings, family photo shoots, graduation photos, and more!"

Photography is the closest to my background in print media, but then I think about how nice it felt to be painting again. In a smaller line underneath, I add, "Also available for house portraits and custom oil paintings."

I try to keep the desperation out of the copy but it's hard because, well, I am in fact desperate.

Two hours later, I'm downtown, carrying a bunch of photocopied pages. I balance the stack in my left arm, pausing to staple a few to a job board by the library. I have already approached several businesses with my résumé, including *Nantucket* magazine and the local gazette, *The Inquirer*.

There's a small art studio down by the library, and when I walk in and ask if they are hiring someone for the front desk, a snooty girl with acrylics and a bad attitude tells me to come back later.

"When later?" I ask.

"I don't know . . ." the girl says, flipping through a copy of a magazine without looking up. It's the brand I used to work at. We designed everything months in advance, and I recognize my handiwork on the cover. "Just not now."

As I walk through the wide, airy space and stare at the paintings, I feel this tingling sensation in the crook of my elbow, my telltale sign that something is registering with me. Many of the pieces are what you might expect from a beach town: impressionist paintings of sunsets reflecting off the sloping backs of beach dunes, sailboats in the harbor, a rainy rendering of the street right outside the window—all the lights aglow with warmth, and yellow shadows on the brick sidewalks. There are photos of lightning striking water, black-and-white images of women wearing vintage bikinis, a beach van in retro colors, a close-up shot of a wave about to fold—the ocean churning angry froth like the open mouth of a beast.

Others are more of a surprise. Outside the gallery is a large bronze sculpture of a man and a boy. A hippo in a tutu balancing on one foot. Sculpting is the one medium I could never comprehend in school. Perhaps I admire it all the more because of this.

I keep being met with the same noncommittal answers whenever I drop my résumé off at one of the galleries, but at least posting flyers is a start. It feels good to be doing something ostensibly productive, even if it proves to be a dead end.

"Lily!" a voice calls out as I'm pinning a flyer on the bulletin outside of the coffee shop, the Hub. I recognize it immediately.

There, walking across the brick sidewalk, is Becca Stone. I met her the same night I met Henry. She was the coworker who invited me to the party. For the last several summers, we have reconnected like old camp friends, picking back up where we left off despite the winters of not speaking.

I have a somewhat naive theory that almost everyone in the world would get along if only they were locked in a closet together for enough time. Being in Nantucket that first summer was kind of like being locked in one glorious, small closet; Henry and Becca and I banded together and bonded over house parties and bonfires and tanning on the beach and ducking into bars on the wharf through the open windows when no one was looking. Drunk middle-aged men would buy Becca and me drinks, and we would pass them back to Henry, fishing paper wristbands out of trash cans, taping them back together, and sneaking into Cisco Brewers during the day—persuading one of the young oyster shuckers to give us free snacks from the raw bar.

Back then, everything was easier because anything was possible.

"It's so good to see you!" I say when she approaches. "How have you been?"

"I'm good! I'm just here for the week, back and forth between the island and Boston for the summer."

"What're you doing downtown now?" I say quickly, before Becca can get a chance to ask me any questions.

"Oh . . ." Becca looks down at her white sandals. They have handwoven flowers on them. "I'm actually meeting Henry for lunch, and his . . ." She adjusts the glasses up the ridge of her nose before continuing. "His, uh, fiancée."

"Cool." I smile breezily while my heart splits open. I know Becca and Henry have remained friends. She refused to take sides in the breakup, which I respect. "That's great. I ran into them at the grocery store the other day. She seems nice."

"She is, yeah!" Becca grins, clearly relieved. "I kind of can't believe they're getting married already, I feel like we just graduated college yesterday, but I'm happy for them. Real excited for the wedding in August, too. It's going to be at the yacht club."

Miraculously, I keep the smile fixed on my face as shock hammers through my body, landing somewhere in my gut. I know I need to respond, but I can't locate the appropriate words—or, really, any words.

So soon. "Oh, that's lovely," is all I manage.

My voice sounds false, even to me. I adjust the flyers to my other arm. The edge of one of the pages slices across the soft skin of my forefinger, leaving a paper cut. My legs feel strangely weightless, like they might buckle.

"Well, I should be going, but it was good to see you," I add. "Tell Henry I say hi."

Before Becca can respond, I am already walking away, down the brick sidewalk, past the wharf, onto the farthest edge of the dock, where the boats are floating, oblivious. Five seagulls fight over an abandoned turkey sandwich, ripping the bread to pieces. Their squawking drowns out the sound of the ocean, my thoughts, everything. The salt air must be thinner around here, because I can't seem to find the oxygen to take a full breath.

I stand like that until I can no longer feel my fingertips vibrate, watching the ferries come in and out of the port.

It was on one of these ferries that I saw Henry on the last day of our first summer. We were on the way back home, off to college shortly after, and I spotted his curved back on the top deck of the boat.

We had been on dates on and off all summer, but neither of us wanted to start college with a long-distance romance, so we never pushed it past casual. We didn't ask how each other felt or question when we would see each other next. So much was unsaid back then.

The night before the ferry departed, I considered calling him. I even walked by his family's house on Baxter Road and stared at the big white porch, the swing chair that looked over the steep drop of the cliff. I thought about knocking but didn't. I just kept on walking, regretting my cowardice.

Seeing him on the ferry that last day felt like fate, a chance to finally say how we felt before it was too late.

We smiled at each other hesitantly over the tops of seats until I approached, navigating my carry-on bag through the aisle. The waves made everything unsteady as the boat reversed into the harbor, propelling us forward.

There's an island tradition that throwing a penny in the water when you pass the Brant Point lighthouse on the ferry will make your wish come true. We went outside to watch the white lighthouse shrink smaller and smaller and threw pennies in the water, standing back-to-back. My wish came true, and then it didn't. I didn't ask what he wished for, but I used to like to think it was the same.

Imagine us standing there, hair whipping into my eyes, stinging my cheeks, both of us asking the universe for each other. How could it resist? Even the universe can be persuaded.

Henry had the penny framed for our third-year anniversary. As it turns out, he had never thrown it at all.

Maybe that's where everything went wrong.

August. They are getting married in August.

Chapter Nine

Rose

June 1

The ocean mist hangs in the air like a question.

I check my watch again. It's past six and my date is nowhere to be found. I've been sitting on the wooden bench by the docks downtown, waiting for him to arrive for ten minutes already. The sun is now beginning its slow descent into the water. Behind me, people are chattering at one of the many open-air restaurants on the wharf. I can hear drinks colliding, melodic voices rising and falling. But I won't be joining any of them, because William insisted on having dinner on his boat rather than at a restaurant downtown.

My chef is far superior to anything they have here, he texted with a winking face a few hours ago.

If you had told me at fifteen that, decades later, my hands would still get clammy before a first date, I would have given up right then and there. It's exhausting how nervous I still feel each and every time: It's exhausting to continually hope and lose.

And yet, perhaps it is even more exhausting to think about the people I apparently cannot lose. Because if you had told me that

Tommy Wentworth would be spending the summer in my cottage, I would have thought it a cruel, cosmic joke.

He looks nearly the same as he did when we were eighteen. He looks . . . perfect. The years between us have been kind to him, far kinder than they were to me. Besides some strands of gray in his hair and some lines around his eyes, he is much the same as ever. I used to think he was the most alive person I had ever met, every atom of his body tuned to his surroundings like some sort of human barometer. He had the same stoic expression, the same masculine build: impossible to read but somehow still sensitive.

It infuriated me.

Before today, I had not laid eyes on him in more than thirty years. Now we will be sharing a breezeway, a garden, a parking spot.

What sick twist of fate is that? How had he not recognized the cottage when his sister sent him the rental information? How had his sister, Rachel, been so clueless? She visited the house once. Sure, she was only a teen when I met her, but she was a precocious kid, smart even back then, always trailing behind her big brother.

Because my own older sister and I weren't close, the idea of a little sister had been thrilling. The Elliots presented well in public, but behind closed doors, we were like strangers, roommates whom I just happened to be cohabitating with. Tommy's family was the opposite. The summer I met him, his parents and sister came over to visit him for a weekend. He invited me to join them for dinner at a popular dive spot downtown, and everyone fought to be heard over loud recounts of inside jokes and old stories repeated a hundred times with the same relish.

Afterward, I was almost drunk off the fun. "Do you guys ever fight?" I asked.

He said, "Of course we do. Every family fights."

But the difference was that the Wentworths fought because they knew each other. I didn't know my dad or sister well enough to fight with them.

"You look beautiful tonight." I turn to see William approaching.

He's standing in front of the bench, wearing white pants and a starchy tan button-down. His silver hair looks almost orange in the refraction of the sunset. He's objectively good-looking, but the more I stare at him, the more his features seem to grow and warp. Everything distorted now that it's been compared to Tommy.

He offers me a hand to stand up and I take it.

"Thank you!" I say. "You look very handsome, as well. I'm so happy we're doing this."

"Shall we walk to the ye ol' vessel?" says William.

"We shall," I imitate him in a mockingly formal tone, hoping to break the tension. He doesn't laugh, but instead leads us to the farthest pier.

When we arrive at his boat, it is, predictably, ostentatious. Calling it a boat is like calling Buckingham Palace a house. It is three stories high and equipped with a staff of fifteen. On the top deck, William has had dinner prepared for the two of us, complete with a white tablecloth and a bottle of champagne sweating in a silver bucket filled with ice. He leads me up the front staircase and pulls the chair out.

"So, Rose," he says, clearing his throat. "I hope you don't mind my forwardness, but I must admit you caught my attention the other night."

I smile again, placing the napkin on my lap and discreetly wiping my palms on it. It seems a little early for a romantic declaration.

"Thank you. That's very flattering, but I must assure you that I don't always wear my slippers to the bar. It's a long story." I force a laugh.

I hate how formal and high-pitched my voice sounds. William speaks in crisp, complete sentences, as if there is a screenwriter in the room hiding behind the captain's seat, eavesdropping for material. I can't help but unconsciously imitate his tone.

I expect him to ask a follow-up question, but he doesn't. Rather, he says, "Well, you certainly clean up nice. Even better than expected."

"Thank you," I repeat, although I'm not sure if it's a compliment. "This is such a lovely setup. Thank you so much for inviting me."

Lottie once said I am so polite that if I got hit by a car, I would apologize to the driver for the mess and offer to clean his vehicle. Lily once, in a rare fit of teenage rage, called me a pushover. Both comments stuck with me, but I can't help myself. I was raised to be polite.

"So," William says, taking the champagne from the container and pouring it into two flutes. "You have a daughter, right? She was with you at the bar when we met. Tell me about her."

It has continuously surprised me, as a single mother, how many men are scared off by the fact that I have a daughter. Lily is living proof that they will forever be doomed to come in second. Lily is my first priority, always. Hearing William's warm curiosity melts some protective edge in me. I relax immediately.

"She's great," I say, smiling for real now. "Lily is headstrong and creative. She's nothing like me in that sense. I wish I had her independence and her unapologetic nature."

Maybe somewhere Lottie is looking down on us. It was Lottie who comforted me when I first received the letter from my father demanding I end the engagement with Tommy. Tommy was too young, too poor to care for me, he said.

"An Elliot is worth more than a cadet," my father wrote.

I could practically hear the arrogant, classist scoff in his script. Despite the fact that our family has long since lost any generational wealth, he still continues to hold on to this antiquated idea that our name means something. He wants to "restore the Elliots to their former glory," and for sexist reasons, he assumed marriage was the path forward.

"There will be others," he lied. It was only first love. It was only the beginning.

And who was I if not obedient back then? Who was Rose Elliot if not a good girl? A dutiful daughter.

Against all my better judgment, I listened. I've spent a lifetime paying for that mistake.

The summer I met Tommy, I was working at the Lobster Trap—an unassuming seafood grill where the only decorations also serve as fishing equipment—and much of our dates consisted of Tommy biking over to meet me at closing time. The two of us would eat leftover kitchen scraps on the employees-only back stairs of the restaurant, our hands slick with butter and grease. I remember the thrill I got from watching him get off his bike and walk to the stoop, the way his stride itself was like some sort of holy ritual, proof of all the goodness in the world. I loved his voice most of all: the cadence and rhythm of it, the deep bravado. I could have spent the rest of my life just watching him walk in circles and hearing him speak. It was my dearest wish.

I taught Tommy how to crack open the lobster shell and extract the meat from every crevice. He had never had lobster before, and he was disgusted by the tomalley, the soft green mush in the body cavity. I used to tease him by making the lobster dance, which he found inhumane. Everything was funny with Tommy. That's what I remember most: laughing so hard my chest almost split open.

And that's how I feel thinking about him now, split open.

I wish Tommy had just stayed gone.

Appearing here to taunt me after thirty years of no contact is cruel. I wish he would retreat back to his own picture-perfect life, rather than come here to gawk at my failure. I should have moved on by now, certainly. I had a child with another man, after all. His presence shouldn't affect me like this, but some hearts only have it in them to break once before they're spent.

William hands me the champagne. "And what are you like? What makes you and Lily so different?"

Tommy is a phantom now, as irretrievable as Lottie, but William is real. He is sitting in front of me, and he is offering a fresh start. I could be anyone to him still.

I take the champagne from his hand and tell him who I am.

Chapter Ten

Lily

June 3

"My back is killing me," says the old woman next to me.

We are standing under a greenhouse in the perennials section on Friday. Beside us is a long auction table with various items to bid on. Some are potted plants, others paintings or experiences like a sunset cruise or a weeklong rental in Telluride. Josie has donated several bracelets and pearl necklaces at Rose's behest. It is my job to encourage guests to make offers. Mom is somewhere in the back, making sure the hors d'oeuvres and drinks continue to flow. A tray of bacon-wrapped scallops keeps passing by, but I am always interrupted by a question before I can grab one.

"My bunions are killing me," the woman's friend says next.

Both of them are wearing pantsuits in different shades of pastel, like an elderly version of the Powerpuff Girls. They are fabulous.

"You know, my knees are really hurting me lately, too," I chime in. I'm trying to bond with them, but they also do actually hurt. My knees have been hurting since the day I turned twenty-five, another symptom of my interior decomposition.

The ladies stare at me, their eyes narrowed in accusation. "What do you know about knees? What are you? Sixteen?" the first woman, the one in the blue suit, says.

The other laughs heartily.

They walk away without bidding on anything, and I'm left alone again, leaning against the table. I let out a blow of air, stroking the waxy leaf of a plant. The event is the same as it always is, except for some inexplicable reason they have decided to bring in a fortune teller. The lady sits in a little booth in the corner with a stack of tarot cards. A hand-painted sign above her reads "Ten dollars for palm reading, fifteen for tarot cards, and thirty for past-life regression."

The psychic keeps winking at me, ushering me over with a curved finger. It makes me shiver with unease. I have to look away. The woman is wearing a red shawl that looks familiar, but I can't place why.

Before I can worry too much, I spot someone else I recognize by the art section of the auction. She's standing next to a large frame. Inside are three-dimensional cutouts of butterflies flying off the white canvas to create the shape of the island. The price tag reads "Bidding starts at $7,000."

The money seems like an unfathomably large sum: my entire savings.

Her name is Marie Chen, and she's the owner of one of the most popular galleries downtown, the one I tried to drop my résumé at the other day. I know this because I just recently read a profile of her in *Nantucket* magazine. Marie is wearing an elegant blazer dress with gold buttons down the bodice. I consider approaching, but my walk is interrupted by the sight of my mom, barreling through the crowd.

Josie quickly follows her, wearing small, pink kitten heels that make her have to take comically short steps.

"Come on, Rose." Josie shuffles. "Don't be like this."

Rose keeps walking briskly, leaving Josie standing there, resigned. I shoot her an apologetic look and follow my mom, taking Josie's place in the race. I catch up with her by the bar, angrily refilling a bag of ice. There's a harsh noise as the pieces crunch together. Rose's face looks flushed like she's just been out for a long run, except my mom never runs and also never usually looks disheveled.

"What was that about?" I ask

"Nothing," Rose says curtly.

"I thought we didn't keep secrets."

Without looking up, continuing to break the ice, Rose says, "That rule is for you, not me."

"Wow."

Rose finally looks into my eyes. Her pupils are wide as sand dollars. "Look," she says. "I got in a disagreement with Josephine. It's not a big deal."

"About what?"

"I don't need your judgment, Lil. Don't worry about it."

"When am I judgy?" Rose gives me an incredulous look. "Okay," I amend. "I won't be judgy right now."

This makes Rose laugh a little, but then almost immediately, her face crumples back into despair. "I asked her to check with her brother and see if we can get Tommy—I mean, Thomas," she corrects herself, "out of our place, ASAP."

"And what? Leave him homeless?"

"He wouldn't be homeless. I've been doing some research on him and I can assure you that he will be very much okay. After his service, he went on to study engineering and sold a start-up company a few years ago. He made enough money to retire at forty-eight. He doesn't need you worrying about him."

I ignore the admission of Google stalking. "But it's so mean."

My mom shoots me a pointed look. Rose is now breaking the ice apart with a metal rod, using too much force.

"Sorry, sorry, not being judgy. I just feel bad for him is all. I mean, it was so long ago, and he seems like a nice guy now. Also, we could use the money for your new practice. What would you do without the rental income?"

"Time." Rose snaps her fingers in the air. "Went by just like that. It doesn't matter how long ago it was. But Josie's brother assured me there's nothing I can do to break the real estate contract now. We're stuck with him. Josie said I was overreacting."

"Did you tell her why you wanted him out?"

"No, of course not," says Mom. "That would be humiliating."

"Well, if it means so much to you, maybe it's worth it."

Rose pushes her shiny red hair from her face. She's sweating slightly around the temples.

"It's too late," she says. "Just drop it. Okay?"

There's an uncharacteristic tone to her voice. It sours her expression like she's bitten into something rotten and foul. It's such an unusual sight on my mom's delicate face that I decide to let the argument go.

For the rest of the night, I help my mom with the event: wrapping up items that have been sold, pouring drinks, carrying plants and paintings into waiting cars, throwing out discarded napkins with multicolored stains in the corners, whatever is needed.

When the sky darkens and the twinkly lights turn on above, I finally muster enough courage to approach Marie, and to my surprise, it actually goes well. She offers to take a look at my résumé, says they may be hiring someone soon for an associate role at the gallery. By "associate role," what she means is a glorified receptionist, but I'm thrilled. I write down her email in my phone. When I do so, I see a text from Theo, the bartender from the other night.

Hiya, it reads. *I talked to my boss today and they said you can come in for an interview tomorrow between 12pm and 3pm if you're free.*

My chest is warm and light. I haven't been sleeping well in the last few days since I discovered that Henry is engaged. My stomach has been tied up in a constant state of nausea, unsettled, but now, it rests. Maybe I was wrong. Maybe everything will be okay.

It's with this good fortune buoying me that I decide to approach the psychic who has been eyeing me all night. Walking away from Marie, I feel strangely invincible, ready to address my fate, my future, head-on.

There's an undeniable magnetism that has been drawing me closer all night, some mystical aura to the garden with the deep denim-blue sky and the setting sun and the yellow lights reflecting off the greenhouse. Now or never.

"Hi," I say to the psychic. "I'd like to do a tarot card reading, please."

"No need for that." The psychic smiles. It has an eerie effect on her face, like the moon's shadow crossing over the sun. "I already know what I need to tell you. Give me your hand."

I take a hesitant seat on the hard wooden stool. The psychic grabs me a little too roughly, tugging my arm across the booth. She bends my fingers back, pressing her thumb into my palm. Her skin is shockingly cool to the touch, and her nails are sharp and unpainted.

"You have a strong life line," the psychic says, digging into the lines of my hand.

"Um. Well, that's good news."

The psychic's eyebrows are tattooed on, and I find myself momentarily mesmerized by the deep brown color and the few patches where real hair is still coming through. The pigment is so dark it looks red.

"There's a strong maternal presence in your life."

I nod in lieu of answering.

"There is also death."

"Oh," is all I can say.

Sometimes, in the middle of my day, I will be momentarily seized by the idea that my life is not my life. Something has gone wrong. I made one wrong turn somewhere along the road, and now I have ended up in this alternate universe where up is down and my boyfriend is in love with someone else and my dream job is ruined and Lottie isn't around. I think if only I could retrace my steps, I might find that one faulty screw that shook everything loose. I could go back. I could fix it.

"You will have two great loves," the psychic continues without pause. "One greater than the other, but both have a first name that starts with the letter *H*."

I can hear pounding in my ears. My cheeks and teeth throb as if my heart is trying to escape through my head. Then, the psychic says the singularly most ominous thing anyone has ever uttered at a fundraiser for mental health:

"You are at a crossroads in your life." The woman's tone is grave. "Choose your next steps carefully."

Chapter Eleven

Lily

June 10

I feel like I'm at a crossroads, you know?" I hear a teen boy say to his instructor. "Like with my tennis swing. I need to either bulk up and commit to my forehand, or work on getting better at doubles and my net game."

A row of shiny rackets stares down at me with judgment from behind the desk I'm seated at: Wilson, Head, Babolat, Prince. All of which are available for demo. Their grips are wrapped in various shades of pastel. Little green hairs are stuck in the strings, almost imperceptible unless in direct sunlight.

It's a week after the fundraiser and my first day at the job Theo helped me secure.

"We can work on both, but first, I think we need to nail down your serve," says the instructor.

The interview for the position was seamless. The manager didn't care much about who took over this role as long as they could show up on time, keep a schedule, and appear friendly. Theo is apparently a beloved instructor, so his recommendation meant a lot, too. It was generous of him to put himself on the line like that for someone he barely knows. It makes me even more eager to impress everyone, to prove to them that his word carries weight.

I'm scheduled to work the morning shift on Tuesdays, Thursdays, Fridays, and Saturdays for the rest of the summer.

The teen boy stands in his white shorts and athletic polo, apparently oblivious to the fact that his sneakers have tracked in clay on the hardwood floors. A steady trail of his green footsteps follows from the screen doors to the desk. I'll have to grab a mop to clean them up as soon as he is gone.

"So, am I making varsity or what?"

The boy leans against the desk, almost into my face. I can smell an unpleasant combination of his sweat and shampoo, distinctly similar to baby powder.

He has the calm arrogance of someone who has been raised in beauty, good health, and wealth his entire life. I imagine his father as a stout bald man with a mean streak. Maybe he owns a hedge fund in Connecticut, like Henry's family. His mother is probably one of the many professionally skinny blond women who frequent this place: their faces artificially preserved with Botox and whatever magic is in the green juice they suck down like it is a potion, just as God and Goop intended.

"We'll see." The instructor gives him a friendly shoulder slap. "I have a good feeling."

I haven't been officially introduced to the pro yet, but from what I've gathered from the other staffers, her name is Emily and she plays tennis at University of Georgia. Her family is from Hawaii originally.

Immediately, I recognize that she is beautiful. She has sun-kissed brown hair and the kind of collected coolness of someone who has spent a lifetime cultivating self-confidence. She leans against the counter, swinging her racket back and forth, looking at ease in a world dominated by men.

I want to be her friend immediately.

I have loads of friends back in New York, but right now, they feel inaccessible. I have friends from the magazine, coworkers whom I now can't bear to face. Jade is still angry at me for needing to move out and leaving her with a subletter she doesn't know. Becca is busy with Henry's circle, and although I know I could text her, too, I don't want to hear more about the wedding.

Truthfully, with Rose working so much this week and missing dinners, it's been a bit lonely.

"Well, we better hope so," the boy says, spinning his racket in his left hand, copying Emily. "Or else we'll have to see if you get that end-of-summer tip from good ol' mom and pop."

The racket drops to the ground, making a loud, tinny sound against the wood.

I wince as Emily picks it up for him. A cocky grin flashes on the boy's unbothered face.

"I'll see you next week!" he calls as he takes the racket from her hands and heads out to the shell-lined parking lot.

"Can't wait, champ!" Emily yells after him in a good-natured tone. "Screw that kid," she mumbles to me as soon as the boy is out of sight.

I let out a surprised laugh.

Theo walks by and takes the boy's previous spot, leaning against the counter between Emily and me. His farmer's tan looks more pronounced with the contrast of his tennis whites, like a paint swatch.

"Can't wait, champ!" Theo playfully mocks Emily in a high-pitched imitation of her voice, nudging her shoulder. "I'm surprised you kept your cool so well with that little shit."

"He's not worth my time." Emily rolls her eyes, nudging him

back. "Besides, let's be real. He'll make varsity when hell freezes over. You should see him trying to hit my lobs. He looks like a grasshopper."

She does an impression of the boy eagerly jumping up and down in little hops. The bit makes Theo laugh so hard he nearly spits out his water, and suddenly, I wonder if there's something between them. I'm surprised to find myself disappointed by the possibility.

"He's probably in love with you," I offer. The two abruptly stop laughing and look at me. "What I mean to say is that boys that age usually tease the girls they like."

Emily raises an eyebrow. "Yeah, well, that's no excuse. Anyway, I have to go to my next lesson. I have three seven-year-old girls, so we'll probably just play Alligator all session, which is fine by me."

Alligator is a drill in which you line up at the net for volleys, and if you miss a feed, you "lose a limb" to the alligator.

During my precisely four hours and thirty-three minutes on the job, I've already learned that there's a lot that goes into being a tennis pro at a place like this. There's the athletic skill, of course, the technical knowledge of tennis, but that's just the barrier to entry. Perhaps more important is personality—or the performance of a certain type of personality.

You have to be likable, reveal enough about yourself so the members can relate to you, but not too much that they feel you've crossed a line. They don't want to think about you more than they have to. You must be good with kids, encouraging with mothers, fun to be around but tough when you need to be—a disciplinarian who can make anyone laugh. You have to be able to shoot the shit and snap back into business mode.

It helps if you're young and attractive, too.

That's probably why Theo is beloved. He has an easygoing charm that makes everyone instantly comfortable. I've seen him chatting up different members all day, and with each, he makes the individual feel like they're his friend immediately, and it doesn't even appear to be an act. He's like a golden retriever: affable, loyal, undiscerning.

"So, I was thinking," he says to me once Emily is gone. "You should probably learn tennis if you're going to be working here."

The only time I tried to play tennis was in gym class in middle school, and I hit the ball so far into the neighboring trees, the teacher called it a "home run."

"That's okay," I say. "I'm good at the front desk. I love the front desk. It's safe here."

"Come on, you have to try. I can give you a lesson." He winks. "For free."

I roll my eyes. "So generous of you. But I'm telling you, it's better for all of us if I don't try. I'm a danger to myself and others when it comes to sports."

My mind flashes back to the grocery store, the laundry detergent falling.

"Okay, fine. We can start with something a little easier. What about pickleball?"

"Pickleball?" I repeat, considering it. Lottie loved to play with her friends, and I know Mom still has her paddles, but I can't imagine it would go any better than my brief foray into tennis.

"The ball is lighter. The court is smaller. It'll be an easier transition into the racket sports arena. And anyway, I happen to be the reigning pickleball champion of this island, and beyond being gorgeous, smart, funny, charismat—"

I cut him off. "Can we get on with it?"

"As I was saying, in addition to all of those other qualities, I am also an exceptional teacher. You'll be an expert in no time."

"Okay," I agree hesitantly. "Maybe."

"Maybe is a yes! When are you free for a lesson?"

I laugh at his eagerness. "Next Thursday afternoon work for you? We can go after work."

"Excellent." He smirks at the corner of the room, avoiding my eyes. "It's a date."

I open my mouth to protest, but before I can refute the statement, he is already walking away and out the door to the courts.

A few hours later, I wait for the bus home, tired the way only a new job can make you tired—even a half day. It's the memorization of new names, new rules, new social and professional protocols.

In my hands are half a dozen pages of scribbles, doodles I made in the downtime between tasks. They're not much to look at, but I'm proud nonetheless. I'm proud that I created anything at all.

The last few years working for Clive at the magazine, I started to worry that the creative impulse had abandoned me entirely. I used to spend every spare minute sketching, but the longer I worked as his assistant, the less I felt the desire to pick up a pencil or paintbrush.

When I first moved to New York City, I was twenty-two years old and thought I had reached the center of the universe. I could see the Empire State Building from my cramped apartment in Murray Hill, the air through the open window was warm but not humid, and the sun beamed bright and fearless. Later, I would find out that it was in fact the Chrysler Building, not the Empire State, and maybe nothing good happens at the center of the universe.

Clive wasn't outright abusive at first. He never screamed at me, but he raised his voice until I learned to cower, avoiding anything that might trigger an outburst: a wrong coffee order, an email with a minor typo.

"You're an idiot," he told me firmly and often. "Do you even want this job? Do you even want to be here?"

I suspect *idiot* may have been his favorite word.

A few weeks in, I developed a stutter in his presence. I stopped speaking up in meetings. I worked twelve-hour days, and then went home to answer more emails until my eyes were so sore, I couldn't respond to texts from my mom without going cross-eyed. I was easy to work with because I didn't hold enough power to be difficult yet. Eventually, I got so good at playing dumb, some days I even believed my own bit.

That's when the panic attacks started. Every passing day, I felt less and less myself.

At first, I didn't tell Rose or Lottie what was happening, because I knew they would encourage me to quit, but I did tell Henry.

He said, "This is just how you earn your keep. First-years always get treated like shit."

I bit my tongue, wanting to point out that since he had joined his father's company, he probably had a different experience than the rest of us. Regardless, I stuck it out.

Then, the pandemic happened. Lottie's breast cancer came back, worse this time. I moved back to the island and worked remotely for what I thought would be a week but became a year. Henry and I took a "break," because I couldn't risk seeing anyone while Lottie was going through her treatments. What if I got her sick? I'd never forgive myself.

The break became a breakup, I moved back to the city, got fired, and now here we are.

All of it is so tied together in my mind, a spiral of unfortunate events: It's like I lost my career, my great aunt, and Henry all in one fell swoop.

The bus pulls up with a laborious exhale and I get on board. We make a turn onto Milestone Road, and after a few minutes, pass Sankaty Head Golf Club: the site of my first kiss with Henry.

It was an early June night. It felt illicit sneaking onto the course: the absolute quiet, beyond the rumble of the nearby ocean, just over the bluff. The only source of light being the moon and someone's iPhone flashlight. Henry lent me a sweatshirt, and as we were hopping over the tall grass of the rough, he mustered up the courage to reach out and grab my hand, leaning in quick and brief, lips light as a passing prayer.

While I was walking home that night, I spotted a discarded tee on the outskirts of a putting green. Without thinking, I quietly picked it up and shoved it in my purse, a part of me, even at the time, missing the innocence of the moment as it rolled on by. I still have it to this day.

What I wouldn't give to go back to that summer now, before everything got so messed up.

Now Henry is worse than a stranger. In August, he will be someone's husband, and the past will stop being part of an ongoing narrative. It will just be past. And me, the only ghost still betrothed to it.

I know I have to let go of Henry. He deserves happiness with someone else, and his fiancée deserves it, too. I know psychics are silly and probably fake, but last week when the woman said my soulmate's name started with the letter *H*, I'd be lying if I didn't admit that hope the shape of a white lie took hold in my chest.

When the bus drops me off at 'Sconset center and I arrive back home, the renter, Thomas, is outside reading in the garden. It's odd seeing him, given the little I now know about his relationship with Rose, but I'm also surprised I haven't bumped into him sooner. Has he been avoiding us? I wouldn't blame him. I squint at his salt-and-pepper hair and try to imagine him younger. Who is this mysterious man who once wanted to marry Rose? And who was the version of my mom who almost went through with it?

When he spots me, Thomas stands up, placing a finger in the crease of a worn paperback to hold his spot. I notice where he is sitting: Lottie's old bench by the honeysuckle bush. No one uses it anymore. Rose and I never discuss Lottie's chair, but wordlessly, it has remained empty, an unspoken agreement.

"I'm sorry," Thomas says, brushing dirt from his pants. "I thought no one was home."

"Oh, hi!" I arrange my features into my best imitation of a smile. "No problem. I'm Lily by the way. I realize I forgot to introduce myself the other day."

I reach out to shake his hand, inspecting it for signs of the aforementioned wedding band. I don't see one, but perhaps he took it off to go to the beach.

"Thomas." He shakes my hand back. "Apologies, I thought no one was home."

"It's okay, please don't let me disturb you. I'm just stopping by to drop off my bag and change into sneakers to go for a walk on the beach."

Truthfully, all I can think about is Henry and the wedding. Hearing about the engagement had been shocking, of course, but I thought there would be more time. More time for what? I'm not quite sure, but I assumed it would be one of those long engagements—maybe a year or two before the big day. So much can go wrong in a year or two, after all. I know this well. Based on the date of the engagement photo, they've only been engaged for a few months. What's the rush?

"Is there a good walking trail nearby?" Thomas interrupts my thoughts.

He's holding the book with two hands behind his back now. I wonder if it's from Lottie's library, and the thought makes me want to cry again. Thomas's expression is sheepish. He looks torn between staying put and running away, but something keeps him grounded.

"Definitely!" The corners of my mouth hurt from faking smiles all day. "There's the famous 'Sconset Bluff Walk. It goes all around the east shore bluff. It's narrow at parts but super cool. You can see the ocean and the big cliff that leads to it on one side, and then on the other side are the lawns of Baxter Road. It ends at Sankaty lighthouse. I highly recommend."

My face feels tight, effortful after the rambling monologue. Thomas nods attentively and thanks me with genuine gratitude. I take a few tentative steps toward the front door.

"I'd hate to be an imposition, but would you maybe show me it one day?" he asks before I can escape.

"Oh," is my only response. I'm too shocked to come up with anything better. What would my mom think? She's so angry at him for reasons I still don't understand.

"I mean—I'm sorry, that was rude to even ask," Thomas says. "You guys are so nice to have me in your home, I'd just like the company is all. There's something I'd like to talk to you about . . . about Rose. But please don't feel pressured."

His eagerness to please, his deferential manners, tug at my heartstrings. Even if he's a near stranger, even if he made mistakes, who am I to judge? I've made enough mistakes for a lifetime of remorse.

"No, no, it's not an imposition at all. I'd love to show you sometime. Maybe tomorrow afternoon?"

I know Rose will be at the office at that time. Recently, she's been seeing two clients on Saturdays around then.

"Yes, of course, whenever," says Thomas in a rush of emotion. "That would be amazing, thank you so much." He looks around, seemingly debating whether to sit back down.

I nod toward his seat, Lottie's bench. "Please, sit. Don't let me disturb you, I'm leaving soon anyway."

He gives me a small, gracious return nod and then resumes his book. I see he's reading something by Jane Austen, but I can't catch the title because the spine is too worn—an unexpected choice, regardless.

Inside, I throw on an athletic set, slick my unruly hair into a ponytail so tight it makes my brain hurt, and lace up the old pair of running sneakers I reserve strictly for walks on the beach. They still have sand in them from last summer. I decide to grab my camera, a Canon EOS RP Lottie bought me for Christmas a few years back. It's mirrorless, lightweight, with a fast autofocus that makes it particularly adept at capturing nature.

Just as I'm about to dart back outside, two texts appear on my phone. The screen door slams against my body, ricocheting off my backside as I pause to read them.

One is from my mom. With it springs forth a new surge of guilt over agreeing to meet Thomas tomorrow: *Hope you're having a wonderful day, Lily-pad!*

Hi, the latter reads. *Good running into you the other night. Would you be open to grabbing a coffee and catching up soon?*

The sender's name is Henry Wright.

Chapter Twelve

Lily

June 11

The next day, Thomas and I meet in the garden by the old white arbor. The roses have begun to climb, wrapping dark green leaves and thorns around the shingles.

It is afternoon and our Rose is out at work. She seems to be gone a lot now—up with the sun, out until after dinner.

Thomas and I walk down the street to the entrance of the bluff walk, saying little. There's a nervous crackle of energy between us that moves like static.

He walks with his head bent down, hands in his pockets, mouth slightly open as if he is about to begin a sentence before closing it instead and frowning at his shoes. The only sound is the crunch of shells beneath our sneakers. In front of us are the small cottages that stand on either side of the bluff walk like walls. Between the cracks in the periwinkle hydrangea bushes, I can see the ocean. It is hot enough that I have to take off my sweatshirt and tie it around my waist.

The breeze from the ocean is like dew on my skin.

Thomas trips on a loose rock and then regains composure, running a hand through his hair. It's the third or fourth time I've seen him stumble. He must be nervous. I look at his hand and notice he does in fact have on a simple gold wedding band today. Once again, Rose was right.

"Anyway," he starts. "You probably have some questions for me."

It's funny, because I don't. Not really. I've wondered why he's here, how he's doing, what he wants from us, but my own life has been such a mess that I haven't had time to analyze his presence too much. Maybe this makes me an inherently selfish person.

"Yes, of course," I lie.

"Well, as you might already know, I knew your mother a long time ago. I loved her." His voice sound rusty, like he also hasn't gotten enough sleep the last few nights. "I wanted to marry her, actually, but everyone said we were too young."

He lets this revelation wash over me, pausing for dramatic effect. I consider acting surprised, but this is old news. I nod, gesturing for him to continue.

"So I went back to the academy, heartbroken."

I nod again, encouraging him to go on. I know this part of the story. "And then what?"

"I tried to move on with other women." He coughs uncomfortably, glances at me. "But I could never stop thinking about Rose. Seven years later, I looked her up again."

This part is new. Rose didn't mention ever seeing him again.

"I was done with service, beginning my company. I tried looking her up in the phone book but I couldn't find a Rose Elliot anywhere. Out of desperation, I asked Lottie. You see, I still knew where she lived, so I came to the island and paid her a visit. She told me Rose was engaged to a man named James Gardner, your father." Thomas clears his throat again.

He exhales. I can't believe how much my mom hasn't told me.

"So, what happened next?"

"I was too late." Thomas smiles a sad smile. "She was pregnant."

I can feel my mouth slacken with surprise. I've often wondered why Rose was with my father in the first place if she didn't seem to love him. Now I know the reason.

It's all my fault.

The path has begun to narrow. We are entering the cliff side. The thin dirt weaves through the trees and bushes of Baxter Road, once one of the most expensive streets on the island. In recent years, the mansions have begun to fall into the ocean as the face of the cliff erodes.

These days, everyone is moving their houses to lots on the other side of the street to buy themselves a few more good years. This is the great dichotomy of the island in action: the constant battle between the unruly natural environment and the residents' relentless efforts to reshape and control it.

"I don't mean to upset you, I'm sorry. I feel terrible if I've overstepped, but I want you to know the full story."

The hedges here have grown together to create a pathway above us like a tunnel. Enveloped in their leaves, it is dark and quiet like a church. By the bend, there are brightly colored rocks, hand-painted by children. A few of the stones have carved dates and initials on them, some more than thirty years old.

"I always loved these," says Thomas from behind me.

I spin to face him. "You've been here?"

He looks sheepish. "Of course," he says. "I spent that summer here when I met your mother."

"Why did you lie then?"

"I'm sorry for deceiving you. I just wanted an excuse to talk to you."

Something clicks for me. "You didn't rent the cottage by accident, did you?"

Thomas shakes his head. "I did, actually. It was a gift from my sister, Rachel. But I'm starting to suspect that Rachel knew the truth."

"Why would she do that?"

He kicks the dirt. "My wife passed five years ago. I met her after I found out Rose was engaged. A year later, we were married. And then . . ." He goes quiet.

"And then what?"

"Never mind," he says. "We built a wonderful life together. I have no regrets. We had two girls together. My eldest lives in Colorado. My youngest is in college in Michigan. I sold my company a few years back, and now I have too much free time on my hands. I think Rachel worries I'm lonely. Plus." He smiles. "She always loved a setup."

I recognize the grief in his eyes—the splinters in his eyes like cobwebs. "I'm sorry," I say. "About your wife."

"Thank you," he says simply.

"So that's why you wear your wedding band still," I realize in a quiet voice.

Thomas looks down at his left hand, as if surprised to see the ring there. "Well, yes. I suppose I should take it off. It's just . . ." He twists the gold ring off his finger and rests it in the palm of his hand. "It's sentimental to me," Thomas says, twirling the ring around. "We had it engraved with our kids' initials, and I guess I thought that taking it off would be erasing my wife's memory, and I don't want to do that."

Looking at his hand, I wonder what the palm reader from the other night would see. Would she see a line for Rose?

He shows me where the initials are engraved on the inside of the band.

"That's beautiful," I say. "We lost my Great-Aunt Lottie a year ago. I love it here in part because everything reminds me of her."

"I'm sorry," he says sadly, both of us aware of how futile and small the sentiment is compared to the insurmountable fact of grief. "She was a great woman."

"You knew her? I mean, I guess that makes sense. She must have been around the summer you met my mom."

"Only briefly," he says. "But I always admired her."

"It's strange because logically I know she was older. I know she was never going to live forever, but knowing that still didn't prepare me for the reality, you know?" Thomas nods. "Have you ever heard of the lifeboat theory?"

He shakes his head again.

"Essentially, it's the few people who are so essential to your life that you would need them on your hypothetical lifeboat. Even though I knew on an abstract level that we would lose Lottie someday, she was on my lifeboat. She was essential to me. Without her, I feel like I'm drowning."

I'm not sure why I'm telling this to someone who is a practical stranger, but Thomas has a reassuring presence, a steadiness and seriousness that make it easy to confide in him.

He pats me on the shoulder. "I understand," he says. "And I really am sorry."

We continue walking in silence for a moment, down the path. There's a historic home at the end that's been left abandoned. It's dilapidated, falling into itself. Everyone calls it the haunted house. The old rumor is that it was passed down in a family lineage until a rift split the remaining siblings apart. No one could decide who got to keep it, so it sat unused until it became decrepit. As a kid, I would hurry my bike past it, scared to look into the windows lest I see some phantom staring back at me.

I know Henry's house is coming up soon, too. The lot is so large it looks more like a military base than a home. There's a man-made pond meticulously maintained by the landscapers to look effortless. "The grounds," as they call it, must employ a team of thirty just to keep it looking natural, untouched. It's only a few doors down from here. He's the real ghost I should be afraid of. I answered his text last night.

Are you still engaged? I asked.

Yes, he sent back after a few minutes.

Then what do we have to talk about?

I saw the ". . ." of him typing before it disappeared. He still hasn't responded.

"So, what's next?" I ask Thomas now. "I mean, now that you're here. What do you want?"

"Honestly?" he says. "I'm not sure. I guess I wanted to check with you. Do you think Rose is happy? Do you think it's best if I leave?"

I consider the question. I know Rose is angry with him. I know she has resentments and regrets about the past, but does that mean she truly wishes he would leave? She said so the other night at the fundraiser, but I can't help but think that was her hurt speaking.

Here is her past love, miraculously appearing at our front door. Is that not something worth pursuing? Is that not something I would dream of? Henry returning, knocking on the door of the cottage . . .

Maybe Thomas is someone Rose needs on her lifeboat.

"Why did you fall in love with her?" I ask, testing him.

We stop to face each other. To our right, I can see the high hedges of Henry's parents' lawn: the wicker lawn chairs, the purple hydrangeas, the two-story wraparound porch we used to sit on and watch the sunset.

"Because . . ." He pauses to think. "Because she is selfless and smart. She's clever but never uses that cleverness against you. She's patient with everyone, even her father and sister. She's . . . she's good. I trust both her mind and her heart. She made me a better man." He looks toward the water. "Or, at least she used to be all of those things. I suppose I don't know her anymore."

"She still is," I rush to say. "She still has all of those amazing qualities and more, I promise."

His phone is in his front pocket and when it lights up with an incoming text, I sneak a peek at his lock screen. It's a photo of what I assume must be his children on a rocky beach in Maine, all teeth and crinkled eyes. He seems like a good dad, and I know that good dads aren't necessarily a given in this world.

For the first time, I really examine his face. It's a nice face with neat, orderly lines: a nose with a clean, even slope and two straight eyebrows like em dashes. He reminds me of a character in an old movie, someone who might say something like, "Ma'am, you're going to have to trust me."

I decide in that moment to do just that.

At least one of us deserves a happy ending, and there is no one more deserving of happiness than Rose. Besides, it was me who got in the way of their second chance. Maybe I can facilitate their third.

"No," I say. "I definitely don't think you should leave. Actually, I have an idea."

Chapter Thirteen

Rose

"Do you believe in second chances?"

"What?" I ask, trying to concentrate. I was up late last night at dinner with William again, and the lack of sleep is starting to affect me. "I mean, what do you mean by that?"

I'm currently in session with a new client of mine, a young mother who just left her husband. She has a newborn at home and is suffering from postpartum depression.

The first rule of therapy to avoid projecting on your clients. We call it "countertransference," when your own biases, experiences, and thoughts end up coloring the way you see a client. I know how damaging countertransference can be to the therapeutic relationship.

Still, it's hard not to see the resemblance to my own life.

"I know we can't repeat the past, but do you think it's ever okay to try again?" the client asks in a small, inquisitive voice.

Her name is Virginia, and she's in her midthirties. Virginia has dark brown hair, now pulled back into a ponytail, and bright blue eyes that look especially tired today. Her son, Teddy, still isn't sleeping through the night.

"Of course," I tell her. "But more importantly, do *you* believe in second chances? That's what really matters."

The bread and butter of talk therapy is something called the OARS method. Essentially through open-ended questions (O), affirmations (A), reflective listening (R), and summarizing (S), you encourage the client to create change.

It's a simple tool but sometimes it's the simplest stuff that is the most effective.

"I don't know," says Virginia. "I want to but I'm not sure if it's possible."

"What kind of second chance are we talking about here?"

I hope she's not talking about getting together with her ex-husband. Perhaps it's unprofessional to have such a biased view toward a relationship in my client's life, but again, it's difficult not to. Therapists who claim not to care about their clients are either callous sociopaths or liars. And from what Virginia has told me, her husband was emotionally abusive, often berating her about finances, her weight, and generally making her feel "not good enough."

When working with a client who you suspect is in an abusive relationship—or in Virginia's case, has recently left one—it's important to proceed carefully, tread lightly. I don't want to scare her away from opening up to me, and I still need to earn her trust. We've only been working together for a month now.

"I met someone new," says Virginia, looking at the floor. Even in the shadow of the overhead lighting, there's a sudden brightness to her expression.

Phew. "Oh, well that's great! Who is the lucky individual?"

She looks up at me with a sad smile. "He's just here for the summer, so it probably can't work."

The clinician in me takes note of the immediate pessimism. It's not easy learning how to be positive when the world has burned you. I mentally mark down that this is something we can work on together.

But simultaneously, the human in me irrationally thinks of Tommy. My breath somersaults. It's an illogical assumption—it's summer on Nantucket, after all! Of course, there are hundreds, thousands, of visitors. Tommy is by no means the only one. Still . . .

"You never know what a summer fling could turn into," I say from experience. "Tell me more about him. How did you two meet?"

"Well, he's renting in 'Sconset for a few weeks," Virginia says, twisting the drawstring of her sweatshirt in her left hand, a nervous gesture. "His name is . . ."

Please don't say Thomas. Please don't say Tommy. Please don't . . .

"His name is Michael," she finishes. "He lives in Rhode Island and we met while I was walking on the beach the other day."

Another phew. A wave of relief washes over me. I take a deep breath in, shifting in my chair.

"That's wonderful!" I say with real enthusiasm now. "Besides the summer ending, what are you afraid of?"

While I wait to start my own practice, I'm currently seeing clients through a group clinic down by the hospital. The rooms are stuffy and cramped. The carpet is a drab gray color, and despite the sound machines we have blasting, you can still catch snippets of other clinicians' conversations through the thin walls.

Every time I'm here, I'm reminded of why I want to go out on my own. Besides needing my own space, I yearn for the autonomy to make my own clinical decisions. Right now, the group practice I work for is strict about which insurances we do and do not accept. I've had to reject countless potential clients because they're on Medicare, Medicaid, or some other insurance we don't accept. I also have no ability to set my own rates or make exceptions for people who can't afford traditional treatment.

It's heartbreaking to reject someone in need, someone who has gone through the brave, often intimidating and confusing process of seeking therapy. It breaks my heart.

"I guess I'm afraid that he won't like me. Or, he'll be disappointed I have a kid. I just . . . I really don't want to get hurt again," says Virginia.

I settle into my chair. This is where the real work begins. When a client like Virginia is able to admit something vulnerable, we can begin to make change and challenge negative self-beliefs.

This is why I love my work. As a kid, I felt orphaned in the world. My sister and father sucked the air out of the room until I learned to take shallower, quieter breaths, blending in with the furniture. In my house growing up, every other sentence I mumbled was an apology. My father and sister were so alike in their grievances and pride. I was constantly disappointing them by simply existing. My mother passed before I was five. Lottie always claimed that we were alike, and I appreciated hearing that, but the truth is I'll never know. What I remember of my mother is vague, and it's not easy trying to love a ghost.

That's what made those summers with Lottie particularly magical. She asked me to come, and only me, not Elizabeth and not our dad. I was chosen, special for once. Lottie had her own ways of living, her own rules and moral codes, but there was a freedom to her, a wildness that was caged in my childhood house. Lottie could be strict. She would lecture me on ethics and values, but she was also playful. There would be music crooning from her record player, sand on the floor with no effort to vacuum it away. She and Charlie danced at night by the fire, so clearly in love it shone out of their heads like the beacon of a lighthouse. Seashells lined the windowsills, books left dog-eared on the mantel. There was a simultaneous fluidity and rigidity to Lottie that contradicted itself, pulled and pushed at the edges of who she was, making it impossible to get a clear read.

Why did no one tell me that grief would be this physically painful?

It's like my spine is a Jenga tower and every time I remember that Lottie is gone for good, one of the blocks dislodges and my whole body crumples down with it.

Spending those summers with Lottie was the only time I felt close to my mother again. My aunt would tell me stories about her, stories that brought her back to life and confirmed all of my hazy half memories with color. Lottie, my mother's sister, was my sole comfort, my closest confidant. She never had her own children, so she considered me like a daughter. I was grateful for that.

I know what it's like to feel misunderstood, to feel truly alone in the world. If I can give that comfort to someone else—even a fraction of the immeasurable blessing Lottie gave to me of making me feel seen—I know I have done something good with my life.

"Let's explore that thought some more," I say, leaning in.

Lily is gone when I arrive back home three hours and two sessions later, probably still working at her new job or looking for photography clients. I'm proud of how hard she's working. It's no easy feat to start back at square one.

When I approach the front door, I also notice that Tommy is nowhere to be found. The windows of the side cottage are open but no one is inside.

I don't know why I immediately thought of him today with Virginia. It was such a comically illogical thought. I shouldn't care anyway because I have something budding with William, something that could be real. It's been ten days since our first date, and already, we've seen each other four more times. My first impression was wrong. He's been a perfect gentleman. He calls when he says he will; schedules elaborate, romantic, albeit over-the-top dates; and most importantly, he is eager to know Lily. I told him I'll introduce them when the time is right. For now, I want to leave her out of it, even though I feel guilty lying.

I pause on the doorstep of the breezeway, turning to look in Tommy's windows again like some Peeping Tom. One of the only drawbacks of the remodel is that Lottie's bookcase, the one my Uncle Charlie built her, is on the guest side of the property. I've left her books there, knowing she'd be thrilled to have visitors read them, but that means Lily and I don't have access to them ourselves. I've already grabbed my favorites for the summer, but I miss browsing them, flipping through random pages and reading the lines she thought important enough to underline. She always loved the dedications most of all. Some of the pages even smell like her perfume.

Would it be so wrong if I went in now, while Tommy is out, and took a look? Surely, that's within my rights as the property manager?

Moral quandaries battle in my brain as I remain standing there. Eventually, curiosity wins. I'll grab a book, make sure he's using coasters and not leaving wet towels on the hardwood or exhibiting any of the other bad habits renters often display, and be on my merry way.

Quietly, I open his side of the cottage and walk in.

To his credit, Tommy has kept the main room remarkably clean. It must be a remnant of his time in the Coast Guard. There are no stray beach towels or clumps of sand. Everything is pristine. The bookshelf, however, has certainly been used. Lottie's beloved books dot the living room like sunflowers popping out of the garden. An open copy left on the armchair, another on the hallway bench.

Well, if he has this much time for reading, maybe he's not dating after all.

I grab a book from the shelf—one of Lottie's favorite beach reads—and am about to leave when I catch sight of her old desk in the guest bedroom. The drawer is half ajar. Clearly, Tommy has made himself quite at home.

It seems wrong that he'd be here, using her old furniture.

I creep into the room and open up the drawer. What is he possibly keeping in here? There are random receipts, a journal that even I have the boundary to not open, and miscellaneous menus for takeout places.

Disappointed, I go to put the drawer back but it's stuck. I push it again but it keeps sticking. The humidity of the ocean air must have bent the old wood.

I hear someone approaching. My heartbeat quickens.

"I can't wait to see you, too," says Tommy from outside the front door. I figure he's talking to someone on the phone, because I can't hear the response. "August can't come soon enough, sweetie."

I jam the desk again, shoving it in with my shoulder. Shoot, shoot, shoot. He's going to catch me and then he'll know I'm snooping through his things like a stalker. Could he complain to the real estate office? Have me banned from renting out my property? Silently, I curse myself for not looking more into tenant law.

A quieter but more urgent question rises through the panic: Who exactly is he calling sweetie?

"I'll call you again tomorrow?" says Tommy. His keys are in the door. I hear them jingling. Crap, crap, crap. "Same time?"

With one final surge of strength, I shove the drawer closed, but in the process, something else dislodges. From underneath the desk, a piece of paper flits down. It's a bit crumpled, but on it is Lottie's unmistakable handwriting.

Quickly, I grab it from the floor, shut the door, and sprint to the back patio. I make it to the side door of our cottage just as Tommy is entering. Through the wall, I hear a long, belabored sigh.

My chest feels like it's caving in as I lean against the door to our place. Only when I'm safe on my own side of the cottage do I look down at the paper.

"The Last Summer Bucket List," reads Lottie's writing on the top. Underneath it are ten items.

Chapter Fourteen

The Last Summer Bucket List

1. Watch the sunrise at Siasconset Beach.
2. Drive to Great Point Lighthouse.
3. Get onstage at the Chicken Box.
4. Win pickleball tournament.
5. Go whale watching.
6. Visit the Loines Observatory.
7. Have a beach picnic.
8. Name the cottage.
9. Crash a wedding.
10. Do something brave.

Chapter Fifteen

Lily

June 16

Theo is already waiting on the pickleball court when we arrive on Thursday, balancing a neon-yellow ball on the center of his paddle. When he sees the two of us approaching, the ball falls off and rolls to the corner of the court. An expression crosses his face like a shadow, but before I can place it, he is grinning again. He runs to the ball before it intrudes on a neighboring court's game. As he lopes after it, he reminds me, bizarrely, of Josie's old golden retriever, all long limbs and energy.

"Hey, you two." He waves, approaching my mom for a hug and giving me a high five. I meet his hand limply, which makes our palms stick together. "I didn't know I had two customers today."

"We've decided to compete in the tournament in August, so I thought it would be best if we practiced as a team," I tell him. "I'm sorry, I should have mentioned that."

Rose told me about the bucket list she found in Lottie's old desk on Saturday while I was out talking to Tommy.

"And why exactly were you there? In the rental cottage?" I asked.

"Ignore that part," Rose said. "But we have to do it. Right? I mean, I didn't know if you'd ever be back here for a full season. This is our chance to live the perfect summer Lottie dreamed of."

Rose's eyes were wet, and the thought of Lottie writing down this secret wish list brought me to tears, too. Why hadn't she told us? We could've helped her complete the list.

"When do you think she wrote this?" I asked.

Clearly, Lottie thought herself physically well enough to compete in a pickleball tournament, but she was also somehow certain it would be her last summer. The more this summer has progressed, the less I seem to understand Mom, Lottie, and even myself.

"I'm not sure," said Mom. "But are you in?"

Of course I was. Secretly, I wondered if I could somehow incorporate my plan with Thomas into the bucket list . . . if I can use it as a way to get them together. He's skeptical of my meddling, but I'm determined. First, I'm trying to ease Rose into it, figure out her feelings toward him and wait for the anger to settle.

I figured Theo's offer to teach me pickleball was serendipitous, so I picked her up on my way home from work and asked her to join.

"A tournament?" asks Theo now. The ball he's balancing freezes in the center of his paddle. "Isn't that a little ambitious? Have either of you ever even played before?"

"We're quick learners," says Rose. "And it's a long story. Are you sure it's fine if I crash?"

Theo waves off her concern but avoids eye contact. "Of course it's okay." He inspects his paddle, hitting it against the palm of his hand as if to make sure it won't spontaneously combust.

"I just couldn't stay away from my little friend!" Rose pokes him teasingly in the stomach, and her tone makes Theo smile, and then all at once, everything is normal again.

We practice dinking first. I have to bend down in order to get my paddle low enough on the ball. It's strange getting used to how light the ball is. Every time I go to hit a ground stroke, it flies out of bounds.

For this reason, Theo has taken to calling me "Muscles."

"Hey, Muscles!" he calls out. "Take your aggression out elsewhere."

Or, "Hey, Muscles! A little too much strength behind that one."

This makes Rose laugh, a lot. Admittedly, it makes me laugh, too.

He's a good teacher, patient and engaging. I can immediately see why he's in high demand at the club. He makes it fun, inventing silly games and showing overexaggerated enthusiasm whenever one of us hits a good shot. At one point, he tries to lift Rose into the air after her overhead lands directly on the baseline. "We've got ourselves a WINNER!" he screams, running in circles around her.

A foursome two courts down looks up, startled.

It's also amusing to see how he dresses when he's not on the job: neither in his bartender getup nor his tennis whites. Today he's wearing what look to be jean shorts and a white T-shirt with green writing that says, "Sweet Pickle Books: New York's Best Pickle Bookstore."

When I ask him about the ensemble, he's eager to explain.

"These shorts took me forever to find," Theo says. "They're almost exactly like the Nike jorts Andre Agassi wore to the 1988 US Open. But these are a fake denim printed on athletic shorts, so they don't chafe." He winks again. I'm starting to wonder if the winks are meaningless, almost a reflex, or perhaps even a twitch.

About the shirt, he says it's his favorite bookstore in New York.

"And I thought it fit the theme because we're playing pickleball today. Get it?" He gestures back and forth between the shirt and the pickleball paddle, emphasizing the connection in case we didn't get it at first.

"You are such an odd boy," Rose responds, shaking her head with amusement.

After the hour is up, we sit for a break on a bench in the shade. Rose checks her phone, pulling it out of a crowded beach bag amidst a sea of lip balms and old receipts.

"Shoot!" she says. "Client emergency, I have to leave now. Sorry, guys. Lily, any chance you can get a ride home from Theo?"

He nods eagerly. "Oh yeah. It's no problem."

Rose turns to him before running off. "Thank you for everything, Theo. You're a delight." He waves her off with a salute as she hurries to the car.

In the wake of her absence, there's a shift in atmosphere, an intensity. I tighten my ponytail and take a long drag of water. Theo and I have been hanging out during every shift at the club. He'll come by every hour and chat for a few minutes or offer to help me with one of the front desk tasks during his break. He's already become a friend, but still, it feels different seeing him outside of work.

"So, you invited your mom on our first date," he says. He bounces his left knee, shaking the entire bench. "I've got to say, still not one of my worst first dates. What does that say about me?"

His tone is light, but I feel a squeezing sensation in my temples, like I've been stuffed in a vacuum. When will I stop letting everyone down?

"I didn't think you were being serious about that. I'm sorry." I try to look him directly in the eyes but he's squinting toward the sun, just behind my back. "If I had thought it was a date, I wouldn't have brought her."

"Nah, I was just joking," says Theo, playfully punching my arm. "We're pals, right? Coworkers and now pickleball legends."

He lifts his arms in the air, interlacing his fingers and cracking his neck. Afterward, he shakes them loose.

There was a part of me that hoped behind all the jokes was something real. And today, seeing how much my mom enjoys him, it had all felt so natural and easy—more than anything in my life has felt lately. But then I think about Emily, their casual closeness. Maybe she's the one he likes, or maybe he's this flirty with everyone and I'm a fool for thinking there's more behind it. Besides, I'm in no emotional shape to date. It would only complicate everything.

I stand and start to stretch for something to do. "Right," I say, not looking at him. "We're 'little friends.'" The callback makes him chuckle. "Anyway, I should be getting home. I have some work to do. Would you mind driving me?"

"Work to do?" he asks. Am I imagining it, or is there a note of disappointment?

"Yeah," I respond. "I've been getting back into drawing. I went on a walk earlier with my camera, and for the first time in a while, I felt inspired. I want to do some sketching this afternoon and follow up on some more emails inquiring about job openings."

In the two and a half weeks since I've been back on island, I've developed a new schedule: I get up before work and paint. Or I draw. Or I go for a walk and take photographs to paint later. The medium doesn't matter, the point is I'm back in the mood to create. It's a tremendous transformation.

"That's so cool," he says.

Earlier today I felt that familiar quickening in my heart again that comes with excitement for a new project. I used to hum when I was a little girl drawing at the dining room table. I was so happy, euphoric even, I couldn't keep it in. I felt such a sense of joy I would lose myself for hours, not realizing that I had begun to sing. My ankles locked together, swinging to the beat. I loved watching the disparate parts of a project come together; how, once it was created, it felt almost inevitable, predestined, and mathematically perfect.

The other night at the beach, the sun was setting and there were these three little girls playing tag, their parents watching on lounge chairs a few yards away. The girls' small frames became black silhouettes against the orange sun and without second-guessing myself, I took their photo. Later, I approached the parents and offered to send it to their emails so they wouldn't think I was some creep, but there was something in that image that touched me.

Innocence, I realized later when I was editing. It looked like innocence. Strangely, of all things, it makes me think of Theo.

I want to try to paint it today.

On the ride home, Theo asks more questions about my work. I tell him about getting fired, even though I'm still ashamed of the story.

"Getting fired is like getting dumped," says Theo. "Everyone should try it once. It builds character. Besides, you have to stop waiting for permission to create from the outside world. No one's going to give it to you. You have to go out and grab it for yourself."

I can't help but be affected by being in the small car with him. Usually, at work, there's a desk separating us. Here, he feels closer than ever.

Theo is borrowing one of the other instructor's cars today, a vintage beach Bronco with tan leather seats and a bright-blue exterior. For his sake as well as my own, I hope he's a good driver, because every inch of this vehicle would cost a fortune to replace. Still, it's nice being here. I feel a sense of contentment down to my fingertips, with the windows open, the top down, the warm air blowing in. Now that it's mid-June, the island is in bloom.

"When did you know you loved painting?" Theo asks, one hand on the steering wheel.

"I think I've always known, since I first held a paintbrush, but I didn't know I was allowed to really want it."

"What do you mean?"

"I didn't know it was possible to make a life doing what I loved. I still don't. But I've never loved painting the appropriate amount."

"Who decides what's the 'appropriate amount' to love something?" he asks.

"I guess I just mean that the way I felt about it was almost . . . violent."

"Violent?" Theo laughs.

"Yeah, I felt like my ambition, even as a little girl, was somehow wrong. Sometimes, I feel like what I'm doing is silly. I'm drawing pretty pictures, you know? I'm not curing world hunger, or trying to stop a war, or attending a protest, or doing what Rose does for her clients. Often, I'll scroll through my phone and see all of these videos of everything wrong with society, people suffering, and I feel helpless. Does art matter? Can it afford to? But also, can it afford not to? I'm not doing anything tangible that would really matter or help anyone, and yet, it feels urgent to me. When I'm painting or drawing, it feels like the only thing that matters even though I know, logically, it isn't. Does that make sense?"

I'm rambling now, and I trail off at the end, embarrassed, but Theo takes it in stride.

"I know what you mean," he says. "When I was trying to go pro, I felt like the tennis world was the only place that mattered. There was nothing better than hitting that perfect shot, feeling the ball against the racket and knowing I could command it to land exactly where I wanted it to. It was . . ." He searches for the right word. "Beautiful."

I know exactly what he means, too. There's something defiant about creating beauty in an ugly world, about prioritizing it as essential.

"When did you decide against going pro?"

Theo laughs. "It's less like I decided against it, and more that it decided against me. Pretty early on in my teen years I realized my limit. I was good enough to get a scholarship to college, but I was never going to make it to the US Open." He shrugs. "But that's okay. It took me weeks to learn how to love it again even though I know I'll never hit that highest rung. Time to figure out a new dream."

I think about what he's saying. I can picture a younger version of Theo easily: fluffier hair, even lankier limbs. I imagine him at predawn practices, dedicated to his craft, and the crushing disappointment of knowing that no matter how hard he worked, it wasn't enough. I wonder if that's what it's like for me with art, if I just don't have it. At least art is something without such a harsh age limit.

"Have you figured out a new dream yet?" I ask him.

Theo looks over at me, his uneven smile on full display. "Still figuring it out."

There's something liberating in that, I think. Allowing yourself to dream a new dream. I thought the magazine world would be the destination I always hoped for, but now, I realize that it wasn't. Actually, maybe it was holding me back.

We stop speaking, but the silence is comforting rather than awkward. I take the opportunity to ask him about his T-shirt again.

"I didn't know you lived in New York," I point out, almost accusingly.

His eyes remain fixed on the road. "Yeah, I graduated from University of North Carolina in 2018 and moved to the city. I did Teach for America for a year in the Bronx. I worked a few administrative nonprofit jobs afterward in fundraising and such, but I realized that what I really love is teaching."

I nod to myself. "I can see that. You're a really great teacher."

"Thank you." He smiles. "I actually got admitted into a couple master of education programs. I'm taking this gap year before I start my degree."

I look at him, surprised by this revelation. "What're you going to do during your gap year?"

He pauses like he wants to say more, but then just shrugs. "Travel, I suppose. Teach more tennis, like I'm doing here. Lots of places like Nantucket will pay for your housing if you teach, which is a major bonus. I'm hoping to take the time to make sure I really want to do this degree before I invest in all of these loans to pay for it."

"That's amazing."

I've been so busy rushing to the next accomplishment, so hard on myself for not abiding by the strict timelines society has arbitrarily set. My friends in New York are like this, too. They are always in a rush: for a corporate promotion, an engagement ring. It's nice to be around someone who wants to take his time and figure it out. Refreshing.

The roads are growing busier as the summer season deepens. We're behind a moped: A woman in an impractical dress sits behind a man, orange-and-white fabric billowing behind her. Her helmet is the same shade of blue as the car.

I take a mental image to try to re-create the scene later: the angle of the sun hitting the woman's brown hair, the way her dress rumples in the wind. I could use a dark brown to create the shadows, and the blue sky would be a nice mix of purple and yellow and white . . .

"You know." Theo clears his throat, interrupting my planning."There's a big bonfire tonight at Ladies Beach. Some people from work are going if you want to come?"

I haven't been to a bonfire since I was nineteen. We used to sneak out with Henry's friends to the old dump, the landfill in Madaket, at night and scavenge among the furniture people threw away. We would toss wooden chairs over the high metal fence, breaking them into pieces on the asphalt and then use the smaller pieces for firewood. Bonfires are technically permitted on the island during open burning season, but you need to request a permit, which we never did. Someone would drive a car onto a secluded beach, dig a deep pit in the sand. We would drink cheap beers by the blaze.

I didn't feel bad spending nights like that back then. I had all the time in the world. Nothing counted and everything could be undone. It would be nice to feel that way again, to let Theo's ease crash over me. It would be nice to sit side by side, talking just like this, with the fire warming our skin.

"Sure," I say. "That sounds fun. When should I meet you?"

Chapter Sixteen

Lily

My sandals dig into the soft, cool sand. It's just after nine, and the only light is from the stars and the moon, like an eggshell above the water in the distance. The waves are calm as bathwater. I'm wearing an oversized sweater and rolled-up jeans.

The beach looks navy blue in this light, transformed into a foreign planet with unknown divots and grooves. My mom dropped me off here, which felt juvenile for a twenty-five-year-old, so I asked her to pull over a few yards away to avoid being seen. That, of course, only made me feel even more juvenile and also like a jerk.

"Have fun, honey!" she yelled from the open car window as she drove off—my punishment. "Be good, Lily-pad!"

In the distance, I can hear the clamor of the bonfire. I walk past the tall dunes, toward the light of the fire. It's bigger than any I've been to before. About fifty people are milling around, chatting in small groups. Someone brought a speaker, and a popular song from a few summers ago is blasting, drowning out the waves.

At first, I don't see Theo, so I head over to the pit. Even in the thick sweater, I'm cold. I place my hands near the flames to warm up. I spot Emily, the tennis instructor from Hawaii, by the water, but she's talking to a pretty blond girl. I search the crowd for other familiar faces and come up empty.

I'm considering leaving, running back to catch up with my mom, when I hear someone call my name.

"Lily?" says a man's voice. It's deeper and smoother than Theo's. Henry.

Why does this keep happening to me? I know Nantucket is a small town, but these days, it feels more like a movie set: actors popping out from behind props, a jump scare.

"Oh, hi," I say, turning around to face him. "It's good to see you."

He looks good in the dim light. I can't help but notice that he's wearing the faded red sweatshirt I bought him several summers ago when I was still working at the shop.

"What're you doing here?" he asks, smiling through squinted eyes. It's like he's making an appraisal.

The intimacy and intensity of his gaze makes me want to duck behind a sand dune. I can't look at him and not see the past, everything we used to be to one another. That's the weird part about losing someone: the useless memories that no longer serve you. It's like knowing a dead language and having no one to speak it with.

I can still recall the way Henry always spoke with his hands, moving them in circles in the air as if solving a complicated puzzle no one else could see. I know his favorite pair of socks with the soccer balls on them, and the smell of his sweatshirt, stiff from the cold air. I remember the time I saw him hold out his umbrella to cover someone else's dog on the sidewalk when we were paused at a New York City crosswalk in the rain, and how it was the sweetest gesture I had ever seen.

Whenever I hear love discussed in media, it's often described by the concept of tension and lust, dreamy men with "liquid eyes" who smell like pine needles or something else ridiculous. It was never like that for me. When I think about what I miss most about Henry, it's the familiarity, the friendship. It's the intimacy of truly knowing each other, especially the unromantic bits.

I'm so caught up in the past, I forget his question.

"Sorry," I say, shaking my head. "What did you say?"

Henry laughs. "I asked what brought you here."

"Oh, Theo invited me."

"Who's Theo?" he asks.

From behind him, I hear, "That would be me."

Theo walks to stand between us, extending a hand to Henry, which he ignores. Theo drapes an arm carelessly over my shoulders, as if he's done it a hundred times. I try to stop the irrational heat from rising to my cheeks.

"And how did you two meet?" asks Henry, arms folded. He's built more solid than Theo, who despite the constant tennis playing is still skinny, but Theo is taller.

"We work together," I quickly answer. "At the club."

"You work at the yacht club?" His tone is edgier than I'm used to. "What happened to your real job?"

He sounds on the verge of scoffing, and suddenly, I'm embarrassed—not for myself, but on behalf of him. Before I can answer and explain how I was fired, Theo is speaking.

"Oh, she only joined to help us out a bit while she works on becoming the next great American artist." He squeezes my shoulders as if in premature congratulations.

His words are slightly slurred—I wonder how many beers he's already drank. There's a container of Gripah from Cisco sloshing in the hand over my shoulder. "I'm getting my autograph framed ahead of time. It'll be worth more than gold someday."

Theo winks at Henry.

"I know all about Lily's art," says Henry, his stance widening. "And when exactly did you two meet?"

Theo and I answer simultaneously.

"About two weeks ago," I say at the same time Theo says, "It feels like forever!"

Henry laughs again. It's a cold, harsh sound. "Right. Well, Lily and I go way back. We've known each other since we were eighteen."

I look at Theo. "We used to date," I explain, an apology in my voice.

"I see," says Theo. I feel the weight of his arm lift from my shoulders. "Well, there are a few people I want to introduce Lily to, but it was nice meeting you, dude."

Theo takes me by the hand and leads me away from Henry. I turn to see he's still watching us, the fire reflected in his eyes. My sandals catch on the sand, and I almost trip into a log a few people are sitting on. One of the boys looks up to give me a disgruntled look. He's wearing a baseball cap despite the fact that there's no sun to shield.

"Sorry, sorry," I say but my voice isn't loud enough to carry over the music and the roar of the ocean and the crackle of the fast-burning wood.

An hour and two beers later, my insides have loosened. Theo introduces me to a few other employees of the club, and we all talk in a group off to the side downwind from the bonfire. Emily approaches and asks Theo to go on a walk, and as I watch them stroll away I feel a fissure in my chest like the aftershock of a larger earthquake.

In the conversation with Henry, Theo seemed almost like a possessive boyfriend. While I didn't exactly love the obnoxious display of toxic masculinity, it at least seemed clear what his intention was, but now, he's off with Emily. I can't see them in the dim light, but I know they must be only a few yards away.

I check to see if Henry's fiancée is around. I don't see her, but Becca is across the way. Normally, I'd go over to talk with her, but she's sitting with a few tiny girls with tight, slicked-back buns and gold, dangly earrings. I know who they are without needing an introduction: Henry's home friends. The only true upside of our breakup is that I never have to force conversation with any of them again.

I wave Becca over, but she points to the girls next to her as an excuse not to get up. I hope this doesn't mean she's mad at me, too. For not the first time this summer, I wish Jade was here. If Jade was around, we'd laugh together about the awkwardness of the situation. She might have called Henry a jerk or made fun of the way Theo postured, but she would be there for me. I know that.

One of the biggest shocks of my adult life has been how easy it is to lose people, to let them slide away. Keeping someone around takes dedication: It's the exception, not the rule.

"Hi, Lily-pad," says Henry, appearing behind me. "Can we go somewhere to talk?"

The fire softens his expression, rounds out the angles of his face. He looks like the Henry I know, the one I still love. But he's not. He is someone else's Henry now, and I need to remember that.

"Talk about what?"

He steps closer. "I don't know, anything. Let's catch up." Henry reaches for the sleeve of my sweater. "It's been too long."

"You're engaged," I remind him.

"So, that means we can't be friends anymore?"

"We were never friends, Henry."

He throws his hands in the air. "Come on, Lily. You're being ridiculous! Let's just go talk over there." He points to the dunes behind us, half cast in light. "Somewhere private."

"Why does it need to be private?"

I look over at his high school friends, who I can tell are straining to eavesdrop. There was always a distance between me and them. Once, I overheard the ringleader, Julie Evans, say that Henry was "settling" for me. We were at a house party that first summer and I was rounding the corner of the kitchen. "She's a local," she said with a scrunched nose. "I think her mom is a social worker or something."

It took every ounce of resolve I had not to pour a beer over her head.

"It doesn't need to be private," says Henry. "I just don't want a whole audience."

After my father left my mom when I was a year old, he ended up marrying the woman he cheated on her with. They moved to Los Angeles together, and his family bought his way into the film industry as a small-time producer. His wife's name is Maren but I can only ever think of her as "the Mistress." The Mistress sometimes came along on my father's trips to visit us. As a kid, I didn't really know any better, so we got along fine. But once I learned who she was and what she had done to Rose, I was determined to give her the cold shoulder.

Still, I checked her social media sometimes. She posted dramatic, inspirational quotes about fate and destiny with hot-pink lettering. My father has been trying (and failing) to get sober since before I was alive. The Mistress liked to chronicle these various attempts at sobriety on her public page, taking selfies in front of the overpriced rehab centers.

I used to wish the Mistress harm. I didn't want to be the one who hurt her, and I didn't want anything truly terrible to happen, but I would stay up in bed at night and imagine small jinxes: fender benders, hair burning off in a freak accident at the salon, a beer bottle chipping her front tooth. Until one day, I checked her Facebook page and saw she had gotten into a car accident. She was fine, but I was spooked. I stopped with the hexes after that but kept my grudges.

Psychic or not, soulmates or not, I will not play the role of the other woman. I might be a mess, but I'm not a cheater. I will not, I can't—

"Please, Lily," says Henry.

His eyes look red-tinged in the light of the fire, as if he's been crying. I always liked Henry the most when he wasn't feeling well; if he hurt himself or was under the weather, it made him more sympathetic somehow.

"Let's just talk," he pleads.

He points to a dark spot by the edge of the dunes, pockets of tall seagrass sprouting from the sand, creating a covering of sorts.

Behind us, I can sense Theo watching intently, can feel his eyes on the back of my neck, burning like shame.

Every structure is subject to instability. That's what Lottie liked to say. She used to lean on certain phrases to contain truths as if they were the only pillars upholding her moral interiority, keeping her thin understanding of the world from collapsing into itself. Every structure is subject to instability, and sometimes all it takes is one bad decision to make the whole world fall.

"Fine," I say. "Let's talk."

Chapter Seventeen

Lily

June 17

It is well after two a.m. when I return home.

I tiptoe through the cottage, avoiding the floorboards that creak. Curiously, I notice a light still lit on Thomas's side.

My hair smells heavily of smoke and wood. I hold my sandals bunched together in my left hand. Over my sweater is Henry's worn, red sweatshirt.

He gave it back to me on the ride home and insisted I keep it. I wonder why—did he want me to have a reminder of him? Or was he eager to rid himself of any vestige of me? Does the difference matter? Or better yet, should it matter? Can it matter anymore?

We talked for longer than we should have.

At first, we danced around the subject of his fiancée, Mary. I still have a hard time thinking of her name. It's too familiar. But eventually, Henry brought up the wedding festivities, the drama between their two families, Mary's expensive tastes somehow conflicting with Henry's mother's equally expensive taste. It was unavoidable.

"It's been a lot of back and forth about the stupidest stuff," he said, rolling his eyes. "Last week, we actually got into a fight about whether the beige tablecloths should be 'sand-toned' or 'camel-toned.' I don't know. Sometimes, I wonder if it was all a mistake. Maybe we're just too young."

I shrugged, digging into the cold sand. "There's actually a big difference between sand-toned beige and camel-toned beige," I said, thinking of my painting palette. "But should we really be talking about this? It feels wrong."

The beer and the vertigo were making the dunes look jumpy. Their hunched backs moving behind Henry's head like sea creatures writhing beneath the long grass. I worried a panic attack was rising, my breathing becoming shallow. What was I doing?

He nodded in a noncommittal way. "Anyway, I was thinking of Lottie the other day, about that time when we all went whale watching and how she kept trying to take photos with her crappy camera but they turned out all blurry. Remember, how you secretly took your own pictures before you got too seasick? Did you ever frame it for her like you said you would?"

Hearing Lottie's name thawed me instantly. The dunes stopped shaking. It was easy to be carried away by the past, like letting myself be washed ashore.

I told him about the bucket list we found.

"That's wild," he said. "You have to complete it, right? For Lottie."

I agreed. "That's what we thought, too. It's almost like she wanted us to find it."

"Absolutely," he said. "Lottie was always sort of witchy that way. I can imagine her still pulling strings from the other side."

I laughed, feeling a surge of love. Here was the Henry I fell in love with, the one who would sit in the garden with Lottie and help water her flowers while the mist rolled in every morning like an act of God and then scattered into sunshine by noon. When I looked at

Henry, I missed Lottie's laugh, and the soap operas she watched, and the cherry tree she planted in my great-uncle's name and how its little white flowers batted its eyes against the windowpane in the kitchen bathroom.

I missed the levity of a wide-open future, all of our big dreams in a world still big enough to fit them. Anything was possible. We had youthful ignorance on our side—impossible to bet against it.

I miss everything I can never get back.

Toward the end of the night, he asked about my job again. "You know if you ever need help finding a new gig, my father has a lot of friends at Sotheby's. He'd be happy to make some introductions."

"Henry," I said. "Thank you, but you know I can't." He had offered the same to me before, years ago, but I didn't want to take a favor or cheat the system. I didn't want to owe his family like that, either, or always wonder if my success was only because of my boyfriend.

Now I wondered if I was being a fool.

When we walked out of the party, Theo was drinking a beer with the tennis crowd. I waved him goodbye, but he didn't return the gesture, so I let my hand drop back to my side, limp and uncertain.

I hope he's not mad at me.

I try to sleep now, but I can't stop smelling the bonfire smoke that still clings to my hair and skin. I consider taking a shower, but I'm worried it will wake up Rose, so instead, I lie awake in the twin bed. There's a dampness to the ocean air coming through the window.

I keep thinking, What would Mary say if she knew?

I feel guilty for talking to Henry. Even though we technically didn't do anything wrong, it was still a moral trespass.

I imagine when he tells her the story of this night, I'll be erased from the picture, and the thought makes me feel dirty.

I'm done, I decide. I'm not going to talk to him again. What's passed is past, and there's nothing to do about it now. I will not be complicit. I will not be the Mistress.

I was eighteen years old when I met Henry, and I didn't know if I could recognize my own face if I happened across it in a crowd. That's what I really wanted out of romance back then: for someone to hold my face between the palms of their hands and simply say, "I see you." And then in the process of being seen, maybe I could finally catch a glimpse of myself, too.

When I miss him, this is what I miss most: being known, feeling seen.

But it's over. It has to be. Tonight was a mistake, but I'm done. I'm done.

I'm done.

Over the course of the next week, I do everything I can to put Henry out of my mind. I am determined to turn over a new leaf, to become someone Lottie would be proud of. Whenever I recall the bonfire, Lottie's face floats into my mind's eye and I shudder at what she would think.

"If you play with fire, don't be surprised if you get burned," I imagine her saying.

When I return to work the day after, I receive a chilly welcome.

"Hi, Theo!" I call out to him, placing my bag on the front desk. "How was the rest of your night after the bonfire?"

Theo is walking out the door when I catch him, and he pauses, looking torn. He's in his tennis whites again, and he twirls the racket between his hands, catching it before it can fall. I follow the worn yellow tape as it jumps in the air.

"Fine," he says, avoiding my eyes. "I have a lesson, but I'll catch you later."

My next shift continues like this. He isn't ever outright rude, but he's stopped taking his lunch breaks at my desk, and he no longer goes out of his way to tease me. I don't understand what I did wrong to upset him except for talking with Henry, but the absence of his friendship hurts. I was starting to rely on him.

I decide to channel my extra alone time into work. I still haven't heard from Marie Chen, the gallery owner, since I sent her over another copy of my résumé. I still haven't received any responses to my flyers.

Almost out of boredom, I start going through some of my old work on my iPad and come across a picture I took of Lottie a few summers back, before she received her diagnosis. In the photo, Lottie is bent over in the garden, hands in the soil, dirt up to her wrists. The way the light is hitting her face makes it look like there is a spotlight on her, illuminating her in some sort of heavenly, impossible glow, like a halo.

I start playing around with the composition, highlighting certain colors and creating more of a contrast with the plants.

"Beauty takes work to sustain," Lottie used to say, so I write the phrase across the image. With a stylus, I add in some drawings of flowers wrapped around her wrists, climbing up her arms. The earth is rich and dark. It's the kind of photo you can smell: sulfuric and metallic.

Only after I'm finished do I realize it looks like the earth is grabbing Lottie, pulling her under.

The next day—coincidentally on the nineteenth of June, Father's Day, my least favorite holiday—Thomas and I meet again. We're walking the bluff again, this time all the way to Sankaty lighthouse. It sits firmly in the distance, waiting: red-striped, like a lollipop planted by a child.

"I don't know," he says. "She seems happy. We shouldn't get involved."

In the last couple of days, it's become obvious my mom is seeing someone, although she's trying to hide it. She keeps leaving the house for "business dinners," and I once saw her get into a red convertible that was parked on one of the small side streets near our cottage. What I don't understand is why she's hiding it from me.

Besides, she's been too busy for the bucket list.

I spend so much of the year worried about my mom, out here on this island alone, and then when I'm finally able to be back, Rose is off with someone else. This is something people with siblings will never understand. There's the stereotype of an only child being selfish because they never had to share, but they also never had anyone to share the burden of worry with either.

"I know my mom," I say confidently, wondering if the sentiment is true. "She still cares about you."

Thomas looks at me. "Do you really think I should be here? I feel like I'm trespassing."

Behind us, I can hear the roar of the ocean, particularly angry today. As I stare at him, he reminds me, bizarrely and all at once, of my favorite history teacher. Mr. Meyers had scruffy gray hair and thick brown glasses and engaged in easy repartee with the students that never bordered on creepy or inappropriate like some of the younger male faculty. He never felt like our friend but everyone trusted him just the same. Maybe we trusted him more because of it, because of his clearly defined boundaries. I used to secretly wish he was my dad. Every parent-teacher night, I would pray for a connection to spark between him and Rose.

"You can't give up," I say to Thomas. "Remember what you said about my mom? Just give me one chance, please. I'll get the two of you together in a room, you can talk, and if there's nothing still there, I promise I won't interfere again."

"Fine," he says, sounding exasperated. "One chance."

We keep walking. A group of tourists pass by, forcing us into the bushes. The path is too narrow to accommodate all of us at once. I wonder if I should give them one of the flyers I made, offer my photography services.

"What are you doing next weekend?" I ask Thomas.

"I'm going to a wedding, actually," he says. "My old friend from the Coast Guard extended a last-minute invite to his daughter's ceremony. He told me to invite my sister, too. She's arriving tonight for a few days."

In the shade, Thomas looks years younger, the stress lines around his eyes disappearing.

"A wedding?" I repeat, smiling to myself. I have an idea. "That could be perfect."

Thomas frowns at me. "Perfect for what?"

"Well, I told you about Lottie's bucket list, right?"

"Yes?"

"Number nine says to 'crash a wedding.'" I smile mischievously, waiting for him to connect the dots. "Two birds, one stone."

"Lily," he says, sounding suddenly like a stern father. Again, the image of Mr. Meyers returns. "You cannot crash my friend's daughter's wedding."

"We wouldn't cause a scene or anything! I swear. It's a perfect opportunity to get the two of you together in a romantic setting, and we'll be super discreet about it."

"I don't know," he says. "This sounds like a recipe for disaster."

"Trust me," I assure him again. "Please."

He hesitates before responding. The tourists pass, their phones pointed to record the clapboard houses, flags whipping in the wind, and the ocean churning to our left. I can imagine their reactions—seeing the island in all its glory for the first time. A couple poses for a staged kiss. I imagine how quickly their trip is passing, the way summer always flashes forward for those in love.

"Fine," he agrees reluctantly. "I'll send you the information."

I jump up and down. "Yes!" I yelp. "This is going to be so much fun." A few of the tourists look back at us to check out the commotion. I shoot them a wave.

Thomas lets out a small smile. "Okay," he says. "But remember: No drama."

I'm ecstatic. I can feel the certainty glowing inside me like a flame. This is right. Rose deserves to be happy, and I am going to help her get there.

"No drama," I repeat, jumping up again. "This is a terrific idea."

Chapter Eighteen

Rose

June 25

This is a terrible idea," I whisper to Lily.

I'm holding a pair of gold heels in my left hand and the scrunched fabric of a long, pink dress in the other. The dress is patterned with white flowers and has flowing sleeves. I'm happy for the coverage. Lily always dismisses when I complain about my arms, but she has no idea what it's like to watch your body change, become unfamiliar. I shift the fabric down again.

"Of all the terrible, ridiculous schemes you've concocted, this is the worst," I say.

"Relax," says Lily, not bothering to look up. She's fixated on a point farther down the black beach, trying to make out shapes in the distance.

The moon is bright, but it is still not enough to fully illuminate the sand. Moments earlier, we watched the celestial object rise out of the sea. It was beautiful and bizarre, like a time-lapse video in reverse. The moon looked like a creature born of the ocean as it emerged into the skyline inch by inch. For a moment, we were stunned into an appreciative silence.

Currently, we're squatted in a sand dune, partially concealed by the tall grass. A few yards ahead are the distant lights of a wedding.

Lily heard about it while working at the yacht club. There are large white tents, a checkered dance floor, and floral arrangements from ceiling to ground, which must cost more than a college tuition. Rumor has it there may even be fireworks. We're here to cross "crash a wedding" off the bucket list.

"We're going to get arrested," I say, a nervous tinge to my voice.

"Arrested?" scoffs Lily. "What would we get arrested for?"

"I don't know . . . loitering! Or, like, breaking and entering. Actually, yes, I have it! Trespassing. This is trespassing on private property."

"It's the beach, Mom. It's not private."

"Well, tonight it is!" I swat at my ankles, feeling something creeping up my left leg. "And we're going to get ticks and then Lyme disease."

I sound like my sister, who is the epitome of hypochondria. Elizabeth is constantly diagnosing herself with various, far-fetched illnesses on WebMD. I sometimes wonder if it's because our mother died so young—if getting ahead of a potential diagnosis, even an imagined one, gives her a sense of control over the uncontrollable.

"If Vince Vaughn and Owen Wilson can do it, surely we can."

"That was a movie, Lil."

Lily snaps back to look at me, her red hair curly and wild. I'm still getting used to her bangs. They make her look more mature somehow, less like my little girl.

"Oh my gosh, we're doing this for Lottie. Remember? If a seventy-something woman was willing to crash a wedding, what are you so worried about?"

"Fine," I sigh, although I'm still not sure. I suppose I already am dressed, and we came all this way. "What's our strategy?"

"Okay, so I think we should just walk in through the tent, and if anyone asks, we'll say we wanted to dip our toes in the water."

"That's your grand plan? Just walking in? Going for a casual, moonlit stroll in formal dresses?"

"The simplest plans are the best."

"And if they ask us who we know?"

"Let's just make up a generic rich person name. Something like . . . Tripp!" offers Lily.

"Tripp? That's way too specific, what if there are no Tripps?"

Lily looks me dead in the eyes. "There's always a Tripp somewhere nearby on Nantucket."

I laugh. What I don't tell her is that William sometimes goes by Tripp, too. He's the third William in his lineage, so lots of his family calls him Tripp, short for "the third." Lily would certainly make fun of that.

"Okay, true. But how about we say something more generic . . . like Jack!"

"Jack?" Lily looks doubtful. "It lacks a certain je ne sais quoi."

"I mean, realistically, how many Jacks do you know? It's the quintessential boring name. They could unite and form a new country, call it 'New England.'"

Lily laughs. "Okay, you're right. So, we know Jack?"

"We love Jack," I confirm. "He's the best! And then we can say, 'Are you friends of the groom or the bride?' and whatever they say, we say the opposite."

"Brilliant," says Lily with a mischievous smile. "Lottie would be proud."

* * *

Moments later, we are in the tent, slipping our heels back on, attempting to dust the sand from our dresses. Grains rattle to the ground, sounding like small beads hitting the floor. My heart is rattling, too, and the high is illicit and sweet-tasting. Lily was right, it really was as simple as walking in through the flap of the tent.

"Good job, partner," whispers Lily from the corner of her mouth, her eyes trained ahead on the dance floor, waiting for security to pop up. "Now, act normal and maybe no one will notice us."

"Hi," a man says to my left. "I couldn't help but notice you."

"Shit," says Lily under her breath. "That was fast."

When I turn around, I'm shocked to see William standing before us, looking dapper in a tux.

"William!" I give him a quick hug. "What are you doing here?"

We're not quite at the dating stage yet where we tell each other our every plan, but still, this feels like something he would have mentioned.

"I'm friends with the groom's father, Jack. We're old buddies from the golf club. It seems to be the season of weddings for me. My niece is getting married here, too."

Lily shoots me a look at the mention of "Jack," and I suppress a laugh by biting down on the inside of my cheek.

"This is my daughter, Lily," I introduce them, straining to sound casual. This is not how I imagined their first meeting going down. "Lily, this is William, a friend of mine."

She shoots me an inquisitive look but doesn't push it. "Nice to meet you."

William takes her hand. "I'm a big fan of your mother, Lily. It is so wonderful to finally meet you."

Recognition dawns across her face. "You were at Gazebo a few weeks ago, right? You were in the Nantucket reds." She says the phrase "Nantucket reds" like it's a particularly horrifying detail.

"Guilty as charged," says William, bowing slightly. Thankfully, he doesn't catch her tone. "I've been quite infatuated with your mother ever since."

Why does the word *infatuated* make me cringe? There's something slightly ridiculous about his style of speech, but he's also sweet, and he's been nothing but kind. What is wrong with me? Why can't I just be happy with a nice guy, for once?

"So, you're dating?" asks Lily. She crosses her arms against her blue dress—the defiant expression at odds with the ethereal gown. She looks exactly like the headstrong teenager she once was. "You're together?"

I can imagine what she's feeling. I wonder if she's doing the mental calculation, counting back to all those nights I said I was busy with "work" when I was really out with William these past few weeks. Logically, I know I don't owe her every detail of my personal life, but I also recognize that she must feel confused by the secrecy.

William surrenders his hands to the air. "Well, we haven't exactly 'defined the relationship' or however you young people put it, but I'm certainly smitten. I'm all hers if she'll have me."

Is this really happening right now? Is he truly asking for a relationship commitment in front of my kid?

"That's very sweet," is all I say, giving him a pat on his tux sleeve.

To his credit, William doesn't let the awkward tension build. "Say, why didn't I see you two during the ceremony at the chapel or for the seated portion of dinner?" asks William, looking around the tent at the white-clothed tables, as if double-checking to see if he has somehow missed our place cards.

Lily widens her eyes at me. The wind on the beach blew my hair out of its clip, so now it feels tangled and unkempt. I smooth it down to kill time. I can't think of a believable lie, so I go with the truth. "Oh, it's kind of a funny story. It has to do with that bucket list I found from my aunt."

William leans in conspiratorially. "Wait a minute, are you two crashing?"

Lily makes another face at me behind his back, shaking her head no.

"Yes," I admit. Lily smacks a hand to her forehead. "But please don't tell anyone, okay? It was a stupid idea, and we're leaving right now. We can cross it off the list."

William laughs, and the sound is somehow formal, like everything else about him. "Forget that. It's a party, come in and enjoy. No one will even notice."

I'm wearing Lottie's old charm bracelet tonight, and I twist the jewelry around my wrist. Lottie's favorite charm—a red ladybug—jingles. The sight of it tugs at my heart and then snaps back like an elastic band.

"Are you sure? I really don't want to put you in an awkward position."

"Heavens no," says William, swatting the air, as if physically batting the thought away. "You've just made my evening. But, you do owe me a dance."

I look at Lily. I don't want to leave her alone. "Oh, that's so sweet, but I actually already have a date tonight."

"Go ahead, Mom," says Lily. "I'll be fine. I promise."

"Are you sure?"

"Of course, go." She shoos us away. She smiles encouragingly but there's something heavy in her eyes.

On the dance floor, green vines hang from the ceiling of the tent, crawling up the walls and over the archways. Alongside them are hydrangeas in blues and whites. It looks like someone robbed a florist, or more accurately, twelve florists. Tea candles are placed strategically throughout the tables, lending the whole venue a warm, fairytale element. It's the kind of setting where anything could happen.

"Wow, this is incredible," I say aloud as William moves his hand to my waist.

"Did you have a wedding like this?"

I shake my head. "No, I actually never married James. I just took his last name so Lily and I would have the same surname. I was eager to ditch my own. I don't know if I'd like a wedding, though. I hate being the center of attention."

I think of Lily and smile. She would love being the center of attention at her wedding. I imagine walking her down the aisle, giving her away.

William spins me. "Maybe that's just because you weren't with the right person."

I try to catch a glimpse of my daughter through the crowd. When I finally locate her, she's standing by the raw bar, sipping champagne by herself. I feel awful for ditching her.

"What about you?" I ask William, going through the motions. "Was your wedding like this?" I know he was married twice before, once to a girl he met in high school, and again, a few years ago, to a woman in her early thirties. Neither marriage resulted in kids.

"Of course," says William. "I love a wedding. That's why I've had two." I can't tell if he's being sarcastic or not.

The bride makes her rounds around the room, her tight updo growing more unraveled as the evening progresses and the champagne keeps flowing. Guests move out of the way to make space for her long, sweeping train. I hope she doesn't spot me. I'm starting to think this is a terrible idea again—that I've now become complicit in ruining someone's carefully planned day. What if she sees me and gets upset?

William twirls me again, and the music changes, picking up speed. There's a ten-piece band on a large, elevated stage. The crowd is closing in on us, gaining momentum. The dancing becomes more frantic. I spin in William's arms, this time faster. As I'm spinning, I look for Lily again, making sure she's still okay. I'm peering through the moving bodies, searching the seafood station, when William jerks me once more, and this time, I lose my balance. My heels, still sandy, slide against the slippery dance floor. I sense myself pulled down, William's hands losing their grasp.

For a moment, all I feel is the emptiness of air. I brace myself for impact, and then . . . The next thing I know, someone is catching me. A strong pair of arms wrap around my rib cage and stabilize me, so I'm standing right side up again. At first, I think it's William, but when I look up, I see an entirely different set of eyes staring back at me.

"Tommy?" I say, looking into his familiar face. He's wearing a suit and looks devastatingly handsome in the candlelight. His expression is placid and unreadable.

"Apologies," he says. "You bumped into me and I didn't want you to fall and get hurt."

I notice, with some embarrassment, that his hands are still around me. He seems to register this at the same moment and quickly lets go.

We remain like that for some time, held hostage to the moment, staring at each other. I can't believe it's him. Even still, I can't believe he's here, on the island, so close but also unreachable.

"Thank you for saving my date." William appears between us, moving to offer Tommy his hand. In the process, I'm nudged away from Tommy. "I'm William, by the way, and this is my girlfriend, Rose."

I wince at the term *girlfriend*, straining to read Tommy's reaction, but he remains resolute. If it bothers him, he doesn't show it. Besides, why should he care, anyway?

Tommy takes William's hand, gives it a firm shake.

"Girlfriend?" he repeats. "Your date?"

I'm thinking of a good way to protest without hurting William's feelings, when he jumps back in, interrupting. "That's right," he says. "I'm the luckiest guy here."

William pats me roughly on the back, and I feel like an unloved dog sitting patiently by the door, like my loyalty is on display.

"I'll say," is all Tommy responds. "Well, enjoy your night." He looks at me with intent. "And be careful."

I can't tell if he's cautioning me about the slippery dance floor or about William.

As he's walking back through the crowd, someone else spots us.

"Rose Elliot!" yells a tall, brunette woman in an elegant red dress. "I can't believe it's you!" Thin arms wrap around my neck, cold to the touch and strong.

When I extricate myself, I realize it's Tommy's sister, Rachel. She looks remarkably similar, even though the last time I saw her was when she was only a teen. I'm surprised by how easy it is to recognize her; despite everything, it's like no time at all has passed.

"Rachel!" I return the hug. "What are you doing here?"

"I'm staying at the cottage for a few days," she says. "Visiting my big brother here."

William nudges his way forward again. "You two know each other?" He addresses the question to Rachel but his eyes flicker to Tommy, who is still lingering to our left.

"We go way back," I say, forcing a cheery, nonchalant smile. "I met Rachel when she was only fifteen. Right?"

"Fourteen, actually," Rachel says.

William eyes Tommy. "And you two, as well, then? You know each other, too?"

Tommy steps forward, composed as ever. "We do."

"Huh," says William. "What a happy accident this all is. To think, you started out by crashing and now you have all these old friends around."

He speaks too loudly, and a few neighboring guests look our way with some curiosity. I wish he would be quiet before someone tells the bride and causes a scene. His movements are a little more languid than usual, and I wonder how much he's had to drink tonight.

Rachel bumps my elbow and waggles her eyebrow. "A crasher, huh?" she whispers. "Bad girl."

Luckily, Lily appears just then, saving me from responding.

"And this is my daughter," I say, introducing her to everyone. She shakes hands with Tommy, and Rachel leans in to give her a hug.

"How's it going over here?" my daughter asks, looking between the four of us, as if trying to solve a murder mystery. "Everyone behaving?"

Tommy cracks a smile, but William doesn't. "Of course we're behaving," William says. "What kind of question is that?" He wraps his arm around my waist again and squeezes.

I look around at our misfit group, taking notice: Tommy looks annoyed, Rachel seems confused, and I suddenly wish that the tent would collapse on all of us, so I can make a quick getaway.

"William," says Lily. "Would you mind joining me to grab a drink at the bar? I'd feel more comfortable if I'm with someone who knows the wedding party."

"Sure," he says, but he seems reluctant to leave me.

Rachel jumps in. "I'll go, too!"

They disperse into the crowd, William glancing back a few times at Tommy and me, until we're left alone. We stand a few feet apart, unsure of what to do next.

The band changes pace again, decelerates back into a slow song.

Tommy shrugs, gesturing to the crowd, which is now pairing into twos. "Shall we?"

"Why not?" I say, feeling my heart get staccato. It's like the music has crawled under my skin, making everything inside me hum.

He cups my hand in his and we begin to dance.

"I didn't realize you were seeing someone," he says.

I can't tell if he's bothered by the information or simply commenting. His eyes are the steady brown they've always been, and I realize how much about him I've memorized. Despite the distance between us, I've kept a "Tommy folder" in my brain, chronicling every inch of him, so that now it all rushes back with urgency.

"I'm not," I tell him. "I mean, we've been on a few dates, but we never decided it was serious."

Everything has remained strangely chaste with William: a kiss on the cheek goodbye after dinner, and once, even a handshake. It's like I'm in a job interview, stuck forever in the final round.

Tommy doesn't respond; instead he dips me to the beat of the song. Where before I felt unsteady on the dance floor, with him, everything is certain. I let him guide me, trusting him to catch me if I slip. He has always possessed a certain commanding resoluteness. When he tells you to follow him, you do, because you trust he's thought it out. When he makes a decision, he sticks with it, even if it's the wrong choice, even if everything would be better if he just turned against his word.

I wonder what he sees when he looks at me. Is he disappointed? Does he wish I was still the girl of my youth? I adjust the dress again, wanting to cover myself from his inspection.

"Tommy," I ask him. There's a thoughtful look on his face, a line between his brows. "Why did you come here?"

"Tonight?" he asks, but I know he knows that's not what I mean.

"To the island."

He looks behind my right shoulder to where the bride is slow dancing with her groom. There's something pained about the expression. "I don't know," he admits.

"Was it really a coincidence that you rented out the cottage?" I can feel my hand vibrating in his, every nerve ending on high alert for his response. It's like every cell in my body is leaning in.

"No," he admits, and I hold my breath. "I mean, yes."

For once, he appears flustered. "I don't know," he continues. "Rachel didn't tell me it was your place explicitly, but of course, I recognized the address when she eventually sent over the paperwork. I wasn't sure if you were still here, but I—I don't know. I'd be lying if I said I wasn't hoping we'd run into each other."

I force myself to take deliberate breaths. "And why did you want to run into each other?"

He looks at me, and those brown eyes seem to melt, turning liquid. I can see every color in them, and I can see the past. I see the miracle of him being here, in front of me again, hand on my hip, everything changed but also somehow the same. All of the years that stretch between us reduced to nothing in the single crush of an instant.

That's what it always felt like when Tommy and I were together—like a collision.

The music stops. We remain holding each other. He starts to speak, but instead of words, there is the crack of fireworks. Not the crackle of chemistry-induced metaphorical fireworks, but the actual, real-life shotgun sound of fireworks exploding outside on the beach.

"Ladies and gentlemen," the singer croons onstage. "Everyone please gather outside to celebrate the everlasting love of Mr. and Mrs. Martinez!"

Then, before I can do anything about it, William is by my side, taking my hand and pulling me along with the crowd. I try to turn to say something to Tommy, but I'm swept away. Maybe I should fight it, break free of William. But what would that do? What are we to do now, thirty years too late?

Outside on the black beach, I see the first rays of color against the reflection of the cold, indifferent sea. When I turn around to look back at the now empty dance floor for Tommy, he is nowhere to be found.

Chapter Nineteen

Lily

It's midnight and the fireworks are exploding. Thomas is standing alone on the dance floor, looking like he was just robbed in broad daylight. His hands are still slightly outstretched, holding nothing but air. He looks dazed and lost, a little kid abandoned in a grocery store with no idea where to go next.

I've been sitting at an empty table with his sister, Rachel, showing her on my phone some of the sketches I've been working on recently. I still haven't shown them to Rose, but sometimes, it's easier to confide in a stranger. So far, we get along great. Rachel has the stoicism and composure of her brother, but she's also quick to laugh and effusively warm.

When we spot Thomas, we lock eyes and immediately stand to approach him. By the time we arrive by his side, he is thawing.

"What just happened?" Rachel asks, concerned.

Thomas shakes his head, as if to shake the events into order. "I don't know. We were talking and then the fireworks started and William grabbed her."

"What were you talking about?"

I curse myself silently. After the three of us went to the bar, Rachel and I started talking and we forgot to keep William distracted. This whole elaborate matchmaking scheme is new to me, and for just a second, I let my attention slip.

"She asked me why I came to the island." Thomas still looks stricken.

Rachel and I exchange a look. Back at the table, she told me she's been playing a matchmaking game of her own, hoping Thomas would come here and rekindle with Rose.

"Did she say it like, 'Why did you come here?'" Rachel bats her eyelashes in a wistful, flirtatious voice. "Or, was it more like, 'Why did you come here?'" This time, she says the phrase in an angry, aggressive tone.

Thomas looks at her like she's speaking a foreign language. "I don't know?"

"You don't know? It's a pretty big difference," says Rachel.

Thomas shakes his head again. "I guess it was in between? I don't know. I can't read her. Maybe I've never understood her."

I anticipate his next move before he makes it. Thomas starts to walk away. I grab him by the jacket. "Come on," I say. "Tell us more. What happened? Why are you freaking out?"

He keeps walking toward the exit, politely disengaging himself. We follow him, trying to keep up. Even in his frustration, he walks with a determined, steady pace.

"This is a bad idea," he says, exiting the tent.

On the other side, facing the ocean, we hear the pop of fireworks and the pleased applause of the gathered group. The exit where we stand is empty of guests. Everyone is outside in a large clump. Out of the corner of my eye, I think I see the red-shawled psychic, but when I look back, it's just a guest in a long, red gown.

"Why is it a bad idea? Tell us what happened," Rachel pleads as Thomas is beginning to walk toward the sandy parking lot.

My heels are sinking in the sand, and it's hard to keep pace with him.

"Because I can't do this!" erupts Thomas, losing his composure. "Because I'm tired of it. I've been through too much to put up with these mind games. If she wanted me around, she would reach out to me. We could have morning coffee. We could go for a walk. We could do a hundred things easier than this. We share a wall, for Christ's sake! What's the point of all this back-and-forth? I loved her, even proposed to her once, and she rejected me. I reached out again, and she rejected me. All she's done is reject me, and I'm exhausted. The last couple of years have been hard. I lost my wife just five years ago, and before that, I watched her get sicker and sicker with every passing day, unable to help." His voice breaks. "I can't keep putting myself through this."

Rachel and I watch his impassioned speech in a sort of awed silence, neither of us seeming to know what to say next, because he's right. We've been unfair to him, forcing him into this uncomfortable, vulnerable situation with no guarantees of a positive outcome.

"I'm sorry," I say in a small voice, barely perceptible over the fireworks.

Thomas's face softens. "I'm sorry, too," he says. "But I have to move on."

With that, he walks away toward his car. Rachel trails after him, turning only once to say goodbye.

"We tried," she says with a sad smile. "It was really nice meeting you."

I watch them leave until I can no longer make out their figures fading into the dark night.

* * *

On the ride home, Rose doesn't speak. We sit in a companionable silence, lost in our own thoughts. Before us, the beach road is bumpy. It looks ominous without the illumination of the bright sun, all those rolling dunes rocking the car up and down.

I feel terrible for putting Thomas in an uncomfortable position, and even worse for Rose. All I want is for her to be happy—it's what I want most in the whole world—and I thought Thomas was special enough to make it happen. What if I was wrong?

I let my mind drift to thoughts of Henry, about the wedding he's planning, one not unlike the party we crashed tonight.

Before him, I never gave much thought to what kind of wedding I'd like to have someday, or whether or not I even wanted one. After witnessing my parents' failed relationship, I didn't allow myself to envision a future that involved a white dress.

Henry was different. He treated life as if the universe was conspiring on behalf of his every happiness. He took what I thought of as extraordinary blessings—financial stability, a happy home, a loving partner, healthy children—and assumed them guarantees. A happy life was his destiny, and he stretched toward it effortlessly and eagerly.

He once told me that my problem was a matter of mindset.

"If you expect good things to happen to you, they will," he said. "But you always expect the sky to fall."

What I wanted to retort is: "If you expect bad things to happen to you, you won't be as devastated when they do."

Henry with his big family could never understand. Henry with his fifteen cousins, his over-the-top family reunions, the weddings with their own hashtags, his protective shell of money and familial loyalty. He was shepherded through life by a million gracious, outstretched hands.

For a while, I let myself slide into this vision. It was as simple as letting the tide take you.

Lottie was sort of like Henry in that sense. A widow herself, she certainly wasn't ignorant to life's challenges, but she was forcefully optimistic. When I worried about something bad happening, she would offer the opposite perspective.

"What if it all works out?" she'd say. "What if the future is even better than you imagined?"

Even throughout her diagnosis and the subsequent treatments, she remained positive. I guess I thought if we completed her bucket list, if we lived like we were her, this mindset would magically soak into us, too.

But in the end, Lottie's positivity wasn't enough to save her. We still lost her. Maybe, in the end, relentless positivity is never enough.

"Are you okay?" I break the silence.

"I'm okay," is all my mom says. "Don't worry, sweetie. I'll be fine."

We're silent again for several seconds until Rose suddenly says, "Did I ever tell you that I had a creek cat?"

The question is so absurd, I momentarily forget where we are and why we're here. "What on God's green earth is a 'creek cat'?"

Mom laughs, gripping the steering wheel a little too tight, the perpetually nervous driver. "It's just a cat I found in a creek when I was a teen."

Outside the window, the sandy road is gradually hardening, turning solid. I try to process what my mom is saying and why she has decided to bring it up now.

"What were you doing in a creek?"

"I was down at Hither Creek in Madaket. With Tommy," she says simply, eyes still on the road. "When I first found him, he was tiny. Smaller than the kittens you see up for adoption. He was this scrawny, coal-black, helpless little thing. Hardly distinguishable from the mud and plants caked around him."

I have a hard time picturing this, too. This is not the mom I know. The woman I know hates outdoor activities like hiking or camping. She played pickleball with jewelry on the other day and didn't break a sweat. The Rose I know wears uniform outfits of matching sweaters and tailored jackets. Even her pajamas are silk sets that never look rumpled or worn. She is a therapist, a professional people go to in times of crisis. Rose Gardner is not a woman you can easily imagine wading in a creek, searching for stray cats.

"I thought you hated cats? And creeks for that matter."

"I never said I hated cats, Lily," corrects Mom. "They usually hate me."

It's true that cats are not a particular friend to her. One Christmas at my grandfather's house, I witnessed as their family cat, Mrs. Clay, launched itself from the top of the staircase and landed—paws first—on the front of my mom's new sweater. It seemed nothing short of a targeted act of aggression, a declaration of war.

I know a long-lost cat might seem a small thing, but it unnerves me. This confession, while relatively small and innocuous, seems incongruous with absolutely everything I know to be true about my mom.

"Did you really have a cat?" I ask again. "And why did you mention it now?"

"I don't know," she says. "Seeing Tommy reminded me of him."

"Tommy also had a cat?"

"Tommy's sister, Rachel, adopted the cat after we nursed it back to health. I wanted him to go to a good home." Rose pauses. "I should've asked her about him. I never heard when he died."

For a moment, I wonder if the cat might still be alive, over thirty years later. The entire story seems so illogical as to make anything possible.

"I can't believe you never told me this," I say.

Mom looks at me across the car. Another vehicle is passing at that moment, and the high beams cast a strange glow over her face. "It's really not a big deal."

"How can I know you for twenty-five years and you've never mentioned you had a cat?"

She shrugs. "We only kept him for a few weeks. Lottie was allergic."

I think about why this secret is so hurtful. The first word I ever spoke was "Dada." Mom likes to tease me about this, but I once read that babies are more likely to say their fathers' names first because for the first few months of life, our mothers are indistinguishable from ourselves. We do not cry out to them, because we do not think them separate beings.

Maybe that's the problem. I can't imagine a version of Rose that I don't have access to.

The rest of the ride home, I try to imagine this younger version of Rose. I picture her with muddy hands, her hair loose and untamed, scooping that cat from the water. I imagine her before she became the tidy, self-contained woman I know, before motherhood and the pressures of adulthood and societal expectations bent her into her final form.

I like thinking of Rose like that: free, unencumbered, as wild as the island surrounding her.

"Do you think we'd be friends if we met at the same age?" I ask her when we pull into the driveway. The garden is aglow with the solar lights Lottie planted around the edges of the fence.

"What do you mean? I'd be lucky to have a friend like you," is all she says.

For some reason, the answer doesn't satisfy.

There are questions I wish I could ask: what she and Thomas talked about, how she really feels about the situation. But that would mean admitting that I talked to Thomas first. And I'm not sure how

Rose might react if she uncovered the ways I've been interfering in her love life. When I asked Thomas to agree to this plan tonight, I assumed I knew what was best for her, but what if I don't?

As Rose gets out of the car and steps into the dim light of the garden, I watch her pink dress billow around her ankles, blending into the dark greenery, and wonder how much I still don't know.

Chapter Twenty

Lily

June 28

The next Tuesday at work, I decide I'm tired of receiving Theo's cold shoulder. It's already the last week of June, summer is rapidly disappearing, and I'm letting it slip away.

He's standing by the water cooler with Emily when I approach.

"Can we talk?" I ask.

Emily looks at the two of us, raises her eyebrows, and then walks away, arms raised in the air. "I'll let you two have some space."

I still don't know what's going on between the two of them, if anything, but I no longer have the energy to care. I miss my friend, and I don't want to squander the rest of the summer over a silly disagreement. Seeing Rose and Thomas interact last night showed me how easy it is to let a small miscommunication snowball.

"Of course," says Theo. His thick eyebrows bunch together, and he looks concerned as the two of us make our way to the outside porch.

Summer light bounces off the white seashell-lined pathway and is momentarily disorienting. I squint into Theo's eyes and take a steadying breath.

"I know everything has been weird since the bonfire, but whatever I did wrong, I want to apologize. Hanging out with you has been the best part of my summer, and I miss it."

I watch in real time as Theo's face softens. All of the intensity and bravado drops. "I miss it, too," he says. After a pause, he asks, "So, are you back with him?"

He lightly kicks a wayward piece of crushed seashell, sending it flying into the green grass.

For a moment, I'm confused by what he means. "Henry?"

Theo nods. "Yeah, I saw the two of you talking at the bonfire. Did he call off the engagement?"

The idea seems so suddenly absurd that I laugh. "No, of course not. We were just talking and catching up. He's getting married."

"It seemed more intimate than just catching up," says Theo, still looking at the shells.

"Well, maybe we shouldn't have talked at all, but no. I can assure you that there is nothing going on between me and Henry."

As I say the words, I feel a sharp edge in my chest. Even though I know it's true, it's hard to admit that Henry is truly gone.

Theo nods. "Okay, just wondering. It seemed like you were playing a risky game there."

"It's over," I say again, assuring myself as much as him. "I mean, it never really started. Nothing happened. But it's over."

A few members from the club walk by, tennis bags on their tan shoulders. We move out of the way and smile at them. I wait until they're out of earshot to speak again.

"Friends?" I hold my hand out to Theo.

His big, uneven smile is back, the one I've grown to love. "Friends," he says and takes my hand.

* * *

The rest of the week, everything goes back to normal. Theo gives Rose and me another pickleball lesson. We're still awful, but at least this time, we're slightly less awful.

On the Fourth of July, he joins us after practice to the Great Point Lighthouse to cross off the second item on Lottie's list. Rose drives the Jeep on the beach, and Theo helps me take the roof off so we can get a better view. The sun is up, the sky is blue, and the choppy waves are mere feet from the tires. Every couple of minutes, a seal pops its friendly, smooth head above the water.

We arrive at the white-brick, remote lighthouse a little after noon, surrounded by hot sand dunes and sharp green seagrass. We plant beach chairs into the sand. Rose packed Something Natural iced teas and squished turkey sandwiches: a beach picnic. We cross number seven off the bucket list, as well.

Staring out at the water, I think about riptides: how they can take you, quick and fierce, and the only option is to let them. You cannot fight the current. All you can hope is that it takes you far enough out that maybe you can swim sideways back to shore.

Later in the afternoon, Rose has to meet a client, but Theo and I are still off from work. We decide to head downtown for ice cream at the Juice Bar. The streets in town are packed with summer visitors, and every few seconds, a biker or vacationer pops onto the narrow streets in front of the car. It's clear that summer is in full swing. By the time we arrive at the ice cream store, the line is halfway down the block and it's begun to rain.

"Do you want to check out the Whaling Museum instead?" Theo asks once I park. The cobblestones are already becoming slick with rainwater.

"I've never been," I admit, surprised at the suggestion. The Whaling Museum is a small establishment about the history of whale hunting on Nantucket. It's only a few rooms.

Lottie was a schoolteacher and continued to sub the fourth and fifth grade until a few years ago when she retired. She always reminded us that beneath the island's tourist-friendly facade was a rich, surprising, and often devastating history.

Lottie reveled in the island's natural beauty, but she never forgot the suffering beneath her feet: the twelve thousand years of human interaction, the Indigenous people who settled here long before the whaling industry and colonization took over.

I'm surprised that given Lottie's love for history she never suggested a trip to the museum.

"Come on," says Theo. "It'll be fun. I promise."

Five minutes and twenty-five dollars each later, we are standing in front of a giant graphic of a right whale being impaled.

"Is this what you had in mind?" I tease Theo.

The building itself, with its white columns, looks more like a historical home than a museum, but once we're inside, I'm surprised by how much there is to consume.

We attend a talk about eighteenth-century whaling practices, marveling at the intricate patterns of scrimshaw art, reading about the sinking of the *Essex*—the shipwreck that inspired *Moby-Dick*. I'm fascinated by the scrimshaw art in particular, the unlikely combination of brutality and delicate beauty. I try to picture the whalers in the grimy quarters belowdecks, carving intricate designs into the teeth and bones, making gifts for their wives and children back home, all while engaging in the violent practice of whale hunting up above.

In one room is a series of gold-framed portraits featuring prominent historical figures of Nantucket's past: *Island People: Portraits and Stories from Nantucket*. In another, installations about the Nantucket of today include a life-size mannequin of a "modern tourist."

The prop is clothed in pink pastel pants and a gingham button-down, a sweater around its neck. It looks a lot like William.

Theo goes to shake its hand. "Ah, my good friend, Chad!" he says, grabbing the mannequin. "It's been so long, I've missed you." The arm falls out of its socket. "Oh, shit!" He looks around, but no one has seen.

Our wet sneakers squeak against the linoleum floors as we walk around the museum, laughing the whole time. Between exhibits, I tell him about what happened with Rose and Thomas.

"You really crashed a wedding?" says Theo, sounding impressed. "Badass."

"It was a terrible idea," I admit. "I probably shouldn't have gotten involved."

"How has everything been at the cottage since then? Have you talked to Thomas?"

"I've seen him a few times in the garden and waved, but we haven't spoken. I've been trying to give him his space."

Rachel left yesterday. She dropped a note on my windowsill. "Thanks for trying," it read.

I've been wondering if Thomas is going to leave the island early. I wouldn't blame him if he cut the rental short. After all, it was what Rose originally wanted.

Theo and I walk into a room made up of old brick that looks almost soft to the touch, like the entire facade is one bad storm away from crumbling. A sign on the wall tells us that it is a preservation of the original building that stood here, an 1847 spermaceti candle factory. Throughout it are exhibits about Nantucket's other original industries such as boatbuilding, coopering, and blacksmithing. A ginormous forty-six-foot sperm whale skeleton hangs from the high ceilings, open-mouthed.

"Have you ever heard the story of how deer came to Nantucket?" I ask Theo as we stare up at the whale.

He shakes his head no. It's a story I know well from Lottie, and recounting it makes me feel closer to my great-aunt.

"Basically, after Nantucket broke off and became an island, deer were quickly hunted to extinction by the early sixteen hundreds. Then, on a random June day in 1922, three hundred or so years later, some fishermen found a buck drowning in the Nantucket Sound. They took pity and rescued him, bringing him to the island and releasing him into the woods. They named him Old Buck."

I tell Theo the rest of the story, how for four years, Old Buck was alone on the island. Then the town surmised he was lonely, clinically depressed even. They purchased a pair of lady deer for Old Buck to choose from. He impregnated them both immediately.

"Classic male," says Theo. "Disappointing."

When the two does arrived by ship, they were greeted by a cheering crowd at the wharf. And like that, the population boomed, and with it, a long and controversial conversation about hunting season commenced. In 1932, poor Old Buck was killed in a car collision but his legacy continues in his many, many descendants today.

Now the deer population is out of control and Nantucket has some of the highest incidence of tick-borne illnesses in the United States. All because some fishermen took pity on poor Old Buck.

"That's a crazy story," says Theo when I'm done. "It sounds made-up."

"I like it because it reminds me of the best and worst of the island."

I like to think Old Buck is a cautionary tale about the ramifications of man's interference with nature but also a celebration of our uniquely human proclivity toward the sentimental. It is the cheering crowds at the dock when the two does arrive, but also the pragmatic brutishness of hunting season years later—how narratives easily form around the singular but are reduced or ignored in a collective.

As the two of us continue exploring the museum, I feel somehow lighter, more optimistic. When I'm around Theo, I miss Henry less. Or, at the very least, I momentarily forget how much I miss him. The hole in my chest is still there, but it no longer throbs around the edges. I can almost ignore it. I find myself wishing that summer wouldn't end so I can keep him around.

Up the winding, circular staircase, on the enclosed glass roof walk, we marvel at panoramic views of downtown. We look onto the rain-coated streets, the light brick buildings made darker by the water, the gray-shingled roofs almost blackish.

There is a moment when we are standing there, slightly out of breath from the climb, when I think he might kiss me.

I'm giggling at his impression of me almost falling asleep during one of the museum curator's presentations, imitating my head bobbing up and down. My sides hurt from laughing, and I'm holding on to the railing for support. We're bent so close together our heads are nearly touching. We lock eyes, and there it is: an opening, an opportunity. I can feel my heart stutter, and I barely have enough time to wonder if this is something I want before the moment has passed.

Another museum guest walks up the stairs, a man with two young children who are holding large whale stuffed animals.

"Oh, sorry," the man says when he sees us. We break apart immediately.

Once the rain subsides, Theo suggests we take a walk around town.

"Will you tell me about how you first got started with art?" Theo asks as we pass various shops, weaving through the crowds. Straw hats bob up and down, undeterred by the overcast.

"Oh, I don't know," I say, embarrassed. "Do you really want to know about that?"

I'm still waiting to hear back from Marie Chen, and the anxiety is settling in. I reached out again yesterday and she never responded—it's becoming more and more likely that she is purposefully ignoring me.

Theo nods. "I just want to get to know you better."

When he looks at me, his eyes are stained glass. There's something about his expression. I remember how I felt when I first met him and wished I had something to draw with. The light is pure and sharp.

"The first time I really felt moved by art is kind of silly," I say. "It sounds stupid."

"I'm sure it doesn't." His expression is insistent and unwavering.

I give in with a slightly exasperated sigh. "It was at an antiques store downtown. Lottie had taken me there to look for some pottery."

I remember the store smelled of old laundry and stale bread, and a layer of dust coated everything like powdered sugar. Each time Lottie picked up an object to examine it and then placed it back down on the wooden shelves, particles danced in the air like synchronized swimmers. There were old globes and compasses and sailor's valentines and faded sculptures of mermaids with their tops askew. Nantucket baskets woven together tightly like braids.

"Lottie told me to pick out anything I liked, but there was so much stuff to sort through, and honestly, I would have rather gone to the candy store in the back of Force Five." I look at Theo.

He nods. "Of course."

There's a "secret" candy store there in the back room of the popular surf shop, stocked floor to ceiling with all sorts of old brands.

There's always a middle schooler on duty, manning the cash register and using a calculator to tally up your order.

"But that's when I saw it. On the wall to the left, sandwiched between a carved wooden sailboat sculpture and a rumpled American flag was a painting of an old sea captain."

He looked as battered and faded as the flag next to him, but there was a triumphant sparkle in his eyes. Sea sprayed behind his back, the ship's wheel glued to his chest, and a pipe to his mouth. His beard was white and thick as salt water. There was no expiration date on his face. Maybe I liked the man because he reminded me of everything my father wasn't: reliable, sturdy.

I have this memory, and I can't tell if it's real or imagined, but we're watching the fireworks at Ladies Beach on the island—back when Lottie still let my father stay—and he lifted me onto his shoulders so I could see better. I must have been five or six. On the long way back to the parked car, when dusk had turned into night and the bugs woke singing their song, he carried me because I was too tired to walk. It's an insignificant half memory, but I've never forgotten the profound feeling of safety. At some point, I stopped feeling that way around him and never got it back.

"I remember thinking that I liked how settled the sailor looked, all sea and stories. I remember marveling at how much personality the painter had captured. Lottie bought it for me. It cost less than twenty bucks, and upon closer inspection, we realized it was a print of an oil painting created by some anonymous artist, but I didn't care. I was in love."

"Do you still have it?" Theo asks.

I nod. "I keep it in the closet in my bedroom."

"Like a shrine?" Theo jokes.

"Maybe," I admit. "The other day I started a new project, inspired by the painting."

After I abandoned the photo of Lottie in the garden, I decided to try sketching instead. I looked at the sailor's painting and began to wish that I could capture the women in my life with as much gravitas. I started a portrait of Lottie based on the photo, except in the sketch, she is looking directly at the viewer—defiant, as if refusing death.

After that, I did another sketch of Rose, getting ready for work in the morning. In the drawing, she's brushing her hair, analyzing her reflection, her expression difficult to read. Her matching pink sweater and skirt look like armor. They're quiet images, simple, but I liked them all the more for that. There's something beautiful about preserving the ordinary.

"Can I see it?" asks Theo.

"Maybe someday, but not today. It's not ready yet."

The work is still in that precious stage of creation where it's mine alone, shielded from the judgment of anyone else.

"The first time I drew something of my own it was of the cottage. Everything was change back then, but when I drew that picture—when I played around with the yellow hue of the light above the door, the shadow against the bronze knocker—I realized I could freeze time. I could keep everything just the same," I tell him. "After that, nothing felt real until I had captured it."

"That makes sense," says Theo. "What you said about freezing time."

We've stopped walking, caught up in the conversation. Around us, the island hums, the crowd of tourists parting around our bodies, and there we are, swept with the current, swimming sideways.

Chapter Twenty-One

Lily

July 10

Lily!" I hear a voice shout. "Are you okay?"

I'm pressing my forehead against the cold wrought iron armrest of Lottie's bench. I keep my vision fixated on the sunflowers in the garden, half expecting them to blink their large heads back at me. It's been nearly a week since the museum trip with Theo. My heart drops down to my belly button and then back up to my throat, like a yo-yo pulled back after reaching too far a drop.

"Is it a panic attack?" a man's voice asks.

In my disorientation, it takes me a moment to realize it's Thomas speaking.

I nod weakly, confused for a moment about how he knows. The gallery called back. Marie Chen.

When I saw the caller ID pop up on my phone, something quick and frantic fluttered in my chest. I wiped my palms on my jeans, tucked my hair behind my ears, smoothing it down as if she could see me, and took a deep breath before answering.

"Hello?" I said, practicing the chirp of a gallerist. Better to start dressing for the part now.

"Hi, is this Lily Gardner?"

"Yes, it is." The creature in my chest was alive then, batting its wings rapidly against the edges of my rib cage.

"This is Marie calling about your application. I'm sorry to say I cannot accept your request at this time. But thank you for your interest. It was lovely meeting you."

The wings abruptly stopped their flapping. "Oh, okay." Before she could hang up, I hurried to fill the dead space. "May I ask why?"

There was a long, uncomfortable pause on the other end of the phone. I imagined Marie in her undoubtedly fancy kitchen in her undoubtedly fancy home. I pictured her in an iteration of the outfit she wore the night of the fundraiser: all tailored blazers and the type of expensive leather shoes that have never seen grass. Marie is someone you could never picture in pajamas.

"You were an assistant for Clive Bozeman, which is very impressive, but when we asked him for a recommendation, he refused. I'm sorry, Lily, but we value transparency here."

"Well, thank you for your consideration, I really app—" Before I could finish, there was no one on the line left to hear it. Marie had hung up.

How did this happen? How did the three years I worked day and night for Clive come down to this? Nothing? All those late nights, dry-cleaning runs, the coffee spilled on my shirt before seven in the morning . . . I never once complained. I never once said, "This is not in my job description." I never took vacation days, always worked on holidays. I didn't ask for credit for my ideas or complain when he took ownership over them. Now I'm unemployable.

Everything used to be wide open. Now life is solidifying. It is beckoning me like an open door, and everyone else is walking into it, securing a future for themselves, while I stand there, paralyzed by indecision, until all of the doors slam shut.

When did this happen? When did I run out of time to waste?

I think about Henry's offer again to introduce me to family friends in the industry. This time, with some regret.

"Lily, can you look up at me and take a deep breath?" Thomas's voice is closer now. I look up slowly and see that he's sitting beside me on the bench. Everything around us, including him, seems to vibrate slightly around the edges. My heart is speeding ahead of the rest of my body, my hands are shaking, and I can't seem to take a full breath.

"We're going to do a little grounding exercise together, okay?" says Thomas. I try to focus on his voice. "Can you name five things you can see?"

I look at the garden behind him. "A green bush, pink peonies, honeysuckles, shingles, and grass."

"Very good. Now how about four things you can touch?"

I close my eyes and breathe. "The wood of the bench, the iron armrest." I put my hands on my lap, gripping the sleeves of my sweater. "The cotton of my sweater, the dirt beneath my shoes."

"Perfect," says Thomas. He models another deep breath. "Now, how about three things you can hear?"

"Your voice, a passing car, the ocean." I can sense the waves of panic receding. It's not gone, but it's relenting just enough for me to gasp for air.

"Excellent. Two things you can smell?"

"Honeysuckles again, grass."

"And finally, one thing you can taste?"

Regret, I want to say. "Coffee from breakfast."

"Wonderful. How do you feel now?"

I open my eyes and look at Thomas's face, his expression expectant and concerned. "I feel better," I admit. "Thank you."

I know the grounding technique he walked me through is called the 5-4-3-2-1 method—Rose taught me it when I first told her about the panic attacks—but I've never been able to successfully use it before. Thomas was the one to break through.

"Good," he says. "Do you want to talk about what happened?"

The attack has mostly dispersed, but I'm left with a trembling exhaustion afterward like a fever has just broken. I shake my head.

"When did you learn that?" I ask him instead.

"After my wife died, I started having some panic attacks." He looks at the grass when he speaks. "I went to a therapist and they helped me through it."

"Thank you," I say again, because as we both know, *I'm sorry* isn't enough. "Would you tell me about her?" He looks up, surprised. "I mean, only if you're comfortable with it."

A smile crosses his face. Somehow, it still looks tired. "She was amazing," he says. "She was passionate, loving, and had the best laugh." His smile spreads, becomes more genuine. "She always carried around extra Band-Aids or protein bars or candy. I swear her purse was the biggest thing I ever saw. She always made sure to have extra items on hand in case anyone needed anything. I used to call it her Mary Poppins bag, because it seemed to defy the laws of the universe."

Thomas laughs, and I do, too. It's hard not to be in awe of this woman he's described. I can see the full spectrum of the loss on his face.

"She was also an artist like you," he says. "She made these really cool ceramics. Our house back home is covered in them. She was also stubborn. A complete know-it-all." He laughs again. "I refused to be anywhere near her when *Jeopardy!* came on. Plus, she had a wicked temper." Thomas sighs. "I miss her every day."

We sit in silence for a few moments.

"I'm sorry," I say, because even though I know it isn't enough, it's the truth. I'm so sorry for his loss.

"Thank you," Thomas says. "I miss my kids, too. I'm hoping they'll come visit at the end of the summer."

"At the cottage?" I suppose they could sleep on the couch, but the guest side is pretty small as it is.

"I've actually been looking at property here," he says. "I've been going to some open houses. If possible, I'd love to buy a place, and of course, give you two some privacy."

"Oh." I'm surprised. "I thought after the wedding you would want to leave the island altogether, not find a more permanent residence."

"I'm sorry about that outburst, by the way," he says, nodding in my direction. "It was unlike me."

"Don't be sorry. It was my fault for meddling. Does that mean you're feeling better about my mom?"

Thomas shifts on the bench, leaning back. "I don't know. Being back here made me realize how much I miss this place. Plus, I've been meeting with my partner from my old company. He has a house in Madaket, so we've been spending a lot of time together, dreaming up what might be another idea."

Once again, I'm taken aback. "I had no idea you were meeting with your business partner while you're here."

He eyes me teasingly. "You thought I was just loitering around your mom's property, waiting around to take relationship advice from a twenty-something-year-old?"

My cheeks burn. When he says it aloud, I realize how ridiculous my idea of him has been. Thomas smiles, and the expression has a warming effect. My mind flashes to the image of the captain's portrait in my closet.

"Tommy?" I hear from the direction of the cottage.

Thomas stands up immediately, looking flustered. "Hello," he says to Rose, smoothing down his shirt. She's standing in the doorway of our side of the cottage, her straw purse by her side and sunglasses blocking her eyes.

Rose stands there stiffly, looking like there's something she wants to say, until she notices my posture.

"Lily, are you okay?" She rushes to my side. Thomas steps out of her way. "You look pale." She presses a cold hand to my cheek.

"I'm fine," I assure Mom. "I'm just tired. I'll be okay. Thomas helped me."

Rose looks unconvinced but she knows when to drop a subject, a by-product of her clinical training: Never push a patient before they're ready.

"I should be going," says Thomas to her left. "I hope you feel better."

Rose turns to look at him. "Thank you," she says with emotion in her voice. "For helping Lily. I really appreciate it."

He nods solemnly. "Of course."

With that, he returns to his side of the cottage, taking slow, deliberate steps as if he has to intentionally tell his body where to move next.

Rose turns her attention back to me. "Are you still okay to come with me to the ferry?"

Today is the day my grandfather and aunt arrive for their annual two-week stay. I know Rose has been dreading it, and even though no part of me takes pleasure from seeing either of them, my mom needs my support.

"I'll be fine." I force a smile. "I promise."

* * *

An hour later we wait at the dock. We're down by the wharf, standing on the packed cobblestone streets. Tourists mill around, bopping from shop to shop that all sell various Nantucket-shaped merchandise. It's always struck me as a funny phenomenon, the way we plaster the places we visit across our outerwear, as if it says something about our values to advertise the names of locations we've been. Then again, maybe the places we love really are part of us, and I suppose there are worse things to advertise.

It's a hot July day, and even the breeze coming off the harbor isn't enough to cool my nerves. I take my sweater off and tie it around my waist, so I'm only in a white T-shirt. We're early, because, well, Rose is always early.

"Do you think they brought the cat?" Rose asks, adjusting her large sunglasses.

"I guess it depends on the rental. What did Josie find them?"

"There was nothing in their budget, so she's letting them stay in her family's guesthouse downtown for half the price. She's an angel."

"Wow, does Grandpa know that?" I can't imagine my grandfather would like being the source of someone else's pity. His ego would never allow the charity.

Mom rolls her eyes. "No, he still thinks prices are what they were twenty years ago."

"That's awfully nice of Josie. So, the two of you made up?"

"She's the best," says Mom. "I apologized the other day and thankfully, she forgave me."

It makes me think of Jade, whom I still haven't spoken to. I keep waiting, hoping she'll be the one who breaks the ice first. I want to reach out, but she's probably busy. She works as a literary assistant at a small firm in SoHo. Her social media is riddled with book parties and nights out with her boyfriend, Mark. It feels like our lives are farther apart than ever.

"Did you explain the history between you and Thomas?"

Mom's eyes are unreadable beneath the thick shades, but her mouth compresses. "No, I didn't want to get into it. She still has no idea."

In the distance, we see the ferry pulling in, its large, imposing body narrowly navigating the crowded docks. During Christmas, it's tradition for Santa to arrive here by the port, riding in with the Coast Guard. It's one of my favorite island quirks.

"Do I look okay?" asks Rose, suddenly nervous. She picks up the glasses and uses them to push back her hair. It's clear she's dressed up for the occasion: sandals and a nice white linen dress with a belt around the waist.

"You look great. What are you so worried about?"

"You know how my dad can be," says Rose. I watch her eyes flit across the heads of the new arrivals, searching for her family in the crowd. "I bet you the first thing he says to me is, 'You look pale.'"

"You're being harsh," I say, but I know she's probably right. Still, I've found my grandfather to have mellowed in age a little bit.

Toward the middle of the departing line—unmistakable in their nearly identical outfits of matching beige crewnecks—are my grandfather and aunt.

"Hi!" yells Elizabeth, waving above the moving crowd. She's carrying two large suitcases, enough luggage for a yearlong stay, and her blond hair is cut into a short, neat bob.

To her left, my grandfather looks as stately as ever with his tall stature, thick white hair, and proud features. His chin is perpetually haughty, raised parallel to the ground. Both of them are freshly tanned, probably due to another lavish vacation they can't afford or a trip to the tanning beds they adore.

"Here comes the gruesome twosome," Mom mumbles to me under her breath before fixing a smile on her face.

"Lily, my dear," says my grandfather when he reaches us. He leans down to plant a kiss on my cheek. "Looking fine as ever." I try not to wonder if he means the statement more as an insult or a compliment. "And dear Rosie! My child, have you been working away all summer? You're looking even paler than usual."

Leave it to my grandfather to comment first on our appearance. It's the greatest disappointment of his life that we look more like his late wife than we do him. At least he has Elizabeth to fulfill her duties as the great carrier of both his vanity and his genome. The two of them—tall, slender, blond, and tan—look more like twins than father-daughter.

Elizabeth's tiny white Persian cat, named Mrs. Clay, shakes in a pink carrier. Her onyx eyes stare us down, as judgmental as its owner.

"And look who we ran into on the ferry!" says Elizabeth as she leans over to give me a hug.

My grandfather moves aside to reveal their surprise guest. The appearance is so incongruous with my every expectation of the afternoon that it takes me a few seconds to register the sight. There, standing between my grandfather and aunt, is my father.

"Surprise!" he says, jazz hands at the ready.

Chapter Twenty-Two

Rose

James and I face each other in a small restaurant hallway. We're standing with our backs to either side of the narrow passageway, waiting for the single-use bathroom door to open. I called on the way here to see if we could add one more to the reservation.

The restaurant, Brotherhood of Thieves, is a quick walk away on Broad Street, so once we put everyone's bags into the Jeep, we didn't have to give up our coveted parking spot. Although, we received many glares from the passing cars James kept waving away.

"You're going to ignore me?" James says now, arms crossed. "Real mature, Rose."

I imitate his posture. "I'm not ignoring you. Consider me stunned speechless."

"Don't be like this, Rose. Come on, talk to me." He leans closer, but a waiter is passing by at the very moment, and we squeeze back to make room.

When the waiter is gone, I hiss, "What're you doing here?"

"What? I can't visit my own kid?"

"Not like you showed much of an interest in visiting your kid recently."

How long has it been since we've seen him? I rack my brain. Two years? Three? He didn't even attend Lottie's funeral. We've seen him once since the pandemic ended, and that was for a quick dinner in which his wife lectured us on the "negative effects a child experiences when growing up in a broken home," courtesy of her new career stint in child development. Maren is always switching interests, going back to school for different degree programs, all of which she promptly drops within three to six months. Most recently, she was a "spiritual coach" offering mental health advice online for $300 an hour. As a therapist and, more generally, as a rational member of the human race, I find it all a bit worrying.

"Rose, that's not fair. You know, for someone who claims to despise me so much, you've spent an awfully long time wearing my last name."

"It's a good last name. It's a good bit, that's all. James"—I lower my voice—"seriously. What's going on?"

"Something has to be wrong for me to visit?"

It's strange how familiar he is to me still, like a childhood friend I can't shake. Or maybe more like a really annoying cousin I wish would just leave me the heck alone. I know his posture: slightly slanted, always slouching. I know his hair: dark, gelled, and subtly thinning at the hairline but still full and handsome. I know his stubborn expression best of all.

"The timing is a little strange you must admit. You just happened to be on the same ferry as my dad and sister? And you didn't think to call before you came?"

"Okay," he sighs. "You caught me. They invited me to come. They said I could crash at their place."

I slam my palm against the shiny wood-paneled wall. "Damn it, James, there's always something fishy with you. Why can't you be honest for once?"

Dad has always had a soft spot for James, by which I mean he lets him get away with absolutely everything, even impregnating his daughter and cheating. Just once I wish he would stand up for me.

I have a realization and groan again. "James, their rental isn't big enough for you. It's a guesthouse that can barely fit them. I had to call in a favor from a friend to even get them that much space."

"That's fine," says James, but he looks dejected. "I'll just get a hotel."

I think about the prices this time of year, especially last minute. I don't know why I say it, but I do. "You can stay with us."

James smiles his winning grin, and I realize this is the problem; this is why James always gets what he wants, from me, my dad, his parents. There's something about him that's childishly disarming. Lily is going to be furious.

He moves closer, and I have a sudden sense of claustrophobia. I wish the hallway would split open to allow more air in. The ceilings are low with dark wooden beams visible. It has the effect of making me feel like I'm in the bow of a ship.

"Rose," James says, trying to get me to look at him. "I split up with Maren."

"Oh God," I groan into my hands. "What happened?"

James grabs my arms apart and puts them at my sides, staring intently at my face.

I can't help but laugh. "What is this? Please don't tell me you're here to try to win me back or something pathetic."

I think about Thomas and William's almost showdown at the wedding two weeks ago and imagine throwing the absolute disaster that is James Gardner into the mix. There's been enough chaos this summer.

James scoffs, but somehow, it's not a cruel sound. "Jesus, no. We've been there before and it didn't work out. Listen, you're still smoking hot and all, so I'm not saying it's completely off the table but—"

"Now might be a good time to remind you that it didn't work out the first time because you cheated on me."

"Ancient history," he scoffs again. "Plus, we both know we were never a good match."

"So then why are you here?"

"I just wanted to see Lily," says James. "Look at me. I'm a twice-divorced fifty-year-old man with nothing to show for my life except for some money in the bank and a terrible relationship with my only daughter. Is it so wrong to want to remedy that?"

"You didn't exactly catch her at the best time," I warn. "She's extra sensitive right now."

The sound of a toilet flushing makes us move apart again, and out of the stall walks a woman in a ridiculous head-to-toe pink outfit, like an advertisement for Pepto-Bismol. It's fitting since James's surprise visits always give me a stomachache.

"Ladies first," James says, gesturing.

I flip him the bird and open the door. "This conversation isn't over."

Back at the table, a waitress brings around lobster rolls and crispy fries. My dad sits at the head of the table with a plastic bib tucked into his collar. Mrs. Clay, the cat, perches in a kid's booster seat to his right.

"Lily, how's work? Are you still fetching coffees?" asks Dad.

"I am not," says Lily, with some degree of irony.

"Good for you! You were always too good to be someone's lackey," says my dad. "What're you doing for work now?"

"I'm a receptionist at the yacht club here," she says with forced neutrality, clearly anticipating his reaction. "I answer phones. It's all very glamorous."

"Well," says my dad, adjusting his bib. His white hair looks electric in the single ray of bright light coming in through the sunken window behind his back. "That's probably better. Less risk of spilling, anyhow." He turns toward me. "I do wish you had confided in me before turning Lottie's cottage into some sort of lodge," he sniffs. "Now I have to get a rental like a tourist."

"There's not enough space for all of us to stay there at the same time anyway."

"Still," my dad chides. "A stranger staying in your house? Using your sheets? It's a little disturbing, isn't it?"

"It's economical and I swap out the sheets." I pause, debating the next part. "Besides, I know the tenant."

"You do?"

"I'm fine with not staying there," Elizabeth interrupts. "I never liked that cottage anyway. It's too . . . old and moist. I'm convinced I got sick from mold last time we stayed."

I avoid rolling my eyes by digging the nails of my left hand into my thigh. "There is no mold, Elizabeth."

"Tell that to the pneumonia I developed three summers ago. Besides, Lottie got sick. What if it was something in the house?"

"It wasn't anything in the house." My heart aches at the thought; it feels accusatory, like I could have done something more to help my aunt, when in reality, I tried everything I possibly could. Right?

"Who's the tenant?" my dad asks again. "Is it another friend of yours like Josie? I always liked her, and she was so helpful with finding us a place to stay—thank God someone was or else we'd be vagrants, wandering the streets. My own daughter casting us aside."

Lily gives me a pointed look; I can tell what she's trying to communicate. It's like we have special mother-daughter telepathy. *Be careful*, her eyes caution.

"It's Thomas Wentworth," I say, refolding the napkin on my lap to avoid their stares.

Elizabeth slaps the table and Mrs. Clay startles. "No way!"

I look around the crowded room. The space is cramped and dark, like an old-fashioned pub.

"Dear God," says my dad.

James leans back in his seat and smirks. "Well, I'll be damned. Tommy Wentworth back from the grave."

I shoot him daggers.

"Thomas Wentworth, really? Is he still off playing sailor?" my dad asks, leaning forward. Mrs. Clay meows.

"He was in the Coast Guard, Dad," I say. "And no. He founded a very successful business, actually. It's a hardware company that designs chips for computers."

My dad uses a steak knife to cut into his lobster roll. "Well, good for him, I suppose. Maybe you should have married him after all."

Lily guffaws. Her mouth drops agape, and I imagine my expression is a mirror image of her own.

"Are you serious?" she says. I give her a look to tell her to stop, but she ignores me. She's in defense mode. "You're seriously going to say that after you're the one who discouraged her from the engagement in the first place?"

My dad releases an exasperated breath and puts down his utensils. "What are you going on about now?"

"You're the one who wrote the letter, telling Mom to call off the engagement." Lily is leaning across the table now, too, her fork in the air pointing in his direction as an accusation.

Dad waves off her concern, digs back into his roll. "I only wrote that letter because Lottie asked me to. I didn't much care myself, truthfully. I was happy to have someone take Rose off my plate, if I'm honest."

My brain tries to simultaneously process the hurt and confusion and short-circuits. It's like I can hear the synapses forming, the electricity flowing at rapid speeds as the past realigns itself.

"Are you being serious?" I ask my dad. My heart feels like it's trying to escape from my throat, bobbing up and out of my mouth and spilling onto our lunch.

"Of course I'm being serious," says my dad. "Do you really think I cared that much? It's your life to live. I've never stopped any of your bad ideas before or since. Heck, I even let Lily run off and play artist." She glares at him. "Lottie told me she was worried you were too young to be attaching yourself to someone with an uncertain future. She wanted me to caution you against it, so I did." He chews and thinks. "Although, I suppose I did wish he wasn't a Catholic."

"Lottie did this?" I repeat to myself, barely more than a whisper. "This was Lottie's idea?"

I can't imagine it. Lottie was the one who held me as I cried, the one who comforted me when I received the letter. She was even-keeled, impassive, never taking a side in the debate as I went back and forth . . . Or was she?

Did she not subtly encourage me to listen to my dad? Did she not tell me that there would be others, other loves and adventures I had not yet met? Did she not emphasize how young we were, how rash we were being?

Did she persuade me?

This whole time I've resented my dad, but in reality, it was Lottie, my closest confidant, who was really to blame. And most of all, me, for being so foolish and easily molded.

It's like the walls of the restaurant are falling down around me, everything I ever believed in collapsing at my feet. I've held Lottie up my entire life as a role model, a certain feminine ideal, the kind of person I strived to be. And all along, she was covering up this huge secret.

The waitress approaches. She has kind eyes and an optimistically high ponytail that bounces when she speaks. She looks around Lily's age. "Can I get you all anything else?"

"What about your number?" James winks. Lily hides her face in her hands. "What?" he says. "I'm kidding, obviously. Just trying to lighten the mood."

"We'll take the check," says Lily from between her fingers. "Thank you, and I'm sorry."

"I'll be right back with that," says the gracious waitress.

I try to communicate my sincere apologies through my eyes without embarrassing her further. She comes back seconds later with a receipt and places it in the middle of the table.

"What a nice family gathering you have here," she says. "I hope you enjoy your stay."

I look around the table. James is checking his reflection in the spoon he holds in his left hand. My dad is attempting to feed Mrs. Clay a piece of lobster. Elizabeth is scrolling on her phone, no doubt looking up mold poisoning symptoms. Lily is staring at James in disgust, holding her knife upright in the fist of her right hand, ready to stab.

As the waitress leaves us, I think about her words. "Nice family gathering" all right.

Chapter Twenty-Three

Lily

July 11

The following morning, Mom and I decide to complete item one on Lottie's bucket list. We had it on the schedule already, so despite the news from yesterday's lunch, we keep the plan.

I wake up early, restless. I can't believe my father is here, unannounced and uninvited. After years of not seeing him, having no clue where he is or how he's doing, it's bizarre to have him right outside our door, sleeping on the couch.

Sometimes when I was walking around New York, I was struck by the fact of his existence. Most days I didn't think of him at all. His absence was nothing, like trying to miss someone you never really knew. It didn't matter.

Except, occasionally, it did.

Once in a while, when I was crossing a street or forcing my way into a packed subway, it suddenly dawned on me: I have a father. I have a father—living on this very same planet as me at this very same astrological moment—and he doesn't know where I am. He doesn't know if I am well or unwell. He doesn't know if I'm madly in love or heartbroken, if I'm thriving in my career or living on the streets.

I wouldn't say the realization hurt so much as it confused. When we're apart, I call my mom upward of three times a day. She knows every meal I eat. And yet, I have this other parent—this whole other half of my family tree—who doesn't have a clue.

I always hated the term *daddy issues.* It feels like just another way for us to blame women for the sins of men. For most of my life before Henry, I closed myself off to boys. I didn't want to play into any preconceived notions of what people think it looks like to live without a father. Eventually, I didn't want to be abandoned, so I abandoned people first.

Three years ago, when I first moved to the city, my father reached out. We had talked here and there over the years, but I was determined to ignore him—still angry about the Mistress.

Then came the emails. Subject lines with "Can we talk?" appeared in my inbox: malignant ghosts. I couldn't tell if my father was drunk or sober at first, but upon reading more, I realized he had entered into a sober living program in Palm Springs, where the desert had physically dried him out, wrung him out like a dish towel. He realized his mistakes. He wanted to make amends. I marked the messages "Spam" and ignored them all.

Henry couldn't comprehend why I didn't answer my father. "He's trying to make amends," he said. "Why are you closing yourself off to that? You're making your life smaller."

Work with Clive was piling up. One day, I got off at the wrong subway stop and ended up having to run ten blocks to make it to the office on time, arriving in a cold sweat. My clothes sat in boxes on the floor; my furniture from Ikea was only half-assembled, always missing one bolt or screw so everything wobbled, off-kilter.

I was in no shape to have this conversation with my father. I was barely taking care of myself.

"You complain about not having a large family, but then you throw away the family you do have," Henry said smugly.

After the fifteenth email from my father, I gave in. I did this for Henry's sake as much as for my own, to prove to him that I was lovable—that I was trying to let people love me.

My father didn't answer. His emails stopped arriving. I didn't hear from him again.

At first, it made me laugh, like, really laugh: a deep, throaty, soulful bellow. My laughter was rage and it was relief and it was even a little smug, the smugness of being proven right.

Henry didn't like the way I laughed. He found it unsettling, because he thought I should be crying. He thought I should be crying because he didn't know what it is to run out of tears for someone.

Pretty soon after, work got worse. That's when I had my first panic attack. Clive needed me to send out emails to some potential photographers. He needed me to make a dinner reservation. He needed a thousand tasks all at once. It was an unseasonably warm October day when everything first came crushing in. At first, I thought I was fainting.

My old therapist later suggested my panic attacks were "unprocessed grief."

"The emotions you suppress have a way of popping up, no matter how much you try to bury them," she told me.

Now, looking at my father, asleep on the couch—slightly drooling on Lottie's favorite pink quilt, the one with ladybugs printed on it—I wonder if she was right.

* * *

It's early and Rose still isn't up, so I decide to get a head start on the day by going to the local diner, Downyflake, to pick up donuts. It's strange being the only one awake in the house; I'm not used to the feeling. I throw my hair into a claw clip, pull on jeans and a sweater, and grab the keys from the hook in the entranceway.

At Downyflake, I'm one of five people waiting for the owners to open. A few construction workers stand outside in a silent, makeshift line. We can smell the donuts wafting out. My eyes are dry and hurt when I blink, my eyelids sticking together as if in protest of being awake. It is dark outside, and everything looks purple around the edges, humming with energy.

When a young woman with a tall bun opens the door, I select five donuts: some tossed in sugar and cinnamon, others covered in chocolate frosting that sticks to the side of the white bag. The latter are my favorite. The former are Lottie's. I grab two coffees, one for me and another for my mom.

Back at the house, Rose is awake and already ready to go. She sits outside on the small steps that lead to the front door, still in her silk pajama pants and a tan sweater.

"Wow." Her face lights up when she sees the coffees and donuts. "You're a lifesaver."

The sun is already starting to lighten to a color of gray that is all white and only a drop of blue, so we hurry to the ocean in companionable silence. We carry blankets underneath our arms. The grass is dewy beneath our sandals, and when we get to the beach, the sand is still cold. We lay out the blankets by the lifeguard stand, hold the warm coffees between our hands, and stare out at the sea, waiting.

"You're awfully quiet this morning," Rose observes after a few moments.

"Mmm," I say, noncommittal. "You are as well. How did you sleep?"

"Fine," Rose says. There are dark circles under my mom's warm brown eyes.

"Pretty big revelation yesterday," I remark, still staring at the ocean.

"Pretty big surprise guest, too," says Rose.

I turn to look at her. "How are you feeling about the Lottie stuff?"

Mom pulls the blanket tighter around her shoulders. "Betrayed, honestly. But also a little silly. Does it matter who tried to convince me not to marry Tommy? I'm the one who listened. I'm the one who is ultimately to blame."

"It's not too late," I say, trying to keep the urgency out of my voice and failing. "I mean, he's still here. I don't know what kind of conversation you had at the wedding, but if it was bad enough, he would have left."

"It is too late," she sighs. "Trust me. Too much has happened. Anyway, how do you feel about your father being back in town?"

Sick, infuriated. "Fine."

"Really?"

"I'll survive," I say, and feel my stomach turn.

The sun is beginning to peek its head out, like a little kid testing whether time-out is over yet. A sliver of light appears at the horizon, turning the water gold where it touches.

"I think we should abandon the bucket list," says Rose, staring straight and squinting.

I turn away from the view in surprise. "Why? Because you're mad at Lottie?"

"Because I've been trying my entire life to be her, to make her proud. I've put her on this ginormous pedestal, and it was wrong. I need a break from Lottie and her 'Lottie-isms.' I need to make my own decisions now."

"Are you sure? This seemed important to her, and I know you're mad now, but if we abandon the list, we might regret it later."

"I'm sure," says Rose, her voice impassive. "I can't go through the charade right now when everything feels so tainted. Listening to Lottie got me into this mess. I always assumed she knew best, but maybe she didn't." She pats my hair and smiles. "Maybe some other time."

"I understand." I nod, but inside, my heart is heavy.

We fall into silence. When the sun rises, it is big and brilliant. It emerges from the waves triumphant, bathing the sand, the water, and our blankets in orange light. I watch the color dance across Rose's face, turning her aglow.

When we walk back to the cottage, my father is awake and waiting for us in the small kitchen.

"Coffee?" he suggests, holding up Lottie's old turquoise pot.

I ignore him and go straight into my room, getting dressed for the day. I picked up an extra shift at the yacht club and have to leave soon. Afterward, I'm going to spend the rest of the afternoon working on my new portrait project. I started to add paint to them, including some of Lottie's sayings into the backgrounds. I used only the most exuberant colors for my great-aunt. "Good writing should feel like singing and reading like dancing," she once said, and I felt that way about the painting process of this project, too. I want the colors to sing. I want to resurrect Lottie's ruthless laugh, her vibrant clothing.

On one, I included my favorite Lottie quote: "We're all under the same rain. Some of us just have better umbrellas."

The problem is that after yesterday's revelation, it doesn't feel right to celebrate Lottie's advice. Rose is right. Maybe the problem is that Lottie was my umbrella, and I can no longer trust that it will hold up against the storm.

As I'm walking out the door, my father stops me, blocking my path. He's wearing plaid pajama bottoms and a Lakers sweatshirt, another reminder of his life without us.

"Lily, before you leave, can we talk? You barely looked at me yesterday."

There's something pathetic about a grown man in his pajamas begging like this, but I refuse to fall victim to his trap. "I'm busy," I tell him.

"Come on, just hear me out, okay? I came to the island to talk to you. I miss you."

I'm not sure why the sentiment makes me want to punch the wall. I ignore him again and continue walking out the door. He follows me into the garden. The sun is large now, and everything feels hot and itchy. Even the grass looks wilted, like it's tired.

I'm heading toward the gate when my father reaches me, grabs me by my left wrist.

"Lily, please," he begs.

Thomas is passing by on his bike. I don't see him until he's already coming our way. "Hey, what's going on here? Get your hands off her," he calls, jumping off the seat and pushing the red bike to the ground.

"Whoa, man. Relax! This is my daughter," says my father, stumbling back onto the lawn.

Thomas looks between the two of us, as if trying to make the genetic puzzle match: line up our slight noses and green eyes and the impish edge of our thin brows that always made my father look slightly feminine. "Your daughter?"

"Yes, my daughter, you idiot. And you must be . . . Thomas Wentworth." His sarcastic grin is back. "It's nice to finally meet the man my Rose was always in love with."

"Dad," I warn, crossing my arms in annoyance, like a petulant teenager. "What are you doing?" I don't realize until after I've said it that it's the first time I've called him *dad* instead of *father* in what must be years. The word feels wrong in my mouth.

"It's okay, Lil," says my father. "I'm pleased, really. When we were together, it was always 'Thomas this' and 'Thomas that.' I couldn't even do the dishes right without being told a story about a time you somehow did them better." He mocks my mom's voice, using an obnoxious high-pitched tone. "'You know, Thomas once cooked lobster bisque from scratch.'"

Thomas is frozen, listening as if in disbelief. His forehead is still shiny from his bike ride, and his ears are turning red at the tips. There's a strange woodsy smell about him, like sawdust.

"Dad, stop. Let it go."

My father reaches out a hand and offers it to Thomas. "I'm just messing with you. It really is nice to meet you," he says. Thomas looks at the hand like my father has just offered him a dead fish. My father shrugs and retreats. "You know, you're a pretty good-looking guy. I can see the appeal. Very rugged."

"Dad."

He acquiesces, taking a step back and turning his attention to me. Thomas is still standing there, dumbstruck.

"Lily, promise you'll talk to me? I'm only going to stay for a week, but I really want to talk to you. I want to explain," pleads my father.

The garden doors creak open again, and in walk my grandfather and Aunt Elizabeth. They're dressed in linen and carrying Mrs. Clay in a Nantucket basket.

"Hello!" my grandfather says cheerfully. "This is quite the scene. We were just stopping by to see what everyone is up to for the day."

I check the time on my phone and cannot believe it's only nine. I'm due at the club in thirty minutes. There's been more drama in this one morning than I experienced in the last two years combined.

My grandfather notices Thomas, who is slowly becoming reanimated. "Oh, and look who it is! This must be the famous Thomas

Wentworth." He places an arm around his shoulders and guides him toward Lottie's bench. "Say, why don't you tell me about this company of yours. I'm looking for a good investment opportunity."

Thomas looks like he's been suddenly zapped onto an alien planet where nothing follows the rules of gravity.

I force myself to stifle the laugh that is bubbling up. This is one of my grandfather's favorite pastimes. He loves to ask about "investment opportunities," when in reality, the only thing he can afford to invest in is a good haircut and a trip to the tanning beds. I can't tell if he's living in delusion or purposefully being deceitful. He hasn't had "investment money" since the eighties.

Aunt Elizabeth beelines to my father. "Do my arms look bumpy to you?" she asks.

My father is looking at Thomas and my grandfather, distracted. "Hmm?"

"I think the rental we're staying in has bedbugs. I woke up last night with a terrible, itchy sensation and now I have these little red bumps." She lifts the sleeve of her button-down and shows him. The skin looks red but not bumpy.

"It just looks like your skin is irritated from you scratching," says my father, still looking at the bench.

I take advantage of the momentary distraction to slip out.

When my father notices I'm leaving, he stares after me. There's a slightly desperate, wild look in his eyes.

"Later," I mouth to him with no intention of following through. He just nods, looking defeated, as Elizabeth continues to talk.

Chapter Twenty-Four

Lily

Later that night, my feet are sticking to the ground at the Chicken Box.

I didn't plan on coming here. It's Monday night, "Box Monday" as people call it: the night a DJ comes. Everyone is dancing and jostling and bumping into each other. My drink keeps sloshing over the edge of the plastic cup, adding its own layer to the thick grime that already covers the floorboards.

Theo was, of course, the one who convinced me to join the rest of the staffers tonight. Usually, I'd say no, but my mom texted me saying that she was going to dinner with William, and despite my promise to talk to my father tonight, the idea of sitting with him, my grandfather, and Aunt Elizabeth without Rose's backup sounds like a nightmare.

I love this place but I haven't been back all season. I used to come twice a weekend with Henry. My mom won coveted "Box Passes" at a charity auction years ago: two black-and-white cards that grant us access without a cover fee.

By the bathroom, there's two grungy pool tables, covered with beer-stained plastic wraps, a dartboard no one ever uses except in the offseason, and a shuffleboard table that moonlights as a sales area for branded merchandise. Outside, concealed by chicken wire and wood fencing, is the smoking area. And inside, past the large bar, is the dance floor with a small stage. A little booth in the corner reads "Hen House." The ceilings are covered with various paraphernalia: license plates, old posters, quarterboards, a wedding banner from ten years ago.

Becca and I used to dance onstage. Once, Jade was in town and joined us. Looking around now, I can't help but miss them both.

Minutes ago, I went to the bathroom, weaving my way past the bar, past the pool tables, avoiding the cigarette smoke and bad decisions. On the wall of my stall, there was a bulletin board filled with graffiti signatures and names carved with pushpins. I remembered Rose telling me about a time when she snuck in through the bathroom window when she was a teenager. In an irrational flash, I went to check for her name.

I didn't find it, but at the bottom of the board, someone had written, "Laura was happy here" and the date—ten summers prior. For a moment, I was transfixed by the sentence. It didn't just say, "Laura was here," but "Laura was happy here." The distinction seemed significant.

I'm still thinking of this Laura girl now. It reminds me of Rose, oddly: how Rose was a girl at this bar, too, how she is still in many ways just a girl falling in love, figuring out her relationships. It's her first time around the sun, too, and more than anything, I hope she's happy here.

"Your refill, madam." Theo emerges from the crowd, a drink in either hand.

His forehead is damp with sweat and his curls are sticking to it, looking windswept. He has been on the dance floor almost the entire time since we arrived two hours ago.

"Thank you, sir," I say.

"We're going to move to karaoke at the Rose and Crown," Theo shouts. He has to talk directly into my ear to be heard over the music. Someone next to us drives a sharp heel into my pinkie toe as she shuffles closer to the stage.

"Okay," I shout back, moving away from the girl. "I'm game for whatever."

"Cool," Theo is saying when I spot them across the crowd.

A strange hot flash spreads across my face, as if I've just stepped into a cloud of steam. My legs become wobbly. Of course, I knew there was always a chance of running into them, but for once, I let my guard drop. For once, I wasn't thinking of him, but there he is . . .

Henry and Mary are dancing toward the stage. Becca is there, too, with some of Henry's friends from home. Henry spins Mary and she laughs. They look happy, carefree. They look, somehow, already married. It's the connection in their eyes, the effortless nature of it. All of the oxygen abandons the room, like I've been sealed in a vacuum.

When Becca sees me, I smile, but she turns her back. So much for not choosing sides, I think. Then, pushing through the crowd, I see the red-shawled psychic again. She moves past me and winks, wearing the same mischievous smile. Before she can disappear again, I tear my eyes away from the sight of Henry and Mary dancing and grab her shoulder.

"What are you doing?" I demand in a hiss. "What do you want from me?"

She's been haunting me ever since the night of the greenhouse fundraiser. I keep thinking I see her in crowds, like at the wedding. I keep hearing her warning: "Choose your next steps carefully." What business did she have scaring me like that? And why did she tell me that my soulmate's name starts with the letter *H*? It's making it even harder to move on from Henry.

The lady jerks under my touch, but when she turns around, it's not the psychic. It's a young girl in a red top who looks nothing like her: a young girl who, under my grasp, looks at me with terrified, wide eyes.

"What?" she says. "You're crazy." She hurries away to her friends, and I lose sight of her in the crowd.

Maybe she's right. Maybe I am losing it.

"I need to get out of here," I say into Theo's ear, trying to keep the panic from my voice. Luckily, he seems to have missed the exchange. "I need to get out of here," I repeat.

I don't wait to see if Theo follows my line of sight. Instead, I head right toward the exit, handing my new drink to a drunk college boy standing by the bouncer.

"I didn't drink out of this, if you want it," I say to him.

The frat boy shrugs and eyes the drink with glee. "I wouldn't care if you did. A free drink is a free drink!"

I can hear his friends cheering as I exit the bar and walk into the cool mist outside.

"What was that about?" asks Theo from behind.

In my panic, I find it difficult to look him square in the face. It's like I'm only viewing him from the periphery, squinting at the sides, so his features are blurry and watery: the view out of a passing car. Sometimes, when I'm having a panic attack, I'm left gasping for air. It's terrifying how physical the sensation is, like I really am drowning.

"Nothing," I say, trying to calm my rapid breaths. "Just something better off avoided. Let's go to the next place."

* * *

We take a taxi downtown to Rose & Crown with Emily and a few other coworkers. It's karaoke night, and on the way there, we tease each other with dares about different songs to sing. I silently pray that no one makes me get onstage.

The interior of the bar is purposefully kitschy, all deep wood and decorations of mermaids, fish, big white sharks. A light machine near the stage casts the entire space in moving blue dots.

Compared to the crowded bar we came from, the place is near empty. There are only a handful of other groups. A couple sits in a circular booth in the far right corner, deep in conversation, so I can't see their faces.

The lady running karaoke is wearing a sweatshirt, leggings, and glasses, but when she sings, she sounds like she belongs on Broadway. She belts through a few ballads to kill time while waiting for people to sign up. Theo walks right up to her immediately, writes something down on a slip of paper, and returns to our table triumphant.

"What did you put down?" Emily asks, touching his arm. My eyes follow the embrace.

"You'll see," is all Theo responds.

When it is his turn, we all stand up to cheer and clap. Strangely, I feel nervous for him, protective. Theo clears his throat onstage, pushes his hair back, turns around, and starts to snap. I cover my eyes. A guitar riff begins. Some people recognize it immediately and begin to holler. Theo spins around.

"Love Grows (Where My Rosemary Goes)" by Edison Lighthouse starts playing.

Emily jumps on the top of the booth's vinyl cushions, cheering. I draw an invisible line between the two of them with my eyes.

As Theo sings the lyrics, his voice is deep, and soothing, and surprisingly good. Everyone is singing along as he dances across the stage. I stand up, too.

Each verse, he seems to gain even more confidence, if that's possible, dancing and snapping, dipping the microphone and then grabbing it just before it hits the ground.

I yell at the stage like a fangirl, laughing. He has never mentioned that he can sing before, but there he is, sure as sin. People have begun to enter the dance floor, couples spinning each other, mothers and daughters dancing.

That's when I notice them, the couple from earlier. As the crowd shifts and the lights dot across the bar, they appear to me in momentary focus, knees bent toward each other in a deep, intimate discussion. I recognize the woman first. It's my mom's best friend, Josie.

It takes me a second longer to identify the man, but when I do, I can't believe my eyes. From across the bar, Thomas looks up. He has a scared, guilty look. It's not too far off from how he looked in the garden this morning being sucked into my grandfather's narcissistic orbit.

At the sixth verse, Theo walks into the crowd, microphone still in hand. He approaches our booth and sings the last chorus, except this time, he replaces "Rosemary" with "Lily."

Emily squeezes my arm. My heart dips to my stomach. Is he doing this now? Is this happening?

I try to stay in the moment, but I can't tear my eyes away from Thomas and Josie. What is he doing here with her? Are they on a date? Even if he's done with Rose, this seems cruel. Going for her best friend?

Theo stands beside me on the booth, still singing. He's close to my face now, and at the end of the last sentence, he leans in and closes the remaining two-inch gap. My stomach performs gymnastics. The whole room erupts in applause as he kisses me, and I can feel his hand on the small of my back, his mouth urgent, and warm, and serious, but a smile just beneath it.

When we pull apart, I smile at him. I look back toward the booth but Thomas and Josie are gone, the door of the bar banging shut behind them.

Chapter Twenty-Five

Lily

July 12

I'm going to vomit," says Mom the next morning. "I actually think I may puke."

She leans against the back door of the cottage, pressing her arms against the screen like she's physically holding it back from being barged open.

"What?" My voice is rusty with sleep, hands wrapped around my coffee cup as if in prayer. I made it in a groggy state a few moments ago with robotic precision: chilled espresso, ice, milk, cream. I kept thinking about the lyrics "Clouds in my coffee . . . clouds in my coffee."

Henry texted me this morning. *Hey, did I see you at The Box last night? Why didn't you say hey?* he wrote.

I haven't responded, but the text unnerved me just the same. Why is he still reaching out? It's over. It has to be over. I can see that now. No matter what any psychic has to say.

Mom's face is red, and she begins to frantically move about the room, picking up a teapot and then immediately placing it back down, scooping crumbs into her hand, and then looking around dazed, as if suddenly uncertain where the trash can is. "I mean, I didn't think he'd be in there—I had no idea."

"What?" I repeat. "What are you talking about?"

"Tommy, of course!" she says, like I'm being intentionally obtuse. "I just walked in on him in the outdoor shower." The redness across the ridge of her nose looks like a sunburn.

"You walked in on him showering?" I suppress a laugh, relieved that this is all that's wrong. But then I remember what I saw last night: Thomas and Josie leaning in close at the karaoke bar. My smile drops.

Rose continues to busy herself, fanning her face with an oven mitt. "I mean, it's not my fault, I was just trying to water the flowers, but I ran straight into him as he was exiting. His towel nearly fell off."

Now I can't help but giggle. Mom narrows her eyes.

"It's not funny!" she says. "Poor Matilda was outside, watering her garden and heard my shriek. She could have had a heart attack."

Matilda is an eighty-year-old widow who lives across the street. She and Lottie had a famously contemptuous relationship—Matilda always complaining that Lottie's rosebushes were extending over the property line, Lottie complaining that Matilda had "a broom-sized stick up her ass."

"Matilda probably got her binoculars out," I say, still laughing.

I debate telling her about what I saw last night: Thomas and Josie together in the booth, evidently on a date. I start to speak but then chicken out. I don't want to face her wrath. She's already agitated. Maybe now isn't the best time. Or maybe I'm just a coward.

"Do you think I should go next door and say something? Apologize?"

My brain is still slow, the coffee just beginning to work its magic. "To Matilda?"

Mom narrows her eyes even further. I'm impressed she can still see. "No, obviously not. I mean to Tommy," she whispers, nodding her head in the general direction of the guest quarters. "I must have scared him. And I mean, it is his right to use the shower. I said he could in the welcome packet. But of course, that's before I knew who the renter was . . ."

She trails off, wringing her hands around a dish towel and looking out the window, torn. "I should apologize," she decides. "It's common courtesy."

"Maybe wait until he's clothed this time," I say. Mom rolls her eyes. "But actually, what good would that do? I would just leave it alone."

Thomas and Josie's image from last night bobs back up to the surface of my brain: him leaning in, her throwing her head back laughing. Their knees touching. I understand if he wants to move on from Rose after the disastrous wedding setup, but Josie is far too close to home. I can't believe he would do something so . . . careless. It feels wildly out of character.

Rose is still staring out the window with an anxious expression. "No," she says. "You're right." But her lips are pursed.

A knock startles us both, and I turn to see Thomas standing outside the screen door, hands behind his back, looking exceptionally polite.

Mom turns to me with frantic eyes and whispers, "Be cool."

"Hi!" she says, smoothing her pink button-down when she opens the door. "What can I do for you?"

Thomas speaks in a calm, deliberate manner, but his cheeks are reddened, too. "I just want to apologize for a few moments ago. I didn't know you were outside."

Mom laughs too loud and waves the dish towel at him playfully. "Oh, that?" she says, trying for nonchalance. "That was nothing. Don't worry about it."

Thomas is now, mercifully, dressed in a plain white shirt and tan pants. His hair is still wet. When he nods his head, a few longer strands fall into his face. "Of course," he says. "Again, my apologies, however. I'll be more mindful in the future."

They stand for a moment in silence, just staring at each other. The tension is a physical presence, weighing the air down. I half expect the clocks to start running backward, the stove to magically turn on.

Rose opens her mouth like she's about to say something more, but then closes it, back to wringing the towel. The blush on Thomas's face deepens, but he too stays silent.

I'm confused. I know my mom is with William and said that she and Thomas would never work, but looking at them now, it's impossible to deny the pull. I've never seen anything like it. Rose is usually so composed, and yet here she is, speechless.

"Do you want to—I mean, no pressure, of course—but do you want to maybe come in for a coffee?"

Thomas's eyes lift. He teeters on his feet, looking into our small, crowded kitchen like he's just been invited to the White House.

"Are you sure? I mean, I wouldn't want to intrude . . ."

"No! Not intruding at all, please. Come in." She opens the screen door for him, but as he is about to enter, my father appears.

"Hey, Tommy boy!" he says. "It's good to see you again, you handsome devil."

If it's possible, Thomas's face turns even more red. He was about to take a step forward, but he leans back on his heels.

"Oh, hello," he says. "I didn't know you were here."

My father makes an exaggerated, performative yawn. "The rumors are true. I'm still couch surfing."

"I really should get going, anyway," says Thomas to Rose, one eye still trained on my father behind her copper-colored hair. "Thank you for the offer."

Mom looks like she's about to stop him, but before she can say anything, he's gone again. She stares after him for a moment and then returns to our small coffee table, slumping down on a seat, dejected.

"What're you ladies up to tonight?" asks my father, oblivious. He takes out Lottie's favorite porcelain mug. It has a chip on the lip. "Am I finally going to get to see my Gardner girls tonight?"

He leans against the kitchen sink, looking disturbingly at home. I'm irritated by how carelessly he's taken up space in our house, like he has some sort of natural right to everything that is ours. A smaller part of me is also mad at Mom for allowing him here. All throughout my childhood, this would periodically happen. My father would deign to appear in various states of sobriety, and Rose permitted the disruption. I never understood why. Especially for a therapist, it should have been a clear boundary.

"I have plans with William tonight," says Rose. She hands him the coffeepot. He takes it, and for a moment, I see a glimpse of what they might have been like as a couple: the same routine and rhythm that I saw last night between Henry and Mary. Effortless.

"You have plans with William again?" I ask.

"Yes, again," says Rose, her tone still a little sharp. "Is that a problem?"

"No," I say, although I do wish she would be around more often. Besides, she seemed a little eager to invite Thomas inside for someone who has a date tonight. "I have plans tonight, too, actually."

An excited, mischievous expression overtakes Rose's face. "With who?" she asks, hope evident in her tone.

"Theo," I admit, sheepish.

Rose yelps. "I knew it! Yes! This is exciting! I adore Theo."

I tell my mom about karaoke and Theo's serenade, ignoring my father's presence and his increasingly disgruntled expression.

The memory makes me smile again now, but I'm also nervous. I've suspected there might be something between us, but I was enjoying living in the in-between period where we could still claim to just be friends. It's like when I have a new idea for a painting and I'm struck over the head by the inspiration. It explodes out of me, fills every inch of my being. But then, as soon as I paint the first stroke, the doubt seeps in.

Dating is like that, too. Right now, Theo is sunshine on my face, someone I look forward to seeing every day but I'm not overly anxious about. Once we take this next step, that will change. Relationships always end, and I was hoping to keep Theo around.

Regardless, I can't back out now. He made me promise to go on a proper date tonight. I hoped he would forget or go back on his word, but he texted again this morning: *7 p.m. reservation for two at Galley Beach.*

I covered my face with a pillow when I read the message and let out a loud groan. Galley Beach is one of the nicest restaurants on island. Obviously, he's trying to be a gentleman and pull out all the stops. Located right on the beach, Galley has the best sunsets and a menu neither of us can afford with our pay.

"Who's Theo?" asks my dad. "Should I give him the talk?"

Rose and I both give him a look. "When's the last time you gave anyone 'the talk'?" asks Rose, amused.

"Is this research?" I ask in a mock-supportive voice. "For a new movie you're producing? Are you trying to learn how to be a real dad?"

"You girls are pretty but you're cruel," says my dad, retreating back into the hall. "Don't worry about me. I'll be entertaining Aunt Elizabeth's latest rash again." He cracks his back. "And this couch sucks, by the way."

"We won't worry!" Rose calls out to him. She turns to me and squeals again. "What time is your date? Because I promised William that I'd pick him up, but if you need the car, we'll figure something else out."

She has considerably calmed down some since her freak-out about Thomas, and she is now sitting at the kitchen table, tugging open a sugar packet to pour into her coffee.

"It's at seven. Galley Beach."

"Well . . ." Rose chuckles and stirs her coffee. I watch as the sugar dissolves. "That's a funny coincidence because mine is at Galley, as well."

"Excuse me, sorry," Theo says as he scoots into the back seat of Lottie's Jeep several hours later. "I must have opened the wrong door."

William moves across the seat, making room. The friction of his Nantucket reds against the leather makes a long squeaking sound. "No problem, boy. Lovely to meet you. I'm William."

He extends a hand for him to shake, but Theo is busy trying to enter the car and misses the gesture entirely. William's mouth screws up in a taut, sour expression.

I'm driving and my mom is in the passenger seat.

"Hi, Theo!" Rose calls out. "How's my favorite coach doing?"

"Good," Theo responds, pulling the seat belt across his chest. "I get to see both of you tonight, so I can't complain."

He's wearing a wrinkled button-down shirt and patchwork shorts that look at least two sizes too big on him. It's clear he borrowed the outfit from someone at the club. I'm wearing my best outfit, too: a long yellow sundress. When I warned Theo that we'd be sharing a car tonight, he took it characteristically in stride.

No way! he texted back. *A double date? Let's go!*

I explained that it was just about sharing a ride. At the restaurant, we'll go our separate ways. It's an economical, eco-friendly move. The added benefit being that I finally get to interrogate William, who has been making uncomfortable throat-clearing noises ever since he first entered the back seat.

"Just a warning, I don't believe you're allowed to wear shorts here," he says to Theo now.

"Oh, shoot!" Theo exclaims, slapping his palm against his forehead. The noise is shocking. "I borrowed these from my friend, too. I thought they'd be fancy enough."

"You're fine," I jump in to quickly assure him. "You look great. There's no formal dress code. This is Nantucket. The restaurant is literally on a beach." I try to mask my annoyance but know I'm failing. William stays silent, but I see his jaw flex in the rearview mirror.

"So." Rose claps her hands together to break the tension. "How about some music?"

My mom turns on the island radio station. "Love Grows" is playing. I catch Theo's eyes in the mirror and we both smile.

"We have to invite them to join us," Theo says twenty minutes later when we are at the restaurant. "Come on, it's weird."

"No!" I whisper. "It's already weird." We're sitting at a table in the sand while Rose and William wait for a spot to open up.

"But there's not even seats at the bar and your mom is wearing heels, and they look sad."

I turn around to glance at them. Rose is politely smiling, tottering from foot to foot, holding a full glass of Chardonnay, while William moodily sips a martini and scans the crowd. His eyebrows are pulled together like they're magnets.

William never made a reservation. "They know me here," he said confidently as he walked up to the hostess stand, flexing his white blazer. "We don't need to call ahead of time."

Well, it turns out you do need a reservation, even if your family is rich. It's late July on Nantucket. Everywhere is packed. Just getting down here took twenty minutes due to traffic. And almost everyone—perhaps with the grand exception of the three of us and the waitstaff—is rich.

"If we invite them to sit with us, we'll have to listen to William drone on about his yacht all dinner."

"Hey, he's not so bad. Might be nice to have a stepdad with a yacht. There are worse things, Lil."

My nickname in his mouth is thrilling. "Please do not call him my stepdad. For all he talks about sailing, I'm surprised he hasn't started calling you 'old sport' yet. Besides, it's not like he's even the one sailing. He has a crew of like twenty, apparently."

"Well, I feel bad," says Theo. A thought seems to occur to him. "Hey! Wait, do you think he'll pay for our dinner if we invite him over?"

"You're shameless," I laugh, but he's already waving them over.

Rose and William walk through the tables to where we are sitting on the beach. A waitress pulls over two additional seats and place settings.

"Care to join us?" I ask.

"Oh, yay!" says Rose, immediately pulling out a chair from the soft sand and sitting down. "Thank you! This is so much fun, it's like a double date!"

William's frown deepens while he examines the table. Rose pats the cushion of the chair until he too sits down.

"Thank you for letting us join you," he says. "Although, I usually prefer to sit inside on the porch, where the wind is blocked."

"But the sun is just about to set!" I point out, nodding to the ocean. "This is the best view on island." Behind us the sky is orange sherbet, melting into the impossibly smooth, flat beach.

"I have to politely disagree. My slip downtown has the best view on island."

It takes every inch of willpower I have to keep my eyeballs fixed in their sockets.

"So, Theo." William shifts in his seat and changes the topic. "What do you do?"

"I'm a tennis instructor at Great Harbor and I bartend at the Summer House. But I'm going back to school to become a history teacher."

"You're going back to school to become a teacher? Isn't that a little ironic. I'm going to give you a bit of advice: Don't waste your time. You'll be up to your knees in debt, and you'll be lucky if you make eighty grand by the time you're forty. That's no income to support a family."

I open my mouth to retort, but before I can speak, a sharp pain in my shin gives me pause. I look up to see Rose staring at me, wide-eyed, an imperceptible shake to her head.

"No," my mom mouths to me silently. "Don't."

"You make some interesting points, William. I appreciate the advice, but I think I'll be okay. It's what I love," says Theo. "And isn't that enough?"

Rose interrupts him before the conversation can continue. "That's lovely, Theo. Anyhoo," she says. "I have that gala the last weekend of July, and as the honoree, I get a few extra tickets! Theo, you should come and join our table."

"I'd love to. If that's okay with you, Lily?"

I nod so vigorously my earrings shake. It'll be nice to have a friend there.

"I'm excited to hear this big speech," says William. "I'm sure you'll look stunning up there."

"People will be too blinded by the beauty of her words to evaluate her looks," I say. Rose gives me another kick. "But yes, you will, Mom."

William adjusts the cuff of his jacket. "I'm sure that's true. But I wish she didn't have to work so hard."

"What do you mean?" I ask. "She's opening her own practice. Soon, she'll be busier than ever. Mom, how did it go with the offer on the office space?"

I should've asked about it sooner, I realize, but everything has been so hectic.

"I didn't place it," Rose answers. "It's a long story."

"What? Why?"

Before my mom can respond, William is saying: "Therapists and teachers. I'm with a bunch of bleeding hearts here."

He lets out an exaggerated chuckle and slaps his knee, like he's auditioning for the role of a villain in an old Western. No one else laughs.

"Don't worry, Lily, if my Rosebud sticks around long enough with me, she won't have to work anymore at all. I'm thinking Palm Beach all winter. Your mom's too good to be here full-time. She's not really a 'local.' Time to cash in, sell the house, and get on with it," he continues.

Sell the house? We've discussed the idea as a general concept over the years, so it shouldn't come as a terrible surprise, but never before did my mom act on it. The cottage is Lottie. Saying goodbye to it would be like laying her to rest once and for all. And what would my mom do if she quit her job? She loves her career.

"Sounds like trading a job for a way shittier job," I mumble.

"Lily!" Rose's voice is sharp. "I have to go use the ladies' room. Will you join me?"

The waitress has appeared to Theo's left, a short woman with a choppy pixie cut. I recognize her as someone who comes back every season. "Hi, I'm Maddy and I'll be your server tonight. Can I get you started with any drinks?"

"Yes," all four of us say in complete synchronicity.

After we have ordered, Mom and I excuse ourselves, placing folded napkins in our seats.

In the back of the restaurant, Rose drags me into a single-person bathroom with seagrass wallpaper. A noise machine hums in the corner, imitating what is surely supposed to be the soothing sounds of an artificial beach—waves, a seagull cawing—but it's too loud, unnatural. Everything smells of lavender soap and rosemary. The seagull on tape is squawking, the waves crashing like the sound of a tambourine.

"What the hell was that?"

"What do you mean?" I ask, a little too innocently.

Rose's neck is red, the way it always gets when she's either angry or embarrassed. "Why are you being so rude to William?"

"Did you hear what he said out there, insulting 'locals'? He's being a jerk."

"You're being childish and dramatic."

"You're being classist and spineless." We are silent for a few long seconds. "Are you going to pee or not?" I ask after enough time has passed.

"You know that was just a ruse to get you alone," Rose says, but she's glancing at the white porcelain toilet. "Okay, fine. When in Rome, I suppose. Can you run some water for me?"

I turn on the faucet and look into the seashell-lined mirror, examining my reflection. My hair has grown slightly frizzy in the ocean air, and my gloss could use a retouch. "Hey, can I borrow your new lipstick? I love the shade you chose."

"Oh, thank you! I thought you'd like it. It's in my purse, here." Rose tosses over her straw clutch.

"Thank you!" I say, applying it. "What's it called?"

Rose rises and walks to the sink to wash her hands, grabbing for the purple bar of hand soap. "I think it's called Berry Crush or something," she says, checking her own lipstick.

"Love it."

"Right?"

We are getting ready to leave when Rose spins around again. "I'm serious, though, Lily. Please try to be nice. For me? I like him."

I think of Thomas. Before last night, maybe I would fight this harder, persuade her to ditch William. But I was wrong about him. I was wrong about Henry, too, and who knows what else.

I look at the soft crinkles around the corners of her eyes, too few laugh lines, and I see another version of her face, a younger one that never knew grief. I know I will do my best to be good. I cannot compromise my mom's happiness, not again. Never again.

The rest of the night passes quickly. I'm on my best behavior for Rose. Nonetheless, in the privacy of my own thoughts, I officially decide I do not like William. He proves every negative stereotype about summer people right. I'm grateful Theo is here to break the tension. His practice at the club has made him an expert at people-pleasing. He's like a chameleon, blending into his surroundings.

William has insisted on ordering for the table, and I watch Theo's face tighten as he places order after order. The menu is prix fixe and includes an appetizer and entrée, but William decides that is simply not enough. He orders the most expensive items on the menu in addition: jumbo lump crab cake, miso-butter-poached lobster, grilled octopus.

"For the table," he says. "To share."

I try to do the mental math of the increasing check, but after a certain point, the numbers make my head spin and my stomach drop out. I lose count.

Something I've observed about the rich is that they seem to order food compulsively, only to have a few bites of each dish and say they're "stuffed." It seems to be a status symbol to spend money without enjoying it.

"I'm surprised you two met in person," William says after ordering three more desserts, which he also does not touch. "Doesn't everyone in your generation resort to meeting online these days because they're too scared to have real-life conversations?"

Theo has taken on the responsibility of making sure there is no food left on the table. He must be about to keel over, but he dutifully tears into the tiramisu as well. His mouth is too full to respond.

"Do you have kids?" I ask in lieu of answering.

"No, why do you ask?"

"Hmm, wonder why," I say.

"Lily," Rose warns.

"I think," Theo starts, swallowing another bite. "It's nice to meet someone in person, but it's also nice to meet someone online. It all comes down to dumb luck in the end."

I turn to look at him, surprised. There's a smudge of chocolate on his upper lip, and I resist the urge to wipe it off by sitting on my hands.

"What do you mean about 'dumb luck'?" Rose asks.

"Well." He wipes his mouth with the tip of a white napkin. "Let's do a little live social experiment. It'll be good for my teaching practice." He winks at William.

"Let's say the average beautiful girl like Lily has at least three hundred matches on a dating app," Theo starts, and I blush. "The average date time is around ninety minutes. If Lily were to go on a date with even half of the profiles she matched with this week, it would take approximately thirteen thousand, five hundred minutes. Even if she booked two dates a day, it would still take seventy-five days to go through her matches, and that is if she were to pause her profile today and only sort through the responses she already has, excluding all other potential connections, online and in person, forever."

Everyone is quiet as we take this in. I'm simultaneously dumbfounded and impressed by his quick math skills.

"I think it's the opportunity cost that paralyzes us. So hear me out. In microeconomic theory, the opportunity cost of an activity or decision is essentially the loss of whatever value you might have derived from the option you didn't choose, right? So, let's say you buy a slice of pizza, the opportunity cost is the hot dog you could've purchased with the same money. When faced with too many choices, we either become paralyzed by indecision or we end up less satisfied with the choices we do make," he concludes, his words ringing in the silence.

"Interesting," Rose says first. She leans across the table, a wry smile on her face. "But unromantic."

"Not necessarily," says Theo. He's leaning on the table, too, subconsciously mimicking her posture. "I think that part of the reason why ideas of fate or serendipity or 'the one' are so pervasive in our society is because of this decision fatigue. If we torture ourselves with opportunity cost, if we spend too much time pondering the flavor we didn't choose, we'll be malcontent forever. We have to believe, at least on some unconscious level, that there is a higher power at play in the universe: that the person we do meet is somehow meant to be, predestined."

"And you're saying that's bullshit?" I ask, curious.

"No, I'm just saying that people like being told what to do, who to be. It's why we fall for astrology and personality tests and psychics . . . At a certain point, all this free will gets to be exhausting. We have to package life into smaller and smaller boxes, categorize and organize it until it becomes manageable. We survive by making sense of the senselessness, by assigning meaning to the random."

"So," I reiterate. "To put it simply, it all comes down to dumb luck. But dumb luck isn't inherently unromantic. Dumb luck can actually be incredibly romantic, in my opinion."

"I agree," says Theo. "That's why every time I used to pass this one bodega in the East Village called Heavenly Market, I'd buy a lottery ticket."

Rose laughs. "You would? That seems unlike you."

"I believe in investing in luck."

The sky behind us has darkened, replacing the sunset with a blanket of cool, indifferent stars. The wind has picked up, and I'm thankful I packed a sweater.

"Ah," says William, folding his napkin in his lap. "This academic banter reminds me of my time as a boy at Avon Old Farms School."

"'O Captain! My captain!'" I mock.

"What?" William looks around, disoriented. "Captain? What captain?"

"Never mind," I sigh, but Theo is laughing, and I realize I love his laugh, how unselfconscious and contagious it is. Even Rose lets out a quick snicker, but she quickly covers it up by bringing a napkin to her face.

After dinner, we part ways. Rose and William go to his yacht, and Theo and I decide to take a walk downtown to grab ice cream.

We stroll through the docks with the boats lit up like Christmas lights, past the weathered brick sidewalks and cobblestone streets, peering into different storefronts. We trade stories about our time on the island—Theo's impression of Nantucket during his first summer here versus my perspective as someone who calls the island home.

"It's beautiful," Theo says as we walk past a line of teens waiting for their ice cream cones.

I choose a flavor called Cobblestones, vanilla ice cream with chocolate-covered cranberries and pretzel pieces. Theo buys a chocolate Oreo cone and then decides he is too full from dinner. "A first for me," he says before offering some to me and dumping the rest into a trash can.

He continues. "It's beautiful but it doesn't seem real. It's too idyllic, like a street in Disneyland. The proportions are all off." He pushes against the clapboard face of a real estate office. "Like, I wouldn't be surprised if this was all cardboard. Movie magic."

I shake my head. "You have to come back in the winter. It feels more real when all of the vacationers are gone and the weather gets cold again. It still looks like a Hallmark movie, but less like you're on a movie set and more like you're traveling back in time."

I consider William's insistence that my mom should move. Would she miss this place? Or is it too isolated in the winters? Would she be happier elsewhere? Am I selfish for hoping she stays?

It's like Theo can hear my thoughts. "Would you be sad if your mom left the island?"

"I want her to be happy, but I also really don't believe William is the person for her."

I tell him about Thomas, how I planned to set them up, the disastrous wedding, and how I saw him with Josie the other night.

"You have to tell her," says Theo when I'm done. "She deserves to know."

We walk away from the town, toward the lighthouse. I've memorized these roads, the stop signs, the curves in each bend like the lines of a favorite poem. It doesn't hurt that Nantucket is actively preserved, quite literally frozen in time. The entire island is considered a National Historic Landmark District, making it by acre the largest historic district in the United States. Replacing Jeeps with horses and buggies, downtown looks almost exactly as it did in the 1800s, when it was still a small fishermen's village: brick and clapboard storefronts, cedar-shingled sea captain houses, and stately white church steeples.

"You know," I say to Theo, changing the subject. "The funny thing about Nantucket is that it wasn't originally preserved out of some sort of preemptive nostalgia or foresight about its future aesthetic value. Although now it certainly is. Originally, it was left alone simply because it was forgotten. Shifting sand bars made it difficult for larger ships to dock in the harbor. For years, no one bothered to change it. Now that neglect is exactly what gives it charm."

Right outside of town is the Goose Pond, where Lottie, Rose, and I once fed the white Pekin ducks that roam there. We ripped pieces of bread and threw them into the grasses until the fat birds became aggressive, dozens flocking behind us, squawking. The ducks chased after us as we ran back to the car. We laughed all the way down the bike path and across the long, flat wooden bridge. Between laughs, I kept checking to make sure Lottie didn't fall. There was no logical reason behind the feeling. Lottie was comparatively young back then, a healthy and active seventy. But even then, even before, I was always worried something bad was going to happen. It was as if I could sense a shift in the air, a ticking clock.

"Do you think I'm being too harsh about William?" I ask Theo.

He shrugs. "I really can't answer that. That's for your mom to decide." He pauses and then grins. "Although, I will say, I was surprised he didn't offer to split the bill."

When the check arrived, Rose, Theo, and I all quickly whipped out our credit cards and placed them in the black sleeve. We looked at William, and he was sitting on his hands, smiling a vacant, unselfconscious smile.

Later, when the receipt was returned, we saw they had only charged Rose. She snuck away and must have asked the waitstaff.

"Jeez," I say. "I feel so bad for my mom about that. I'm going to pay her back, put some money under her pillow like a visit from the tooth fairy."

"I'll pay her back," insists Theo. "And she won't have to lose any teeth over it."

I laugh, and we pause on a lamplit street. We're close to our destination, passing Children's Beach and winding the corner past the White Elephant, the nicest hotel on island.

Here is another one of my favorite spots on Nantucket: Brant Point lighthouse. It's the lighthouse you see when you're arriving on the ferry, the one Henry and I threw pennies at: a squat building amidst a sea of jagged rocks, the first sign that you're almost home. There's a long white wooden walkway with frayed slats. The lighthouse is always getting dressed up for holidays: an American flag for the Fourth, wreaths for Christmas with big red bows.

"Wow," says Theo when we reach it. "I can't believe I haven't been here yet."

It's empty now, and the stars and the moon are the only source of light beyond the fixed red beacon at the very top. It draws a circle over the dark water like a spotlight in a theatrical production.

"It's funny," Theo says as we walk closer. "I feel so comfortable around you, like I've known you forever, but there's still so much I don't know."

I hop onto the railing and sit with my legs swinging. It creaks but remains stable. "Well, what do you still want to know?"

It's so easy to be around Theo, sometimes I forget to feel embarrassed. But when he looks at me now, I remember his mouth on mine last night and have to look away.

"What's your favorite food?" he asks, breaking the tension.

"My favorite food?" I'm laughing. "Easy. Peanut butter and Marshmallow Fluff sandwiches."

Theo pushes his body onto the railing opposite of me. "That's so basic."

"It's nostalgic," I defend. "Anyway, what's yours?"

"Mine? Definitely pizza."

"Oh, and that's somehow more sophisticated than peanut butter sandwiches?" I tease. "Like Domino's? That's boring, too!"

"My favorite is Modern Apizza in New Haven. Have you ever been?"

"Of course. We used to live in New Haven."

"You did? How did I not know this?"

He's right, it is a little odd how it never came up. "I guess because Nantucket has been home for so long, I never think about where I grew up. I always wanted to leave."

Besides, once you live by the ocean, nowhere else can ever really be considered home. The ocean always calls back to you.

Theo looks up at the body of the lighthouse, the boulders by the water.

"By the way," he says. "I get it, about Rose. She reminds me a lot of my own mom actually. She passed away when I was kid. The lottery ticket thing I mentioned earlier . . . I do that because of her. I know it's stupid, but she always loved scratch-offs, and whenever I do one, I think of her."

The sudden confession takes me by surprise. "I'm so sorry," I say. "I had no idea." In the silence, I can hear the sound of the ocean churning and children laughing, blocks away.

It's evident Theo feels regretful about the confession, and I want him to know it's okay. It's okay to talk about his mom, to not always be the funny, cheery one in the room.

"Will you tell me about her?" I ask.

Theo tells me more then about what happened, how she struggled with her mental health for years, postpartum snowballing into a deeper, more persistent depression. She took her own life when he was only ten. When Theo speaks about it, he transforms into someone else. He tells me about his father remarrying, and his little sister who has Down syndrome.

"She's my favorite person in the entire world," Theo says, smiling at the thought of her. It makes me smile, too. "She's this huge ball of energy and joy."

I move toward him and reach for his hand, but after a quick squeeze, he drops it. Behind us, the lighthouse continues to blink red, guiding the ships in the harbor, warning them of the dangerously shallow waters and letting us all know that we're almost home.

Chapter Twenty-Six

Rose

July 15

My neck is strained as I stare at the constellations. If you look up at the stars long enough, they lose their meaning, like reading the same word over and over again until it no longer holds any language at all. My favorite course in college, second only to my psychology classes, was astronomy. Coincidentally, it was also my daughter's least favorite.

We're currently at the Loines Observatory, standing on the porch sandwiched between two great domes. The ridged silver tops of the telescopes look like giant soda bottle lids, but the cylinder bases are covered in the same gray shingles as the rest of the island. Even science must adhere to the beauty standards of the Nantucket Historic District Commission.

It was my dad's insistence that we come here on a "family bonding" trip. It's been three days since my accidental double date with Lily and Theo.

"You two have been busy every night since we arrived," my dad chided. It's not like him to want to spend time with me, so I was surprised by his frustration and even felt a little guilty.

Luckily, James stayed home tonight. Lily has been avoiding him all week. I wish she would give him a shot. He's certainly not a wonderful father, but at least he's trying.

She stands to my left now. "You know, this was number six on Lottie's bucket list. Just saying."

"We're doing this because Grandpa wanted to, not because of her," I remind her.

I'm still mad at Lottie. Even though logically I know I should let it go, a part of me wishes she was here so I could tell her how I feel. It's not easy trying to love a ghost, but it's even harder fighting with one.

"Still," says Lily, looking smug. "It technically counts."

The sky is clear, every constellation visible in the darkness. The air is brisk but not chilly. The whole universe is open above us.

A few people in line shuffle ahead until we're right at the edge of the telescope's entrance. A staff member in a black windbreaker puts out a hand to stop us from going any farther. In the smaller dome we have just come from is an antique eight-inch Alvan Clark telescope from 1908. In the one we're waiting for now is the modern twenty-four-inch research telescope they use for active projects. A slit in the ceiling of both domes allows visitors to look up into the cosmos.

"I'm cold," Elizabeth complains, even though she's wearing a thick fleece she borrowed from my closet. "We're going to get sick standing out here like this."

"It's almost August, Elizabeth," I say, trying to be patient. "We're not going to get sick from being outside."

I've often wondered why Elizabeth never found anyone. Growing up, she was always the more beautiful of the two of us. With her pretty blond locks and heart-shaped face, she was constantly admired in high school. She's six years older than me, and I remember how much I admired her back then, too: her poise and self-assuredness, even when it bordered on vanity. When our mother died, Elizabeth was older than me, the ripe age of eleven, the age a girl needs her mother the most.

The doctors called what happened to our mother a "berry aneurysm," a term that disturbed me even as a child—the word *berry* so light and fanciful. The world ended on a random Tuesday. The sun was hot and bright; Thanksgiving was two days away. The cause of death was compared to a fruit.

"You don't know that," whispers Elizabeth now. "You can't know that."

I soften my tone. "You're right, I'm sorry. Do you want me to get an extra blanket from the car?"

She looks happy to have her suffering acknowledged, a faux-stoic tilt to her chin. Her exaggerated shivering slows. "No, I'll make it through."

Minutes later two young female research fellows take our group through a brief history of the astronomer Maria Mitchell's life: how a Quaker education and a mother who worked at the library contributed to making her the first internationally recognized female astronomer. She went on to open her own school, becoming the first librarian of the Nantucket Atheneum, as well as a professor at Vassar College. She befriended suffragist Elizabeth Cady Stanton and met other prominent intellectual figures and activists, including Ralph Waldo Emerson, abolitionist Frederick Douglass, and writers Herman Melville and Nathaniel Hawthorne.

And it all began here, just a few blocks from where we stand. Maria Mitchell observing the sky from the top of Pacific National Bank, the same imposing, grand brick structure that still sits above Main Street downtown today like a king overlooking his subjects.

At one point, the guide mentions that Maria went to a school named after someone called Elizabeth Gardner, and I feel the nudge of my daughter's elbow against my rib cage. Is James related? It's possible.

Seeing the two young astronomers talk about the cosmos gives me the kind of goose bumps I only get from watching someone genuinely passionate pursue their interests. I imagine what it must be like to be them: working every day on this island, researching in Maria's footsteps, before heading back to finish their own educations.

Despite my best efforts, it's impossible to be here without thinking of Lottie. My aunt loved history, science, anything to do with learning something new, and most all, strong, groundbreaking women. Lottie was fiercely independent, a feminist who regularly wrote op-eds in *The Inquirer* about current events. She was never afraid of ruffling feathers. Like Maria Mitchell, she was a trailblazer.

The line shifts forward, and my dad and Elizabeth head into the telescope, leaving Lily and me waiting outside.

"So," Lily says when we are alone. "I have to tell you something. I know it's not the best timing, but we haven't had a moment alone in days, and it's eating me alive."

I look at her, alarmed. Her red hair is wavy and her freckled face looks serious. Her small, determined mouth is pressed together, like she's physically keeping the secret in. She always had the worst bedhead as a kid. Even as a toddler, she would wake from her nap frenzied, flushed, dazed, as if she had just emerged from a coma.

"Is everything okay?" I ask.

One of the young astronomers starts giving the rest of our waiting line a tour of the constellations, pointing a razor-sharp green light at the sky. It looks as if it could reach the moon. She circles Orion, Aquarius, Ursa Major, the North Star, and a W-shaped constellation in the sky behind the domes.

"This is Cassiopeia," the guide says. The line nods in appreciation.

Lily's eyes look pained but she doesn't look away from me. "I saw Thomas with Josie last weekend. It looked like they were on a date."

She says it all in one quick breath, like she's rushing to expel the information. Afterward, she takes a gasp of air. "Are you okay?" she asks.

I struggle to understand the sentence. Thomas and Josie? Together? It can't be right. The shock feels more like heartbreak.

The young astronomer is speaking again, her voice the practiced diction of a professor. "The star cluster Cassiopeia was named after the mythological Greek queen. She was characterized as so vain that she once taunted Poseidon that her daughter was more beautiful than the sea nymphs. Her punishment was being turned into a constellation and forced to rotate around the north celestial pole constantly. At some points Cassiopeia is completely upside down, left hanging from her throne for hours."

"Are you sure it was them?" I ask Lily. I can feel my heartbeat in my fingertips.

"Yes," she says. "I'm sure."

I want to ask more questions—where were they? Is she certain it was a date? When would they even have the opportunity to have met? Through the real estate office? Is it because I asked her to break the lease? I suppose I can't technically be mad because I never told Josie about my past with Tommy, and I can't be angry at Tommy because I'm with William now. The same way I shouldn't really be mad at Lottie either.

Still, the thought of all of it makes me want to hide in the bushes behind us and never come back out.

The line moves up, and soon enough, Lily and I are standing together around the edges of the circular dome. The guide tells me it's my turn, and I take robotic steps, walking up a rickety metal standing ladder—"It'll stop wobbling once you settle onto it!" the astronomer promises—and place my left eye against the instrument.

I do it because it's expected, because it's what the line needs to happen in order to keep moving forward. At first, it's hard to make anything out: a scattering of white dots in the midst of deep black. As I stare out at them, all I can see is Tommy. Tommy and Josie together. Tommy and Josie kissing, holding hands.

I think about the legend of poor Cassiopeia, spinning and spinning and spinning. Punished for her vanity, her poor decisions, forced forever to circle the same limitless point.

Spinning, and spinning, and spinning.

Chapter Twenty-Seven

Lily

July 19

I'm in the middle of painting when my father confronts me. He knocks on my bedroom door, and I have to find a towel to wipe the paint from my hands before I can answer. I'm wearing old jeans and an oxford shirt, both of which are covered in paint splatters from various projects over the years.

Mom is out today, preparing for the mental health gala next weekend.

"Lily, you have to stop ignoring me," he says as soon as we're face-to-face.

I have the door only half-open, but he must catch a glimpse of my setup. I've thrown an old set of linens on the ground and covered the floor with canvases, palette knives, and brushes. It's an absolute mess, and for a second, I wonder if he'll yell at me the way a father would in a TV show.

Instead, he just says, "Wow," because I suppose he has never acted the way a dad should act, and it's not his place, anyway. "What is all of this?" He nudges the door open so he can see more of my work.

I've refined the original two portraits and added three more. They're all of Rose and Lottie, except I included one of Jade back in our city apartment. In the image, she's eating popcorn on our old shabby tan couch. Her pink-streaked hair is lit up in the yellow glow of the television, and her mouth is full with laughter.

I'm not sure what the common theme is yet, except that it's an ode to all of the women I love. Portraits—such as the one of the captain—are often formal, like images you see of people when the camera was first invented and everyone had to sit still so that the picture didn't turn out blurry. I wanted something more casual but still grand: a celebration of the everyday. I've been getting up early in the mornings to work on them before my shifts. This is a major change from my usual habit of sleeping until noon on my days off, and it makes me feel strangely proud.

"Lily, these are incredible," says my father as he walks in the room, careful to avoid stepping on anything. "How long have you been working on these?"

"Just a few weeks," I respond, all of a sudden shy. He's not who I had in mind when I imagined showing them to someone for the first time, and under his gaze, I worry the magic won't hold.

He leans down to look closer at the one of Lottie in the garden. "It's incredible," he repeats. "You really captured her essence." He smiles, looking at Lottie's stubborn concentration. "You know, she once threw that turquoise coffeepot at me."

"She did?" I've never heard this story before.

He laughs, and I remember how he got away with his addiction for so many years. He has always been too charming for his own good. People let him off the hook. Except, I suppose, Lottie.

"It was after she found out Rose was breaking up with me." He shakes his head. "She was livid about the affair."

"She had a right to be," I remind him.

"She did," he agrees. He turns his gaze away from the painting. "Lily, I'm so sorry. I know you're angry at me, but you have to know that I hate how strained our relationship is."

I don't do anything except stand there, which he takes as a sign to continue.

"I'm a flawed, messed-up person. I haven't been a good father, or a good partner for that matter. But I do love you. I came here to do right by you."

I keep my arms crossed and stand at the opposite end of the room. "Then why didn't you answer my email? When I wrote you back, you didn't even respond after weeks of begging me to talk to you."

My father runs his hands through his hair so aggressively that I worry he'll pull out the remaining strands. It's already thinning. "I fucked up," he says. "I had just gotten sober. I was in a good headspace, so I reached out. And then the funding for the project I was working on fell through, and . . ." He starts to pace. "I panicked. I relapsed. I didn't want you to see me like that."

I force myself to remain stony, even though there's a part of me that feels sorry for him. I don't want to go through this again: the rise and fall of my expectations whenever he flits in and out of my life.

"You could have told me that," I say. "I can handle it. But instead, you just ignored me."

He stares at the painting of Lottie again, as if he wants her to chime in. "I'm sorry," he says in a quiet voice. "I've always assumed staying away was better for you. I thought it would make your life easier, but you have to know that I was there all along, cheering you on."

"What do you mean?" I keep my arms crossed.

"Rose and Lottie would send me everything you did, every piece of art you created, every test you aced. I paid for college, of course."

The mention makes my limbs grow heavy. I know how lucky I am to have had his assistance, along with the few academic scholarships I was able to scrape by on. Without him, we couldn't have afforded tuition on our own, but the reminder of it feels like another way to use money as a means of control. It reminds me of Henry, who is always throwing around his family's influence.

My father quickly continues. "I saw how well you were doing, and I didn't want to ruin that." He smiles sadly. "I tend to ruin stuff. Even the stuff that's been handed to me by my parents, like my career. Or my marriage. Both of them."

"You and Maren are done?" I have a difficult time calling her by her real name instead of the Mistress.

"She left me a month ago," he says, swinging his arms. He laughs in a self-abashed way. "Can you believe it? You're a wonderful kid, Lily. You deserve a better dad than me."

For some reason, the emotion of the summer overcomes me. My lips have been pursed in frustration while he's been speaking, but all at once, a strangled sob escapes. The cry feels almost entirely separate from my conscious self, like my body has gone rogue.

Dad comes over, avoiding the paintings like he's in a game of hopscotch, and gives me a hug. "I'm sorry, Lily. I really am."

"I . . . don't . . . know . . . why . . . I'm crying," I stutter through my sobs. "It's been a long summer."

He asks what I mean, and for some inexplicable reason, I decide to open up. I tell him about getting fired, my estrangement from Jade, Clive refusing to provide a professional reference, Henry getting married. When I'm done, I'm slightly breathless and hot in the face. I feel emptied out and exhausted.

"That bastard!" shouts my father.

"Who?" I ask, thinking through the variety of options.

"Clive, of course. Your old boss. He can't do this." He begins to pace in circles, careful not to step on any of my art supplies or canvases. "He can't fire you with no concrete cause and then make it impossible for you to be rehired." He stops in his tracks, an idea apparently occurring to him. "You should confront him."

"I should?" I'm sitting on the floor, holding my knees. My face feels tight from crying.

"You absolutely should!" He sits down across from me. "Here, I'll help you compose an email. That jackass can't get away with this. I know a fair amount of lawyers who would sue his ass."

I sniff, laughing a little. "Aren't they all probably entertainment lawyers, though? Not exactly employment law."

"Doesn't matter!" rages my dad.

He gestures for me to hand over my phone, and I do so after a moment of hesitation. He opens up a blank email draft and begins typing. When he's done, he gets a satisfied look on his face and places the phone back in my lap. "There!" he says. "That should show him. You're going to send this to him and he'll be shaking in his boots."

"I am?" I open the message.

It reads:

Dear Asshat,

It recently became evident that you have refused to give me a professional reference. After three long years working at your firm, I'm shocked and hurt by this decision. We both know that I worked tirelessly to contribute to the success of this publication and I deserve to have those contributions respected. My future employment opportunities should not suffer because of a personal grudge. Please give me a call to discuss or I will have no choice but to escalate this matter with litigation.

It's not terrible besides the need to soften the language a bit and, of course, delete the word *asshat*.

"Maybe I am," I repeat, nodding to myself as I type in my edits.

I think back to the myriad of ways Clive's personal life seeped into the professional: the vacations he had me book, back waxes (as Clive inappropriately once put it, he likes to be "hairless as a dolphin"), and even once, the time he asked me to drive his car from the city to his house in the Hamptons because his teenage daughter wanted to borrow it. All of this despite the fact that I was hired to be on the editorial art team, not as his personal assistant. He never asked any of the male staff to do this extra work.

"You're right," I say. "If Clive wants to talk about being unprofessional, let's have that discussion. He knows he owes me better than this."

I adjust the language and push send. When I hit the button, a rush of adrenaline surges through my veins.

"That's my girl," says Dad proudly. "No one treats my daughter like this."

Once again with no forewarning, the waterworks return. I realize, with some embarrassment, how much I've been secretly craving this protection, how much I've wanted my father to stand up in my defense and act like . . . well, like a father. It's humiliating, but after years of striving to be hyper-independent so that he could never hurt me again, I feel overcome by the small assistance.

"What did I say this time?" my father asks, rushing over to me.

"It's nothing," I say through hiccups. "Like I said, it's been a long summer."

When I'm done, we both sit on the floor, quiet together.

"I've missed out on your entire life," my father says after a few moments. "You're grown now."

My cheeks feel waxy from the tears, and my limbs are still shaky. I wrap my arms around my legs, as if I can curl into myself and disappear.

"I'm not so sure about that," I say, my mind flitting to Henry, Theo, the mess of this entire summer. "I still have some growing to do."

My dad smiles. "Do you think you could forgive me? Not today, but someday?"

I think about it. It's not enough. This one apology certainly isn't enough to make up for a lifetime of his absences: the school dances, and soccer games, and art shows he's missed. Rose has given me everything I need. She has single-handedly raised me from the ground up. I do not need my father, but maybe I can still afford to let him in a little.

It's not enough. But it's something. It's a start. And maybe a start is better than nothing.

"Let's try." I return his smile.

"What are you doing the rest of today?" he asks eagerly. "I have to return to LA tomorrow for a meeting with my lawyers. I've already outstayed my welcome here. But do you have plans this morning?"

Today is my first shift back at work where my schedule will align with Theo's again. We've barely seen each other in the week since our date. I'm worried he's avoiding me.

We talked about heavy subjects, after all: loss and tragedy. I never would have guessed that behind his easygoing demeanor lived such a heavy weight. It certainly wasn't the most romantic topic, so I wasn't surprised when we didn't kiss at the end of the night. We were friends first—this was our natural state.

Still, perhaps he regrets opening up. I was looking forward to seeing him at work and sussing out his feelings.

"No pressure," my dad says now. "If you have plans, it's okay. Of course."

I know I should go to work, but then again, it would be nice to spend the day with my dad, getting to know each other again. Life is short; we know this now. That's what Lottie used to say: "Life is too short, even when it's long."

So much can go wrong, you might as well savor the good moments while you can. You might as well accept the olive branch when it's extended.

"No worries," I tell my dad. "I'll call out sick."

A few hours later that afternoon, I pull up to the sandy parking lot of Cisco Brewers, driving over the deep ridges in the ground. The hood of my car points in the air nose first like the bow of a ship.

This afternoon, everyone with a morning shift from Great Harbor is expected to come to Cisco after work, the local brewery out near Bartlett's Farm. After calling out sick to spend time with my father, I considered skipping, but I want to see Theo. Dad and I spent the morning together just walking around 'Sconset and catching up. I showed him the cliff walk where I took Thomas, and I filled him in on everything that has happened this summer.

"I think he's still in love with her," he said when we reached the end of the cliff. The long drop was only feet away, and the ocean expanded into what seemed like infinity.

"But what about the thing with Josie?"

"You're not sure that what you saw was a date, correct?"

I shook my head no.

"Maybe it's not as simple as it seems. But I'll tell you this much, for as long as I've known your mother, she's been in love with that man. Even when we were happy, I could tell she was thinking of someone else. I'd bet he feels the same." At the next part, he grinned. "Rose is not the kind of woman you move on from. Take it from my experience."

I wondered what he meant, since he was the one who cheated, but decided to drop it. It was nice to get along, and as I confided in him, I realized what a relief it was to talk to someone else about the situation. Because of his own mistakes, he was oddly easy to confide in, devoid of judgment.

"Do you think I'm a horrible person for getting involved?" I asked.

"I think you're the best daughter a mother could ask for," he said. I hated how much the praise meant to me.

Now I park the car by the fence to the farm, walking down the pathway that is half sand and half dirt, and enter the line for the brewery. Sometimes on holiday weekends, the line can stretch to the street, but today, there are only a handful of people ahead of me.

Inside, past the wooden barns where they brew the beer, is a stone gathering space with picnic benches and two bars. Food trucks crowd the exterior: lobster rolls, a pizza oven, a raw bar with shucked oysters and tuna poke. There's a stage where a live band is now playing a country song I don't recognize, and a pagoda near the garden in case it rains or you need an escape from the sun.

I spot the tennis group to the left of the stage, half-covered by the pagoda. Emily is in a sunlit seat, shading her forehead with her right hand. Theo is next to her, and the two of them are talking close. Abruptly, I feel nervous. I decide to get a drink first.

The brewery distills their own liquor and they're famous for their blueberry lemonade cocktail, a deep purple-blue spirit that tastes vaguely like cough syrup. I order myself a blueberry lemonade. It's delicious but the color is dangerous—how many pairs of white jeans have I ruined here over the years?

I'm about to approach the Great Harbor crew when I see another familiar party: Henry and a few of his guy friends.

"Lily!" He waves when he sees me. He walks over to the bar and grabs me by the shoulder. He's rough enough that the blue liquid nearly escapes from the edge of my plastic cup. "Lily, I'm so happy it's you!"

His eyes are half-lidded, and he looks somewhere between consciousness and elsewhere, like a sleepwalker who is still deciding whether or not to wake up. "I have to tell you something," he says. "Why didn't you answer my text?"

It's the drunkest I've ever seen him, and after the dramatic morning of reconciliation I've had, I'm not in the mood. He kind of reminds me of my father the few times I've seen him drink, the way he's stumbling and the dead, distant look in his eyes. I only saw my father like that a handful of times when he relapsed during one particularly bad Christmas and an ill-fated surprise birthday trip that ended with seven-year-old me in tears and his white T-shirt covered in a disturbing mixture of vanilla cake and punch. For most of high school, I never touched alcohol out of fear I would turn out the same.

"Are you okay?" I ask, concerned. He's tottering like an unstable toddler.

"It's my bachelor party week!" he cries, slurring his words. "Isn't that exciting?"

I look around at his friends, who are a few feet away, sitting on barrels. There's about seven of them in total, most of whom I recognize, except for an irritated-looking blond man who is glaring in our direction. He has slicked-back hair and looks vaguely familiar, but I can't place him. I assume he must be the fiancée's brother.

"That's very exciting," I tell him in a friendly, maternal voice. "You should join your group and celebrate."

He places both hands on my shoulders. I can feel the weight of him as he uses me like some sort of human crutch. To our left, Theo is at the table with the tennis staff, his blue eyes watching intently. I wave, but he looks away.

"I'm good, I'm so good. I'm getting married, Lily-pad! Can you believe it?" yells Henry into my ear. "You know, I used to think it would be me and you up there, but I think it all worked out good in the end. You know?"

Someone has drawn their number on his arm with the message "If lost, call this number!"

"That's great, Henry. I'm happy for you," I tell him, and as I'm saying it, it rings true.

Looking at him now, I can tell that he's a different person than the one I fell in love with. He's not my Henry anymore. His hair has that foreign crop. His face is puffier. His eyes no longer stare into my soul like they know everything about me either. Instead, he looks at me like I'm a stranger, which maybe I am. I've changed since I met him. Heck, I've changed this summer alone.

"I like the bangs, by the way," he says. I touch them, realizing that they've grown, too. They're just below my eyebrows now.

He's not perfect, but he deserves happiness. As does Mary.

I look for a way to strategically extricate myself from his grasp without him face-planting into the dirt.

"I love you." He lowers his voice, looking around conspiratorially. He stumbles again. I catch him by the armpits. "But I don't think we would've made each other very happy. I always felt like I was disappointing you or something, I don't know. Or like you didn't think I was good enough. I never feel that way about Mary."

He leans back a little, the pressure on my shoulders lightening. I know he's right. Still, it hurts to hear. We just weren't right for each other. It's as simple as that. With the nostalgia veil momentarily lifted, I can see that clearly.

"I'm happy for you, Henry," I repeat. "You deserve to be with someone who appreciates you."

He leans in and gives me a fat, wet kiss on the cheek, like a dog. I resist the temptation to immediately wipe off the slime. "You deserve it, too."

Despite the drunk accent on his words, the sentiment strikes me as profound. It's as if the alcohol has burned away all of our complicated emotions down to the simplest, rawest ingredients. I remember what the psychic said about my soulmate at the fundraising event, but psychics can be wrong. Psychics are often wrong, actually. That's kind of their whole business.

"Hey." Henry turns around, suddenly alert. He looks down at his chest, dazed, as if surprised to discover himself out in the world and not in his bed. "Is there something on my arm?" He rubs the skin but the words stay in place.

"Don't worry about it," I tell him. "Have fun."

After he walks away, it's as if he's siphoned a bit of me with him: taking the parts that are still stuck, the pieces that still love him in all the ways I'm not allowed to anymore.

What's left is something more peaceful, steady.

"Hi, everyone," I say, approaching the Great Harbor bench. Theo is noticeably avoiding eye contact, but I sit on a stool next to him, anyway. I refuse to let this be weird. I will shoulder through any awkwardness until we're normal again just like I did after the bonfire.

"Lily!" Emily reaches across the table to give me a high five, almost spilling her drink in the process. "Where were you today?"

"It's healthy to play hooky sometimes," I joke. For obvious reasons, I don't want to explain the full story: my dad's sudden appearance and the history between us.

"Right on, Ferris Bueller," says Emily.

"It's not cool to just call off like that last-minute, you know," Theo mumbles into his beer, not looking at me. "They had no one manning the desk all day. It sucked."

"I'm sorry," I say. He's tying knots out of a straw wrapper. "Something came up."

"Yeah, well. As the one who recommended you for the job, it reflects poorly on me as well. And you looked pretty healthy and fine just now when you were kissing your ex."

"Jeez, Theo," I say, hurt. I notice how little I've actually said his name aloud—it sounds foreign in my mouth, like a language I haven't fully mastered yet. "I really am sorry. Tough day, trust me. I would never want to make you look bad. I'm really sorry."

The rest of the group is talking among themselves, but I can tell Emily is eavesdropping by the position of her crossed legs. Theo lowers his voice.

"Whatever." He shrugs. "So, what did he want?"

"Who?" I think of my dad.

"Henry, obviously. Is he magically calling off his wedding or something? You finally getting the rom-com ending you hoped for there?"

I'm offended by his anger. He has no right to it, especially after days of us not speaking. "Wow, the vitriol is a little dramatic. What do you care anyway?"

"I just don't like being messed with."

"That was never my intention, Theo. I like you, I had a great time the other night." I reach to touch his shoulder but he pulls away. "I'm sorry I've been such a mess this summer, but I've always liked you. That never changed. I've just been working some stuff out."

I can tell more of our coworkers are listening in, and I know I should be embarrassed, but this feels too important to ignore. Not saying how you feel is what went wrong with Thomas and my mom. It is always better to put everything out there, be as honest as possible.

Theo rolls his eyes, knitting his thick eyebrows together.

I remember the first time I opened up to Henry about my dad's alcoholism, and how hard it was to speak aloud. It made it more real somehow. When I was done, I wished I could take it back. I hope Theo doesn't feel the same after talking about his mother the other night: a vulnerability hangover.

"Are you congratulating our boy?" Emily interrupts in a booming voice. "Can't believe he's heading out in less than two weeks. What's first, my dude? Thailand?"

"Cambodia," he mumbles, playing intently with the wrapper again, knot after knot in a chain until the paper frays.

"You're leaving?" I feel a weight near my collarbone drop.

"Yeah." He's still not meeting my eyes. "I'm teaching English abroad for a year. Going to be traveling to a few different places. I'm supposed to leave the first week of August."

"Why didn't you tell me?" I ask, my voice cracking a little.

Everyone at the table is watching us, but I don't have the energy to care. I only care about his answer. I assumed we had all August together. Time to figure out what we are to each other.

"I don't know," he admits. "Maybe I thought you wouldn't care."

There's a buzzing at the edge of my brain like a hive of bees, the first sign of impending vertigo, my panic attacks. It is rising again and there's nothing I can do to stop it except brace for impact.

Two hours and three blueberry lemonades later, I'm too drunk to operate anything larger than a Razor scooter, so Theo takes my keys and offers to drive me home. He practically drags me out of the brewery like a disappointed parent. He made me do this, I think. After his revelation, drinking was all I could do to keep the panic attack at bay.

"I want to stay!" I pout.

"You're drunk, Lily."

"You're right," I giggle at his serious face. "I'm drunk as a skunk! But look, I didn't spill on my jeans!" I twirl to show off my pristine white pants, but then the twirling makes me dizzy, and I trip on a loose stone, and the rest of the blue drink seeps down my body. "Oops."

"Come on." Theo tugs my arm again.

We pass Henry's bachelor party on the way out. He is now nearing catatonia, head sloped over, wobbling dangerously on the uneven cobblestone.

"Goodbye!" I call out to the group, waving. Now that I'm drunk, we're like kindred spirits.

"What're you doing?" Theo hisses.

"They're my friends." I scowl again. "Hi, friends!" They wave back. "See? I have other friends besides you."

On the drive home, we settle into silence. I open all of the windows so the wind smacks my face. The air is sobering. It hurts but in a good way, like a hard-learned lesson, like the muscle ache after a long workout.

It's been a long day. It's been a long summer. I think about my morning with my dad and realize how stupid it was to get drunk after a conversation like that. My dad confides in me about his sobriety journey, and I immediately head to a brewery? Of course, I didn't plan it like that, but the irony isn't lost on me.

"I'm an idiot," I say aloud, laughing at myself. "It's just hilarious how I can fail at so many things at once, you know? At work, in relationships, even my friendships. My art." My laugh is somewhere between a scoff and a bark. "Art! I'm an idiot. Who do I think I am?"

We pull up to the cottage driveway. The car stalls. With the alcohol, my life feels distant. It's like I can take a bird's-eye view of the entire summer, see all my mistakes lined up: rows of dominoes about to fall. I remember the email I sent to Clive this morning.

"Oh God," I groan against the leather console.

"Go inside, Lily," Theo says. "Drink some water."

"You know," I say, staring at the blue stains on my white denim. There's something pretty about the pattern. "I really liked you. I just thought you should know since you're leaving."

He doesn't say anything back, and if it weren't for the numbing effect of the alcohol, I'm sure his silence would have hurt. A lot. Instead, it falls on me like the fog that is beginning to form outside the window in thick, slow swirls, alarming but harmless.

When I'm halfway out the door, another thought occurs to me. "Wait! How are you going to get home?"

"I'll take the bus."

I stumble onto the green grass of our lawn.

Theo gets out of the driver's seat and hands me the keys, placing them in the palm of my hand and closing my fingers around them.

"Get some sleep," is all he says before walking away, head down.

Chapter Twenty-Eight

Lily

In the bright, liminal space of my profound drunkenness, the garden is spectacular.

All of the colors look brighter, more animated. The universe is off its axis, but everything makes better sense at this angle. The sky just starting to darken into evening.

The hydrangeas are as purple blue as the blueberry lemonades I drank. The sunflowers as high as my thighs. Everything lush, alive, the full spectrum of color like a candy store. Growing season, Lottie always called this time of year, everything in full bloom.

There's a ladybug crawling on the edge of Lottie's bench. I place my hand down so it can climb onto me. I examine its spots while it marches across my hand. I count eleven in total.

"Hello, little guy," I whisper.

"Hi," a voice responds.

I'm so startled, I jump in the air. "Jesus," I say, turning to where Thomas is standing by the rosebushes. I suppress a hiccup, which turns into a small burp.

"Sorry to startle you," he says, approaching me slowly. The ladybug has fallen back onto the bench, and it looks so still, I worry it's dead. Did I accidentally kill it? Tears well at the thought.

"I—I wanted to talk to you about that actually," says Thomas.

"About startling me?" I'm still staring at the ladybug, praying for it to move.

"You saw me with Josie the other week," he says. "I need to explain."

The ladybug begins to crawl again, its small, determined legs moving. I feel an enormous sense of relief. I've screwed up this summer, but at least this small, innocent creature won't suffer at my hands. That has to count for something, right?

"Okay," I say to Thomas, because I'm too tipsy and exhausted to argue.

"What you saw the other night with Josie wasn't what it looked like. The truth is, she's been helping me out these last few weeks."

A blue jay lands in the tree behind his back, where he seems to be holding something out of view. Absurdly, I wonder if the bird is Lottie in reincarnated form, checking in on us. The thought makes me both incredibly happy and deliriously sad.

Thomas continues. "I reached out to her a few days after the wedding, when I ran into your family here in the garden. I knew I had to get out of Rose's way, but I also didn't want to leave the island entirely, especially with the progress we're making on the new company.

"Her family has been helping me find a place." He smiles sheepishly. "And, well, it worked! They found me an incredible property on the water in Madaket. The owner agreed to sell it fully furnished. We closed today. I've just come back from the office to sign. I'll be out of here after next weekend, but don't worry, the rest of the lease has been paid in full."

I want to feel shocked, but my capacity for shock has been drained. Instead, I feel stunned: numb and dumb. The garden spins.

"So at Rose and Crown you were . . . ?"

"Just celebrating," says Thomas. "But I also told her about my history with Rose. I probably shouldn't have, since it's Rose's story to tell, but you must forgive me that it just slipped out. I ended up telling her the full story—Josie can be quite persuasive, you know—and she wanted to help me out. She told me about the private practice Rose is working to start. The other night at Rose and Crown, that's what we were talking about."

Of course, I think to myself. It was all a misunderstanding, but I've gone and ruined any chance of their happiness by once again intervening and telling Rose what I saw.

When will the mistakes stop?

"You were just talking about Rose?" I repeat, making myself process the sentiment. "You were just doing business."

"Well, that. And I've been working on this and wanted to show her." He pulls something large and vaguely rectangle-shaped from behind his back.

As he steps closer, I get a better view and realize that it's actually two objects. Both are large pieces of polished wood with lettering that was carved into them and then painted gold. The smaller of the two reads "Lottie's Way." The other is still unfinished. It has a blank spot in the center, but underneath it are the words "Psychotherapy Practice."

"I figured Rose would need one of these once she signs the lease Josie was talking about," he says with a shy, endearing smile. "I left the name blank for now."

Something twists in my chest. "And the other one?"

"I noticed 'name the cottage' was on Lottie's bucket list and I figured I'd give it a try. No pressure if you don't like it, of course. I got carried away at the shop."

I think about William and how he would prefer if Rose didn't work at all. Their incompatibility is obvious. I know my mom—I know Rose better than anyone else on this planet. And I know William is not her person, but there's a chance Thomas might be.

"Did you hand carve these yourself?" I ask, awed. I walk over to run my hand along the smooth wood. It looks professional.

"I've been practicing at a workshop downtown," he says, still looking slightly embarrassed. "New hobby."

My fingers trace Lottie's name. It's such a kind gesture, and the truth is, I love it. It's the perfect name, the one we've been looking for this entire time. But Thomas doesn't know that the woman he is honoring is the same woman who kept him and Rose apart.

"It's beautiful," I tell him. "But I'm not sure my mom is too happy with Lottie right now."

To my surprise, Thomas says, "I know. Your grandfather told me what happened at lunch." He laughs. "He's quite the talker, too."

"And you're not mad?" I'm confused by the even expression on his face.

He sets the quarterboards down and sits next to me on the bench. "I've known this whole time," he admits. "Your great-aunt wrote to me after your parents split up. She wanted to know if it was too late. She admitted everything, explaining how she persuaded Rose against the engagement. But by that point, I was already with my wife. We kept missing each other.

"There's something else," Thomas says. "I found these inside a compartment within Lottie's bookcase."

He hands me two large yellow envelopes, surprisingly heavy. Lottie's unmistakable handwriting is on the top. I notice my hands are trembling when I take them from him.

"Did you read them?" I ask. I look down at the envelopes in my lap as if they are religious artifacts.

"No," he says. "I figured they were meant for you and Rose to find."

"If you knew all along that Lottie was the one standing between you and Rose all those years ago, then why did you suggest naming the cottage after her?"

Thomas looks at me intently. His eyes are intelligent and kind. "Just because someone made a mistake, doesn't make them a bad person. Lottie was a wonderful woman. That one action doesn't define her."

I think about his words, letting them seep in. Another Lottie-ism comes to mind: Wisdom is just regret dolled up in a party dress.

"What are you going to do now?"

He takes a step back. "I'm going to pack up," he says, clasping his hands behind himself.

I realize that it's now or never. I can't watch him walk away without saying what needs to be said.

"Don't leave!" I blurt out. He turns around, a puzzled look on his face. "Don't leave yet. I mean, you can obviously move into your new place next week, but not without telling Rose how you feel. I know the wedding plan didn't work out. But give me one more shot."

I'm surprised I'm able to get through the entire impassioned speech without slurring. Thomas stares back, looking torn.

"Please," I say. "One more shot. Next weekend, Friday, she's receiving a big award at a mental health fundraiser. I'm sure it would mean a lot to her to have you there."

"You think so? You don't think I'd be intruding?"

The garden is still spinning. I need to lie down. "She'll be so happy and relieved when the speech is over that I'm sure she'll be in a good mood. She'll be busy and distracted all week preparing. Maybe you can pull her aside when she's done."

Thomas nods, considering it. "That could work," he says. "Thank you. You're a great daughter. I hope you know that."

He gives me a pat on the shoulder and walks back to the cottage, leaving me alone in the garden, hoping he is right.

Chapter Twenty-Nine

Lily

July 29

The morning of the gala, a tremendous fog rolls in covering the island in a cloud.

"Pea soup," Rose calls it. It's like the view from the very tip of a tall mountain. Everything is gray, and the air is thick with moisture when I go for my morning stroll, somewhere between walking and swimming.

Even in the fog I know the way to my destination—I could sleep-walk here. I'm surprised I haven't already.

I haven't opened the envelopes Thomas gave me yet—the ones from Lottie. I won't until after the gala is over. I know I'll be emotional when I see whatever is waiting for us there, and I don't want anything to detract from Rose's day.

I haven't spoken to Henry since the brewery, either, but in the back pocket of my jeans right now is a letter penned to him. After our conversation, I want to leave everything on a good note, solidify the closure we had last week with a sober goodbye. My sincere well-wishes. I'm on the way to leave it at his mailbox. Then I will be clean of the past, fresh as the mist on my face now, the cool droplets curling the hair on the nape of my neck.

Theo and I haven't spoken since he dropped me off. At work, we ignore each other. It's awkward, but at least Emily is still friendly. Part of me is filled with regret, but another smaller, weaker part is relieved. If he's leaving in a few days, there's no point worrying about it anyway. I messed it all up once again, but at least no one got too badly hurt in the process. Theo was a near collision, a close call, but ultimately, I am walking away from the accident still intact. It is only a sideswipe.

One bright point of all the alone time this week is that the collection I've been working on is finally coming together. The paintings are scattered around my room. There are six portraits in total. I had to use far too much of my Great Harbor paycheck to buy the extra canvas and paint, but it's worth it. Looking at the images, I realize it's the first time in years I've felt proud of something I've created.

Sometimes I think life is really just a process of realizing how unremarkable you are, in your heartbreak, in your joy, in your hopes. And then continuing anyway. I know that these paintings are not groundbreaking; they are not changing the world. But I'm proud of them regardless. I'm proud to have contributed a verse, tried my hand at capturing something that is important to me. In the paintings, the women I love are rendered eternal.

Finishing the paintings made me miss Jade. I kept looking at the portrait of her, her mouth curved with laughter, and thinking of our mutual stubbornness in letting this cold streak continue to grow. Someone has to be the one to break it. I texted her last night asking if she could talk.

So when I hear a text come in during my walk, at first, I assume it's Jade already responding, and my heart lifts. When I see it's from Theo, it lifts even higher. Maybe we should talk, I think. Maybe our relationship deserves a proper ending after all.

My screen reads, *I need to see you. There's something I found out about William.*

It's certainly not what I was expecting, and the mystery makes my heart plop back down with a splat. I feel slightly deflated and not a small bit scared.

Is he a serial killer or something? I joke to break the tension.

I see Theo typing and then stopping. After a minute, he writes, *Let's talk in person.*

Not exactly the reunion I had in mind.

Are you still coming tonight? To the gala? I type frantically before the communication loop closes. *We can talk there. We still have a ticket for you!*

Once again, the ellipsis of him typing appears and then disappears. I wait for him to say something, but no message arrives.

I look up and realize I'm just about at my destination.

Through the fog, I can barely make out the red door to Henry's house, but the lawn is wide and green, and I know that behind it is the cliff to the water, a straight drop.

Everything is going to be okay, I think, as I place the letter in Henry's mailbox. I nestle it between other envelopes tenderly, like I'm tucking it into bed. Everything is going to be great.

Chapter Thirty

Rose

The paper in my hand shakes as I practice the speech one final time.

"Thank you all for being here tonight," I mumble into the mirror. "I am so honored to be here with you raising money for this important cause."

It sounds false and hollow, even though I really do mean every word. I read it again, trying to infuse more emotion this time.

"Thank you so much for being here," I say again. "It means the world to me to be with you here tonight."

Now I sound like a bad actress reciting an acceptance speech for an award I don't deserve. I put the paper down, close my eyes, and try to stop the nerves that are spreading throughout my body, making my knees unsteady. I can do this, I tell myself. I can do this. Tonight is the big night. I will announce my new private practice, and I will start my next chapter, a better one.

I've always detested public speaking, looking out at a crowd and seeing their expectant faces slowly grow bored. I imagine what I would say to a client of mine: "No one is scrutinizing you that closely. We overestimate other people's imagined critiques of us and underestimate their positive thoughts."

It doesn't help.

A knock on my bedroom door startles me. I still need to shower and get ready, but my dad and sister asked if they could come over beforehand. "The shower in Josie's guesthouse has terrible water pressure," my dad said. "There's mildew," claimed my sister. James left last week. It was actually nice to see him in the end, and I'm happy he and Lily are on a better path. I just hope his sobriety sticks.

Currently, my dad is using up all the hot water, singing a show tune. He brought over a pressed white linen suit and will no doubt spend the majority of the next two hours before the gala in our one bathroom, perfecting his hair.

"Can I come in?" I hear Elizabeth's voice through the door. I open it and watch as she enters.

Elizabeth is already dressed, looking beautiful in a tan wrap dress and heels. When she sees me, still unshowered and in jeans, she audibly gasps.

"Rose," she chides. "Please tell me you're not wearing that."

I make a face at her. "Obviously, I'm not wearing jeans tonight. I'm just waiting to get into the shower."

"Thank God," says Elizabeth, overdramatic as usual. She stands in the doorway, still scrutinizing me. "You really do need a tan."

"Is this what you came in here to discuss?" I ask, trying to suppress my growing annoyance.

Elizabeth shakes her head. "I came in here to talk," she says, but she eyes my disappointing appearance again like she still finds it distracting. "I wanted to hear how you were feeling before the big speech."

This is not what I expected. The last time I can remember Elizabeth looking for any sort of heart-to-heart was at my engagement party. It was at our family's home, just James's parents, Elizabeth, my dad, and a few close friends. Everyone was disappointed we hadn't opted for a larger affair, but I could barely stomach that. Maybe, I knew somewhere that we were already doomed and didn't want an audience. I was getting ready in the bathroom, putting on our mother's pearl earrings. Elizabeth came in to help me fix the clasp.

"Is this what you really want?" Elizabeth asked with her cold hands on my ear. It was the first time someone had asked the question so blatantly, and at first, I didn't know how to respond.

"I think so," I said, which was true at the time. I wanted to stop thinking of the past. I wanted to take a step forward in my life, even if it was the wrong one. At least it would solidify my life in a direction. Besides, Lily was already on the way. Even though I wasn't showing yet, I could feel her there, tossing and turning, my precious little secret.

"Okay," is all Elizabeth said. "Then let's fix your hair. It looks flat."

That was the closest since childhood we had come to a sisterly moment, and of course, it ended in an insult. I didn't call it off that day, or even that week, but ten days later, we were no longer engaged and I felt a sort of breathtaking relief.

"I'm nervous," I admit to her now. "I don't want to disappoint anyone."

Elizabeth comes closer, stands behind me in front of Lottie's antique mirror. The wood is carved into the shapes of seashells. The steam from the shower is seeping into the room, making the mirror fog around the edges.

"You'll be fine," she says confidently. "You've always been fine." She twists my hair behind my back in a tender gesture.

I look at our reflection in the mirror and am surprised to see the years on our faces. We look similar to our childhood selves, but the lines of time are unmistakable. Maybe it's the nerves or the unexpected sentimentality of the moment, but I see my eyes start to fill with water.

"What's wrong?" asks Elizabeth, turning away from the mirror to look at me directly. She wipes away a tear from my cheek, and the gentleness of the action makes me cry more. "I was always jealous you got our mother's brown eyes," she says with a long sigh.

It strikes me then that everyone is gone; all the adults have left the room. After all, my father has never acted like a true "adult." Now it's just the two of us, holding down the fort. And we're doing a shitty job at it. We barely even speak, besides the occasional text about her hypochondria and a forced holiday gathering.

"Are you happy?" I ask, looking at her heavy makeup, her bright, optimistic hair.

She's turning fifty-six in October. She has friends, and she and Dad travel more than they can afford to, but is this what she wanted? She's never been able to hold down a job or find a career she's passionate about. I picture us as kids. She was the same egotistic, bossy girl of our youth, but there was such determination about her. I thought she would grow up to be a CEO, or maybe a dictator, but after our mother died, it's like she left the window open and now, the fear has come in with the draft.

"I'm okay," is all Elizabeth says, and for the first time in years, I can sense a mask has slipped off, leaving her vulnerable. "Someone had to take care of Dad, right?"

I hear him, in the shower still, continuing to sing: a long, operatic belt.

"Oh, Elizabeth," I say, putting a hand on either side of her shoulders. "Is that what happened? You thought you had to stay to take care of Dad?"

"Of course," she whispers, and her pretty eyes look sad. "Besides, you had Lottie. The two of us were never close."

I look back at the past from this perspective, imagining what Elizabeth might have thought. I felt neglected in our home, she and Dad always so alike and critical. But maybe she felt abandoned, too. Maybe she was jealous of how untethered to it all I seemed.

"I'm sorry," I say with warmth. "I'm sorry you felt that way."

The flatness is back in her eyes, but when she looks away, a tear slides down her left cheek. "Relax," she says. "At least my hair doesn't look like a greasy mess."

I laugh as she takes the twist of my hair again and pretends to cringe.

We hear the shower turn off in the bathroom. My father still whistling. I wonder what will happen when he's gone, how Elizabeth will cope. He's the foundation on which her life is built. I need to be a better sister and check in more, let her know that they're not alone. Maybe she can come here more often, use the guest half of the cottage once the summer is over.

When we hear the door shut behind my father and the sound of his large footsteps departing, Elizabeth pushes me into the small bathroom. "Now, please, for the sake of our family's good name, get yourself together."

I laugh and follow her orders. In the shower, the hot water works wonders on my stress, untying all of my knots. Tonight is going to be okay, I tell myself. It's going to be great.

Chapter Thirty-One

Lily

After leaving the letter at Henry's, I spend the rest of the day helping my mom prepare for the event.

I get dressed early, letting my grandfather and aunt use my room to get ready. I pick up Rose's dress from the dry cleaners, a gold silk gown with a matching wrap. I'm wearing a midnight-blue one my mom picked out.

I make sure the pamphlets for the event are printed and stack them all neatly in cardboard boxes. The auction items for the fund-raising portion have been packaged and delivered to the venue, the ballroom at the Great Harbor Yacht Club, downtown.

Now it's almost six, less than half an hour before the event, and I have just dropped off Rose. She is making sure the sound system is in place, the microphones work, the tables are laid out with the items on sale, and most importantly, that the bar is fully stocked. Rich people always donate more when they've had a few too many.

My fingertips are lined with stinging paper cuts from the pamphlets. Upon arriving, we realized there wasn't enough ice, so I was sent on a mission to grab some at the supermarket just two blocks down the road.

That's when it happens. As I'm driving back with the ice, my phone rings. The car shows on the dashboard the caller's name: Clive Bozeman. I've been waiting for this call. I knew it would eventually come once I sent the email, but I forced myself to ignore the impending confrontation. As soon as his name appears, I feel the thump of my heart racing. My hands become slick on the steering wheel.

I let it ring for a few seconds before answering.

"Hello?" I swallow.

"Hi, Lily," says Clive in a neutral, calm voice.

I try to picture where he might be. It's Friday, so I assume he's at the office. Are his legs crossed atop his desk? Is he playing with the fidget spinner he always used? Or is he back at home in his Tribeca loft?

"Hi," I repeat in a less certain voice.

"I received your email," he says. He sounds almost amused, sardonic, and maybe even a little . . . impressed? "Quite the theatrics. I must admit I didn't know you had it in you."

His tone is smug and condescending—it's how he always sounds. But at least he doesn't seem particularly resentful.

"Yes," I say, clearing my throat. Bikers pass in front of the car, and I try to stay focused on the road. "I was told you had some choice words when Marie Chen called. It's one thing to fire me, but you and I both know that it's not fair for you to ruin my future career prospects after all I did for you." I do my best to sound confident and stern.

"Interesting," says Clive in that same amused voice. It immediately takes me back to how it felt to be his assistant and personal punching bag for three years: the snide remarks, his perfectly manicured eyebrows always raised in a snobbish expression. The belittling.

I'm expecting him to fight back, to yell like he used to, or threaten to get HR involved, but to my surprise, he just laughs.

"I suppose you're right," he says. I can hear the shrug in his tone. "I wasn't always fair to you."

I'm too shocked at first to compute. "You weren't?" I repeat. "I mean, no. You certainly were not."

Clive gives another airy chuckle. "I know I wasn't the best boss. In my defense, I was going through a divorce, so I wasn't exactly my best self either. But regardless, you're right. If I ever get asked for a professional reference again, I will be sure to sing your praises."

Is it possible that it was this easy all along? I can't believe he's agreeing without a fight. I knew he was going through a divorce, and while I also know what heartbreak can do to a person, it's still not an excuse.

"Thank you," I say. "I appreciate that. And I'm sorry, too. I mean, about the divorce."

Clive sighs. "Don't apologize, Lily. You were doing so well! Stand up for yourself. It's tiresome."

That pisses me off again. "You're right," I say with more strength. "You were a terrible boss, and I am honestly thrilled to never work for you again. I hope we never cross paths."

He laughs, almost a snort. "There you go," he says. "Way to finally grow a backbone."

A thought occurs to me. "Wait, can I actually get this in writing—"

Before I can finish the request, the conversation is over. I hear the beep of the call ending. In the front seat of the car, I let myself breathe a relieved laugh. It's over. No, Clive didn't exactly make amends for his atrocious behavior, but at least he won't affect my future going forward. He won't hold me back. Nothing will. Maybe my dad was right.

It is on this short drive back to the venue—the big bags of ice secured in my back seat, the satisfaction of settling the score with Clive making everything feel lighter—that I see the deer a second too late.

I spot the antlers first, emerging from the gray fog only three feet in front of the windshield. It is a surprise to see a deer here, so close to the busy town center. I'm used to them appearing on Milestone Road or out on the sleepy side streets in 'Sconset, but not here, in the middle of civilization. I wasn't on guard.

I stop just in time. My heart jolts along with the brakes. The head of the deer is visible before the rest of its body, like one of those already dead trophies on the walls of hunting lodges. The car keeps sliding on a puddle. I slam even harder on the brakes. The deer doesn't move, just keeps looking at me, blinking, before walking away at a leisurely pace, unbothered.

It takes several seconds for my heart to restart before I can move. When I hydroplaned, I ended up a few inches onto the sidewalk in an effort to avoid hitting the buck. Now I cautiously pull out, but the fog is too dense. There's a car parked behind me on the side of the road, but I can't see much else. I move slowly, or at least I think I'm going slow, but the adrenaline is pumping through my muscles, and all I want to do is get to the safety of the parking lot.

That's when I feel a bump and the hideous, grating sound of metal on metal. The noise is awful, haunting. I think I will hear it forever: the sensation of my car colliding, scraping along the one behind. When it stops, all I can think in the silence is, No, no, no, no.

I get out of the car to inspect for damage, but there are still people whizzing by, honking. My legs are shaking and it feels I've been punched in the sternum. The other car, thankfully, mercifully, looks fine. The license plate is a tad askew, but when I go to adjust it, it lifts back into place. There's a line of paint on the front bumper, but

I wipe this off easily, too. It's as if nothing happened. Our spare tire must have cushioned the blow.

Then I turn my attention to our car. Lottie's car has fared the worse by far, taking on the brunt of the damage. There's a long, silver scrape of chipped paint on the back, probably from the other car's plate. I have a hard time looking at it directly, as if it'll become less real if I only squint at it. I consider leaving a note, but what would it say? The damage is only to Lottie's car. The wind of passing traffic blows back my hair, and I realize that if I stay put like this, I risk getting into a worse accident. I get back into the driver's seat and pull out hesitantly, quietly. I drive the remaining two blocks back to the venue, scanning the mist for hidden threats.

When I am safely parked, I examine the scratch again. It's bad, as if someone has scraped a giant fingernail against the rear end of the Jeep. Childishly, I want to cry. A few moments ago, the car was perfect, intact, and now here it is: damaged, changed. It is all my fault. It is always, in the end, all my fault. Lottie's Jeep will never be the same again.

I fix my makeup in the rearview mirror, waiting for the blotchiness on my neck to settle back to a uniform color. I adjust my hair, now in unruly curls.

Tomorrow, I will deal with everything else, but tonight is about Rose. With a deep breath, I enter the yacht club.

I can still fix this. I can, and I must.

Inside, the event is already in full swing. I carry the three bags of ice, cold against my chest. One is blocking my vision, so I have to keep adjusting it. I spot my grandfather and aunt by the raw bar. They look like twins: artificial orange tans and the same bored expression, as if even the champagne flutes they hold are disappointing somehow.

The yacht club is directly on the harbor, and outside the water is still, the fog rolling off it in wisps. Behind the wide glass windows of the dining room sits a handful of lawn chairs. The grass is uniform, freshly clipped; the sailing flags ripple in the wind.

"Lily?" I hear, but I can't see past the ice to who is speaking.

For a second, I assume it must be Theo—did he decide to still come despite everything? Instead, when I move around the bags, I see William. The image of him is slightly warbled, like opening your eyes underwater.

William is wearing a ridiculous white suit. He looks like a cross between a Miami club promoter and a sailing captain. I'm so alarmed by the sight of him that I drop the ice. I forgot he would be here when I invited Thomas. I still don't know what Theo wanted to warn me about, and the possibilities are chilling.

The bags fall together, landing in a pile with a loud crashing noise. One splits open. Ice slides everywhere, some cubes flying as far as the stage. All of the fancy guests turn around, holding their cocktails up in the air, their eyes embarrassed on my behalf. The band cuts the music.

I drop to my knees and try to scoop up as much ice as possible. My hands go numb as I pile more and more together until I can no longer feel the paper cuts. The ice begins to melt from the warmth of my body until I'm holding half water. The band restarts.

"Here, let me help," says William, kneeling in his suit.

"No," I insist, feeling sorry for him. In the end, he's just a man in love with my mom. He hasn't done anything wrong. "I'm fine, please. I'm sorry."

I heave the remaining intact bags together and what remains of the split bag, rushing to the kitchen. I drop them onto the metal table by the industrial fridge, and lean against the edge of the countertop.

"Lil?" Rose says. "What are you doing back here?"

My mom is standing by the door next to the freezer, her back pressed against it. She looks beautiful: a golden statue. There are a few pages of printed paper folded in her left hand.

"Uh." I empty the split bag full of dirty ice and listen to the clink as it lands into the industrial sink. "I'm just dropping off the ice. There was an accident."

The word *accident* makes me think of the deer, and the scratch, and all of the many irrevocable mistakes I have made this summer. I close my eyes tightly, forcing the image away.

"Are you okay?" Rose approaches. "We have five minutes to showtime, but I can talk if you're upset."

"I'm totally fine," I say, faking a smile. "I'm just going to give one of these to the bartender. Sorry for interrupting you. You're going to do great."

Before she can respond, I am out the door again, thinking only of escape. I locate the bar in the right corner of the large, elegant hall, and hand the ice bag over to the bartender. I pause to catch my breath.

"Lily!"

No, no, no, no. What now?

Approaching to the left of the ballroom is Thomas, eager and handsome in a dark suit. In his hand is a cluster of white hydrangeas. "How are you doing? I can't wait to see Rose! Do you know where she is? I'd love to give her these."

"Oh, yes! So nice of you, really. Thank you for coming. I think she's going to take the stage soon, but I can hold on to them for her."

I reach for the bouquet. At that moment, Rose walks by, a practiced smile on her face, all grace. William trails after her in a slinky, sulky manner. I wonder if they've had a fight.

"Oh, perfect!" says Thomas. "I'll give them to her myself!"

He waves to Rose as she makes her way through the crowd, gesturing to the flowers in his hand. He mouths, "For you! Good luck."

Horror flashes across my mom's face before it is wiped clean. I turn to see William staring at Thomas with his hands clenched. His eyes are hard and black like buttons. Rose shoots me a wide-eyed glance.

Uh-oh, I think. Now I've really done it.

"Thanks, Thomas!" I grab the flowers from him quickly. "I love them!"

William squints in our direction.

Thomas looks confused but goes with it. On the podium, Rose clears her throat, brushing loose strands of red hair behind her shoulder. She looks thin. Too thin. Has she always been this small and breakable? I'm nervous for her, the way I was nervous for Theo at karaoke but amplified by a hundred.

"First off, I want to thank all of you for coming here tonight," Rose starts. Some guests are still mingling, and their voices carry to the stage, drowning out her soft words. "There is nothing more important than prioritizing our mental health, and there is nowhere more important to me than this community. I was so thrilled when the organizers of the Dragonfly fundraiser asked me to speak tonight. As many of you know, it has been my great honor to serve this island. But perhaps my greatest honor is—"

"YOU BITCH!" A yell echoes across the room. Every head swivels to catch sight of the source, myself included. That is when I see Henry's fiancée, Mary, barreling toward me.

My blood runs cold; not in a figurative sense, but in a very literal, physical sensation, as if the ice bags have bled into my veins. This can't be happening; this can't be happening.

"You fiancé-stealing, cheating, lying, ginger freak!"

Mary pushes through the crowd. People jump out of the way to avoid her. She is wearing a long white dress as if it's already her wedding day. It strikes me then that I have never seen her in anything but a white dress. In one of her hands, Mary is clutching a letter.

No, no, no, no.

"You had the audacity to leave a love note in my fiancé's mailbox this morning? What did you think was going to happen?"

Mary waves the envelope so close to my face, I have to step back in order to not be sliced. In my mind, Mary has been like a fictional entity, more concept than person, some perfect girl next door who radiates sunshine, and warmth, and smells of fresh cookies and vanilla extract. But here she is, red-faced, furious, shoving me back into the wooden counter of the bar. Is it weird that I respect her even more for it? Under different circumstances, I might be cheering her on.

"It's—it's not a love note, I swear. It was a goodbye." My voice comes out weak.

"Oh, so you have to say GOODBYE to my fiancé? What—were you screwing around with him all summer and now you're finally done?"

Henry stands three feet behind her, inspecting the ground, conveniently silent.

"No, no, I swear. Nothing ever happened, I wouldn't do that. Henry wouldn't do that. Tell her, Henry."

"I told her we didn't—"

"SHUT UP!" Mary yells at him. He becomes preoccupied by his leather shoes again.

"Mary, I'm so sorry. That letter might have been inappropriate, but I swear, if you read it, you'll see I meant no harm. Can we please do this elsewhere? Let's go out on the—"

"Oh, you think I didn't read it already? Of course I read it, you dumb bitch." Her eyes are knives pointed directly at me, her nostrils flaring, her mouth curled up. My whole body is shaking like Mrs. Clay when she gets a bath.

"Then you'll see that I meant no harm! Truly, I'm so sorry. Didn't you see all the nice things I said about you in it? How happy you seem together?" I look back at Henry in desperation, but he's still staring at the same floorboard. "Please, can we just go outside?"

"Oh, yeah, that's rich. Like I needed your permission or approval. Who do you think you are to talk to my fiancé about our relationship? You don't even know me."

I plead once more, my voice small: "Please, you're right, I'm sorry. Can we just go outside, please, so my mom can finish her speech? Please."

"You've ruined my engagement, so I'm ruining your mom's night. Deal with it."

I feel spit land squarely on my jaw at the same time Mary shoves me, ripping the left strap of my dress. The fabric tears in one long line, and I have to hold the hydrangeas against my chest so I don't flash anyone.

"Hey, that's quite enough. Leave her alone." Thomas steps in between us, his arms holding Mary back. She pushes past him, and slaps me across the face so hard my eyes sting. I feel the outline of Mary's hand radiating on my right cheek.

"I SAID ENOUGH," Thomas yells, restraining Mary's arms.

William comes swinging over, shoving Thomas, who is still holding Mary. "Get your filthy hands off my niece!" he shouts. "Who the hell do you think you are anyway?"

"Niece?" My head is spinning, trying to connect the dots. "You're related?"

I look between William and Mary. There is something there: in the cleft chins, the full lips, the enraged madness in their eyes.

"I'm the guy who is in love with your girlfriend," says Thomas. "That's who I think I am."

The two of them struggle, Mary caught between like a caged animal, until the whole lot fall over, sprawled across the ground. Their bodies spread out—various limbs entangled—like a Renaissance painting I once wrote a paper on in college.

My chest is vibrating, the whole room is toppling over, my panic attacks resurfacing for a grand finale. The hardwood floors become the ceiling, the counter I'm grabbing tilts like a sinking ship. I hold on to it for dear life.

"Lily?" I hear in the crowd for the final time that summer.

It's Theo in another too-big suit, long at the arms. His curls are slicked back. His blue eyes look confused, concerned, hurt, all at once. I watch as he spots the flowers in my hand, my red cheek, and Mary knocked onto the floor.

I know a second before he moves what he must assume happened here tonight. I can see the mental gymnastics in real time. Henry standing there, looking guilty. I imagine Theo's train of thought: Did Henry come here tonight to give me these flowers? Is that why Mary got involved?

"You prick!" Theo shouts before launching himself at Henry, punching him straight across the jaw. He falls to the ground with a hollow, resolute thud. The audience—because that's exactly what they've become, the audience to this spectacle—lets out a collective gasp.

The last image I see before the world turns fully upside down is Rose at the podium. Heartbreak in her eyes. She shakes her head only once, small but clear, and I am sure I have never seen anyone look so utterly disappointed.

I catch a glimpse of a red shawl in the crowd. Then the room goes black.

Chapter Thirty-Two

Lily

Outside on the deck, I hold a cloth filled with ice to my cheek and a pool towel around my shoulders. Beside me, Thomas is icing his right knee. Neither of us speak. The fog rolls off the lawn and onto us like a curtain closing. I lift my face into it, as if it possesses some sort of purifying power.

My jaw is sore, and my lips feel swollen. All of my words come out thick and slow.

"Kill me," I say to Thomas. "Just kill me now."

He gives me a heavy pat on the back but remains silent. A text comes in from Jade. *Let's talk. Tonight?*

Under other circumstances, I'd be thrilled, but I'm too tired to feel the relief.

Theo approaches us, his too-big jacket askew and his hands tucked into the mismatched trousers.

"Can we talk?" he asks, and Thomas nods in our direction before hobbling off to sit on a lawn chair a few yards away. I hear the grunt of him landing in the seat.

I turn to Theo. "I'm sorry," I say automatically. "For everything."

He's looking at the deck. I notice he's wearing sneakers with his suit, and the sudden surge of affection I feel for him makes my chest ache. "I'm sorry, too," he says. "I should've told you I was leaving, but I didn't want to ruin all of the fun we were having."

"I understand," I say, and then smile sadly. "But I do wish I had known. I would have wasted less time."

He turns to me with a surprised, eager expression. It makes him look like a little boy. "So, you're not mad?"

I shake my head. "No. Are you mad at me for getting drunk and making a fool of myself at the brewery?"

He laughs and then sighs. "No, I'm not mad. I'm sorry for getting so weird after our date, too. It just felt like so much pressure, like we were getting too deep, when I knew I was leaving. Maybe I shouldn't have ever asked you out, and we could've just stayed friends. It was selfish."

I grab his hand and squeeze it. He adjusts to face me, and the sneakers make a squeaking sound against the damp deck.

"No, I'm glad you did. You've been the best part of my summer. And you're going to be a fabulous teacher. I'm really happy for you."

He smiles the smile I've come to love: the chipped incisor, his blue eyes bright and filled with optimism. "Thanks, Lil."

"So, friends?" I ask, dropping his hand and then offering it to him again for a handshake.

"Friends." He smiles. "For now."

I try to ignore the butterflies. "For now," I agree.

Our hands stay pressed together for a beat longer than necessary until I hear someone approach to our left. Walking out of the glass doors of the country club is William.

"Hello," he says, approaching. "I, um . . . Well, I wanted to apologize for getting physical out there. It wasn't very gentlemanly."

To my surprise, Theo stands up first, anger making his features look scrunched. "Back off," he says. "The jig is up."

In the chaos of the night, I almost forgot about the mysterious text Theo sent me, but now, I realize that must be why he's acting like he's in some sort of bad detective show. The jig is up? What on earth is he talking about?

William appears confused, too. "I'm not sure what you're going on about, but I assure you, I mean no harm."

Theo scoffs. "Does the name Bunny Andrews ring a bell?"

I look between the two of them, trying to make sense of the nonsensical. Bunny Andrews? The name does sound mildly familiar, and I realize, after some brainstorming, why. She's a new member at the club: one of Theo's more recent regulars.

William backs away a step. "No," he says, but he sounds less confident. "What are you going on about?"

"Bunny moved to the island. Bet you didn't know that, and she told me a little story about you in Palm Beach. How you tricked her into a relationship and then siphoned off her assets."

I feel my jaw drop and have to physically remind myself to close it. Rose appears behind William, looking utterly exhausted and wary.

"What's this now? Please, I can't handle another fight," Rose says, but William doesn't turn around. I watch as his face becomes increasingly more red, almost purplish.

"This is slander," he says, but his voice wavers. "Rose, ignore them. They're talking crazy."

"What?" says Rose. "Theo, what's going on?"

Theo's angry expression smooths when he looks at Rose and is replaced with pity. I can sense him hesitate, knowing he doesn't want to hurt her.

"One of my tennis clients told me that William regularly preys upon single, rich women and uses them for their money. That yacht apparently isn't even his. Bunny bought it, but he convinced her to give over the deed for what he claimed were 'tax purposes.' She's been trying to fight him in court."

William stands frozen, only his eyes moving frantically, like he's a cornered animal searching for a path to escape. "Rose, don't listen to them."

My mom, to my astonishment, doesn't yell or cry or even look horrified. Rather, she just laughs.

"You thought I had money?" she asks, incredulous.

William must finally decide the jig is indeed up, because his shoulders slouch and he sighs. "You have a house on Nantucket. What do you mean? Of course you have money."

Mom laughs harder this time, nearing hysteria. She bends over and tries to catch her breath. I wonder if she's lost it, if the drama of the day has cracked her open and done irretrievable damage to her psyche.

"Yes, I'm lucky enough to have inherited a small cottage in 'Sconset, but that's pretty much all the assets I have," she says between laughs. "I'm a community therapist."

I remember William encouraging her to sell the house and leave the island. This must be why. He always intended to use the profits for himself.

"Rose." William reaches toward her. "You must know that my feelings were real. Whatever misconceptions I had about your financial situation, I care for you. I . . . well, I love you."

Mom cringes away from his touch, her laughter replaced by a disgusted scowl. "Oh, give it up, already! I was trying to break up with you before my speech regardless." That explains his sullen expression, trailing after her before she took the podium. "This just makes my decision easier. Now, get the fuck out of my face."

This might be the only time in my entire life I've heard my mom curse, and I feel a certain pride. Theo and I clap as William slinks off, like a dog with his tail between his legs.

When he's gone, I stand and offer my mom a high five. "Go, Mom!"

Rose ignores the gesture. "You, get in the car. We're going home."

On the ride home, Rose and I don't say a word. Aunt Elizabeth and my grandfather decide to stay out later. Apparently, they ran into old friends from Branford. They said something about "going for a nightcap at Gaslight." We sit in the dark of the car. The fog has turned to rain, and the windshield wipers squeak against the glass, emphasizing the quiet. I didn't show Mom the scratch on the bumper yet. That particular reckoning can wait.

"How did the rest of the night go?" I ask. "I mean after the speech. Were you able to keep going once the fight was broken up and we went outside?"

"How do you think it went?" says Rose. I've never heard my mom sound so cold.

"I'm really sorry. I can't tell you how sorry I am—"

"Can we just not tonight? I'm exhausted. Let's just sit in the silence."

The rain is coming down hard, crashing onto the roof. Headlights flash by, blinding us. Nantucket is unrecognizable in this weather. The island changes during a storm. You realize how isolated it truly is, a sand bank thirty miles out to sea, an anomaly, a miracle. I consider warning my mom to watch out for deer but decide against it. Rose doesn't need the kinds of warnings I need. She always knows what to do.

"I just, I need you to know how incredibly sorry I am. You're the most important person in the world to me and I just—"

"Please! Lily." Rose's voice cracks. "Please. Enough. Can you respect this one thing? I just want to be in silence."

I stop talking, staring out the window at the dark, unknown shapes.

Rose breaks her own vow of silence first. "I just can't believe you would act so irresponsibly. I love you, Lily. You know that. But you have to grow up."

"Mom, that's not fair," I beg, but I know she's right. Tears glide down my cheeks and into my mouth. They taste like the ocean. "I never wanted to hurt you like this."

"Life is hard, Lily. The hits will keep coming and you're not a kid anymore."

The words sting on my skin, like I'm taking a physical lashing. "I know, I'm trying to be better. I made a mistake, that's all."

My mom's knuckles are flexed around the wheel, turning white. "I mean you and Henry broke up so long ago. He's getting married. And you wrote him some sort of letter this morning? What did you think was going to happen?"

The tears are coming faster than the rain outside. "I just wanted to leave everything on a positive note."

"All of this fuss over Henry?" she says, staring at the road like it's somehow to blame. "Why do you even care about him? He's always been a spoiled brat."

I'm confused. "What do you mean? You always liked Henry."

Mom scoffs. "I was nice to him, sure. I pretended to like him because I didn't want you persuaded by my opinion, but really? All of this drama over a boy who wears designer sneakers?"

In another universe in which tonight's events did not unfold, the sentence would make me laugh. But tonight is not that night, and Rose has already moved on to something else.

"And you invited Thomas tonight? What did you think that would do? Like I wasn't nervous enough already? Why do you think you can interfere in my life like that? You're the child, Lily. Not the parent."

I've never heard her speak like this. Even when I was a teen with raging hormones, we never fought. Sure, we bickered here and there. But not like this. The road in front of us is narrowing, the trees curving around the car like hands reaching out at us, grabbing.

"So, what?" I yell back through my sobs. "I made a mistake, and now you're going to ditch me like you ditched Lottie. You abandoned the bucket list because she wasn't perfect. Now you're doing the same to me."

I know my words are cruel, but I sling them at her anyway, wanting to feel the full impact.

Her mouth tightens. "That's not fair. You know, last week one of my patients was a single mother of three who was just diagnosed with terminal brain cancer. I sat with her, and held her as she sobbed into my shoulder, because she doesn't know who is going to take care of her children when she dies. The youngest is only six."

I cover my mouth, horrified. Something solid is stuck in my windpipe, making it difficult to swallow.

"That's why tonight was so important to me, Lily. For them. To raise enough money to keep supporting community programs that are quite literally saving lives. Or, at the very least, sitting with people in their grief at the hardest points of their lives. I know I put on a happy face, but it is hard work."

The indicators beep as she pulls up to the cottage, headlights lighting up the kitchen. I see the reading nook with its soft, tan cushions. It's almost like Lottie's shadow is still visible.

We sit there, neither of us moving.

It reminds me of all the times in my childhood when we would linger in the car after school, sitting in the driveway, just chatting. I told her everything: which girls were bullies, which boys were gross, which teachers were unfair. Rose listened to it all. She never made me question whether a topic was off-limits. She always made me feel seen, heard, validated. Sometimes, in college, I would call her, and when we ran out of topics to talk about, we would let the line go quiet, cleaning our respective rooms or sending out emails. I could always hear her moving on the other side of the line; every ten or so minutes, one of us adding something we forgot to mention before.

Before she opens the door, Rose reaches out to touch my face. My skin is still tender from where Mary slapped me. “I love you, Lily. It’s just been a long summer. Let’s talk in the morning.”

She puts the car in park, switches off the engine, and walks into the house. It takes me several minutes before I can follow her, ducking from the raindrops that land on my head, harsh and certain as bullets.

Chapter Thirty-Three

Lily

Back in my room, wet from the rain and bone-tired, I'm desperate for distraction, for comfort.

I sit against the hard edge of my bed frame and remember Jade's text. Because of the exhaustion I feel from the action-packed night, when I check the clock and see it's only nine, I'm surprised. I decide to give Jade a call, and she picks up on the first ring.

"Lily," she says immediately. Her voice is chipper and kind. "I'm so happy you called. I miss you."

It's the familiarity of her voice, the friendliness and warmth. I've missed her this summer, I realize. I've missed my best friend.

"Jade, I'm so sorry," I say. "I'm so sorry I haven't reached out before this. I was just insecure and being stupid."

She rushes to jump in. "I could've called, too," she says. "I honestly felt a bit abandoned when you left me with the lease. I was angry, and I let that frustration build instead of being the bigger person. I know you were going through a hard time, and I wished I could've been there for you more after you got fired."

In the background, I hear what sounds like the clinking of pots and pans. "Oh, I'm so sorry. Is now a bad time? It sounds like you're cooking."

Jade lets out a short huff, and I picture her rolling her eyes the way she always does. "That's just Mark," she says. "He's cooking very loudly." In the distance, I hear her boyfriend laugh. "I'll go into the bedroom for a bit."

There's the sound of a door closing and then quiet. "Sorry about that," says Jade. "Can we be okay again?"

"Of course," I tell her, relieved at how easy this reconciliation is. Just like it was with Clive—how many things have I avoided out of misplaced fear? "Thank you," I say. After a few seconds, I ask, "So, Mark's cooking dinners now?"

Jade giggles. Her laugh has always had a bright, musical quality: girlish. "After you left me with that random subletter—who, by the way, was super messy and gross and always left hair on the shower wall—" I shudder. "Well, it kind of expedited my plan with Mark. I moved into his apartment."

I can sense the smile in her voice. "Jade, that's amazing! Congratulations!"

Maybe earlier in the summer, I would have heard this and felt sorry for myself, knowing that if I ever return to the city, our relationship won't be the same. We'll never again be roommates. But now, I really am happy for Jade.

"So, what's new with you?" she asks. I hear the creak of her leaning back on her bed frame. "Catch me up!"

"Well, for starters, I instigated a six-person fistfight tonight. Henry is engaged, and his fiancée wants me dead. I met a really great guy but kind of blew it. My dad and I maybe reconciled. I yelled at my old boss, Clive. My mom's long-lost love ended up renting out the other half of our cottage, and I've been on a mission to set them up all summer." I'm breathless when I'm finished. "Oh, and a really creepy psychic lady told me that my soulmate's name starts with the letter *H*. Where do you want to start?"

Jade is nonplussed. "Definitely start with your mom's long-lost lover."

I tell her the full story of the summer. By the end, we're laughing so hard my ribs feel sore. I look over at my bedside clock and see it's already ten. Discussing it all with Jade, everything feels more manageable. She's always had a way of putting the world into perspective. After an hour, I realize I've probably kept her from her dinner plans with Mark.

"I love you, Jade," I say.

"Love you, always," she says. "And don't worry. Your mom will forgive you. You guys are so close. Nothing can break that."

After we hang up, I look around the room, taking stock. The portraits, now dried, are leaning against the right wall. To their right, on a small wooden stool, are the envelopes from Lottie that Thomas found.

Normally, a message from Lottie would have been the first thing on my mind, but with everything else going on, the urgency has been lost. Maybe that's a sign that we're healing, finally moving on.

I walk over and pick them up. The first one is lighter than the second. There must be at least a hundred pages inside.

I sit back down on my bed, open the envelopes, and begin to read.

Chapter Thirty-Four

Lottie

According to the pamphlet I was given at the doctor's office yesterday morning, this is the recipe for what a dying woman should do with her rare, remaining days:

1. Live every day to the fullest.
2. Tell people that you love them.
3. Get your will in order.
4. Let go.

It's not exactly bad advice, but it's generic. I've lived too much of my life by the status quo. Time is thinning, and the last thing I want to do right now is be another cliché.

Besides, it's not easy to "live every day to the fullest" when chemo has made your spine as brittle as crackers, and walking from the kitchen to the reading nook is enough to leave you breathless.

Numbers two and three are good ideas, but four is tricky.

I know I'm close to dying, because most nights, Charlie visits me. It's not as creepy as it sounds. He is not a ghost in the night, floating above our bed. Instead, he appears in my dreams. More often than not, he is waiting for me when I close my eyes. We talk. I ask him about death. He tells me it's strange but okay. He says he's excited to see me, and when he does, I realize that I am, too.

I suppose I have "let go" in that sense. I'm not afraid, but I am leaving too much behind, unfinished.

The other day, I snuck into Lily's room when she was out and used her computer to search "What to do when dying?" Someone suggested making a bucket list. It was silly, but I tried. I wrote out a few ways to enjoy the island anew, but by the time I was finished, I realized it was a doomed venture. These days, I'm not fit to do much besides sit in the garden and think. Besides, a bucket list isn't what I need. I need something grander, more difficult to grasp.

What I need now is to be honest.

There's a lot you already know about me, but there is much you still don't. When I was nineteen, I wanted to be a career woman, a magazine girl. It was going to be glamorous: fast-paced, unpredictable, maybe even a little seedy. I lived a cloistered upbringing and the word *seedy* sounded exciting in and of itself. The plan was to move to New York after I graduated from Sarah Lawrence and work as an editor at a women's publication. I was supposed to intern my sophomore summer, but then that April, something else happened. I met your uncle.

You have to understand what Charlie was like back then. He was all big ideas, and curly hair, and he had this dimple in his chin, and when he spoke, the whole room quieted to listen. He was never a loud man, never domineering or obnoxious, but still, people listened to him just the same.

Charlie was visiting his sister at college when he first spotted me. I was on the quad, and it was one of those rare spring days that are warm and ripe with hope. I was reading a book, and he stopped in front of me, his tall frame blocking out the sun.

He said, "Excuse me, ma'am, I'm lost. Could you help me out with some directions to the science building?"

I pointed at a large brick building across the way and returned to my pages.

That wasn't enough for Charlie, because he followed up with, "Would you mind walking with me? I don't want to get lost."

I really looked at him then, the bright sun on his face like a promise. His smile was mischievous and full of courage. I thought him brave.

But I didn't say that. "It's a straight shot," I said. "I think you'll manage just fine."

He shielded his eyes from the sun, and they were as green as the April grass. "I don't know," he said, smiling. "Looks awfully far."

I must have been feeling particularly bold or in some sort of terrible mood, because "You'll manage" is all I responded before returning to my book.

Charlie tipped his hat at me, and I watched his figure retreat across campus.

That was a Thursday, and I thought about him all weekend. I wondered if I should have accompanied him. It was a short interaction, and I was a bit mystified why I kept seeing his face float up in front of my pages. It was the dimple, his smile, and the way he said, "Ma'am." I assumed he had left campus. I didn't know his sister, but most visitors only stayed in town for a day or two at best.

The following Monday, I saw him again. There he was, cutting across the quad, walking on the stone steps. I was reading on the same bench. Maybe I hoped if I stayed in the exact same spot, he would come by again and I would get another chance. Well, as it happened, I was right. I straightened in my seat, pretended to keep reading, going over the same sentence again and again. I had freshly applied lipstick and pursed my lips as if in pretty concentration.

But this time, Charlie didn't stop. He didn't even seem to see me. He kept walking, his head looking up at the clouds, and his expression serious.

He was just about to pass by me—the moment was ending, the opportunity narrowing—when I stuck my foot out. Charlie tripped over me, stumbled. When he straightened and saw who his assailant was, he was smiling and the dimple returned.

"Did you trip me?" he asked, but from the way he said it, I could tell he wasn't mad.

"That's ridiculous," I denied. "You must be lost again. Where are you headed today?"

It was the way he smiled, the look in his eyes like I was something marvelous and unexpected, a present to be unwrapped. It was the way I was waiting to be looked at my entire life.

"You're right," he said, hands in his pockets. "I am lost. Could you help me find the dining hall?"

We walked together that afternoon, and a few short months later, we were engaged. I later found out that he had just discovered his sister was too sick to continue at Sarah Lawrence. She passed before our wedding.

"You tripping me was exactly the distraction I needed," he told me years later.

After that April day, I stopped dreaming of magazines and big cities. We moved to the island. We bought the cottage. We made a home. I tried to have kids but couldn't. My students became my children instead, and you, of course, most of all. I kept writing but only for myself, and later for the local newspaper. I had once dreamed of a big life, and instead, I found a beautiful one.

I loved Charlie. I adored him. I loved teaching and the rewarding *ping* I felt when my students understood a difficult concept. I loved watching their minds form and their opinions strengthen. I loved when my students graduated and then returned to visit. They always marveled at how tiny the desks looked. They seemed proud when they said it, and I was proud, too.

And yet, even as class after class graduated, I stayed put. My room, my lectures, remained largely the same. Habit took over and, later, comfort.

Sometimes I wondered about that other life. Sometimes I even wished that I hadn't tripped Charlie. He could have kept walking by. We could have easily missed each other. It would be as simple as taking the later train.

You know how I adore nineteenth-century novels from authors like Jane Austen and the Brontë sisters. I love the narrative tidiness, the misunderstandings that get in the way of the love interests and then the inevitable reunion, all the more sweet because it's been hard-earned. I love the comfort of the so-called marriage plot, in which everything is resolved by the end, love triumphing always. And yet, I also rebel against it.

As a feminist, I always resented the false idea that marriage was somewhat a cure, a destination. It made sense in those novels, during a time period where matrimony was socially and financially necessary for a woman. The stakes were high. Where would Charlotte Lucas in *Pride and Prejudice* be without marriage? Destitute? Cast out? Marriage was survival. Now it's not. Now we have the luxury to choose our own path, to make our own names.

Still, we fall in love, and when we do, it feels like the single most important movement in the universe. It seems absurd that everyone around you can't see that the world has changed direction, begun rotating around a new gravitational center.

When Charlie died, I realized that my entire life was built around him. The most important element of a garden is the soil. Without healthy, nutrient-rich soil, nothing grows. Charlie was like that for me, and without him, I was bereft. I didn't want that for you. I'm not excusing my actions, but I didn't want you to make my mistakes. I wanted you to enjoy the freedom of youth unburdened by love. I wanted you to make your own mistakes. When Thomas proposed to you, I saw myself. You were too young. You didn't even know who you were yet. I wanted you to explore. I wanted you to be free. The older you get, the harder it is to take risks.

So, I wrote to your father and persuaded him to tell you to end the engagement. It was cowardly of me. I didn't have the nerve to say it to you myself. You are my only child, and I couldn't bear being on the receiving end of your resentment.

I know now that I was wrong to interfere. I will live with that regret for the rest of my life—however long that may be. You should know I tried to remedy it. I wrote to Thomas after James left, but it was too late. He was already married.

At every stage of our lives, we ask ourselves, "Who am I going to be?" which is really just another way to ask the more pertinent question, "Am I going to make it?"

Try not to be so concerned with the latter that you forget to enjoy the ride. Don't be stingy with your dreams either. Ask for everything out of life and see what you get. It won't be all that you asked for, but it will be a great deal more than if you made your desires smaller to begin with.

More than anything, I hope you get a second chance. Because I know now that love is as important as anything else you may do with your life.

And maybe I can get a second chance, too. Lord knows you have done enough for me already, but maybe you can do me this one last kindness. The following pages are the manuscript I've been working on for over ten years since Charlie passed. It might be bad. I never had the guts to find out.

Maybe in death I can be braver than I was in life.

My dear Rose, this is for you. Do with it what you please.

Chapter Thirty-Five

Lily

July 30

I leave the house early the next morning, Lottie's words held close to my chest.

After last night's storm, it's unseasonably cold, like the first night of the summer back in May. The grass is damp with the morning dew.

Everything in my body feels heavier, as if the strength of gravity has multiplied overnight. My heart hangs low like a long necklace.

I left the letter and manuscript on the kitchen counter for Rose to find. For once, I'm up earlier than her. Now I walk to the village center and across the white wooden bridge, down to the beach. I find the lifeguard stand empty and climb to the top, taking a seat. The sight of Lottie's precise handwriting is burned into my retinas like the glare of the sun.

I didn't read the rest of the manuscript. It's clear the package was intended for Rose, not me. Why would Lottie be this mysterious and leave its discovery to chance? I'll never know.

I keep thinking about the line she wrote about being brave. I've spent this entire summer afraid. I've been scared to be alone, to lose

Henry. Scared to tell Theo how I feel. Scared to let my dad in again. I've been scared to show my work to people and put myself out there. I've been scared to reach out to Jade.

I know I've made mistakes—last night being a major one. But at least I've tried. To Lottie's point, I would rather make mistakes than be too scared to take a risk. I think of the image of Lottie I most remember: working away in the garden, determined. I picture her stubborn, solid back, the shape of it curved like a shovel.

I would never describe her as someone who was afraid of anything, but I suppose I was wrong. We all make mistakes, and we all get scared.

I once heard my mom describe anxiety to her patients as "Too much, too soon." That's what I felt during every panic attack: too much, too soon. All at once. I know now—I probably knew all along, subconsciously—that this was what I wanted out of Henry this last month. I wanted him to make it better, to travel to a time before loss touched our lives.

I close my eyes. It is time to let go. We hold on to some memories just to hurt ourselves because they confirm a long-held suspicion we've always had that we are somehow at fault, to blame, deficient, incapable of the contentedness that others share: unlovable. There's satisfaction in being proven right, even if the thing you're right about is your own unworthiness.

It's time to let those thoughts go.

For a second, with my eyes closed, I feel something on my shoulders: pressing down, warm and spreading. The air smells of Lottie: sweet honeysuckles, and salt air, and warm sand, and freshly mowed grass, and irrational hope.

When my eyes open, there's only one person I want to see.

* * *

Back at the cottage, Rose is waiting at the coffee table, staring into her mug.

"I'm so sorry," I say first.

"No, I'm sorry! I said such awful stuff to you, I should have never—"

"NO! You were right. I was being selfish and reckless and—"

"No, no, you were doing your best. It wasn't your fault that all ended so—"

"I made your special night about me—"

"You were attacked and I should have defended you against that awful girl—"

"It's really not her fault. It's mine—"

We continue to interrupt each other, swapping apologies back and forth until we're both breathless.

"Truce," I say finally. "Can we move on? Can we go back to being best friends?"

"Always," says Rose. I notice her eyes look red. She's been crying. "But just so you know, sometimes I have to be your mother, too."

"Deal," I tell her. "So, how are you feeling about the William of it all?"

"You mean the fact that he tried to swindle me?"

"Yes, that."

"I feel dumb." Mom releases a breathy, light laugh. "I mean, I can't believe I almost fell for someone who is essentially a con man. It's embarrassing. But I'm mostly relieved that he's gone. I wanted to break up with him, anyway."

"A con man who is also somehow Mary's uncle," I add. "Does that make Mary a con man, too?"

Mom laughs, and then changes the subject. "Did I ever tell you about the Advil study I learned about in grad school?"

"No, what's that?"

"I'm going to butcher the science of it, but essentially, they discovered that people who take a dose of ibuprofen report less emotional pain when recalling negative feelings than individuals who were given a placebo."

"So, what are you saying? I should take some more Advil?"

"No," Rose laughs. "I guess what I'm trying to say is that your pain is real, even if you can't see it." We are quiet as we stare out the window. Lottie's nook looks less empty somehow. The sunlight is hitting it directly, making patterns out of the tassels on the pillow.

"I love you, Mom," I tell her. "I'm so sorry."

"I love you, too, honey. We'll be okay." Rose reaches out her right hand to squeeze my arm. "So, what do we do now?"

I look at the yellow envelope on the counter. "Did you read Lottie's note? The manuscript?"

Rose nods. "I read the letter, but I have only just started the manuscript." She smiles softly, and it somehow contains both sadness and happiness. "It's good."

"Of course it is." A thought occurs to me. "Hey, is the pickleball tournament still tomorrow? Can we skip it now that we know Lottie doesn't care about the bucket list?"

"It is," says Mom. "But actually, that gives me an idea."

Chapter Thirty-Six

Rose

July 31

We pack the car with everything we'll need: paddles, beach towels and chairs, running sneakers, a change of clothes, and binoculars.

First off is the pickleball tournament, which starts at nine. Item four on Lottie's bucket list.

We slather ourselves with a thick layer of sunscreen, tie our hair into tight ponytails, and put on white visors.

"Ready to crush the competition?" Lily asks, coming out of her room wearing eye black. The streaks look comically out of place with her white tennis skirt.

"Is the war paint really necessary?"

"It's supposed to reduce the sun's glare," she says in an academic tone. "Plus, it's really intimidating."

I smile. "We're going to do so well. First place, for sure."

"We're going to crush the competition, obliterate them. When we're done, everyone on the island will know the infamous story of the Gardner duo." We high-five.

* * *

Two hours and three defeats later, we are back in the car, out of breath.

"Okay, so I guess we need more than a few weeks of practice to win a tournament," Lily admits.

I take a long drag from the water bottle. In the rearview mirror, my face is flushed. "No kidding. That other team was really good."

In the shade of the clubhouse, our opponents take a break, waiting for their next match. They're both white-haired and look around Lottie's age.

"Beatrice is a killer," says Lily, still struggling to get air in. Her eye black has smeared off from the sweat. "They were totally cheating, though."

"They were not." I pull out of the dirt parking lot.

"I'm just saying, Beatrice's 'bad eyesight' was a little convenient when it came to her line calls."

"Lily," I chide. "We lost eleven to three. And Beatrice has glaucoma."

On the drive to Nobadeer Beach, we regain our energy. A cappuccino later, and Lily is a whole new woman. "I think we could've had them," she says, referring to our last game. "Actually, they were a little slow."

We drive up a sand road and pull over to the side, practically in the brush. My father and sister are waiting in the parking area when we arrive. My dad is in some ridiculous swimming getup that looks like it's from the twenties. There's a matching blue-and-white-striped shirt and swim bottoms. My sister has on a large, floppy hat that keeps almost flying away. In her arms is an elaborate cat carrier, Mrs. Clay inside.

"Quite the spectacle the other night," notes my father when we catch up to them.

"We live to entertain," says Lily.

To my surprise, my dad grabs my shoulders and looks into my eyes. "Are you okay?"

The gesture is slightly marred by the glaring sun and his bizarre outfit, but the sentiment is not. I can't remember the last time my dad asked me a question like this—like he really wanted to know the true answer.

"I'm okay," I tell him, emotion making my words thick.

He gives me a firm pat on my left shoulder, almost knocking me over. Sometimes I forget how tall he is, and surprisingly strong, too. "I'm here for you."

Irrationally, my throat gets tight. "Thanks, Dad."

"So, how does this work?" interrupts Elizabeth. "We just wait and hope we happen across a whale?"

"Pretty much," I say.

"That feels like a tremendous waste of time," she grumbles. Her hat tries to take off again, lifting inches into the air.

Lily grabs it and pats it back down on her head. "Have some faith, Elizabeth. We've got Lottie's magic on our side." She looks at Mrs. Clay's carrier. "Also, don't cats, like, notoriously hate water and beaches?"

"Mrs. Clay is no ordinary cat," says my dad in a solemn, serious voice.

We lug our belongings down the street to the beach path, resting the hot metal of the chairs against our shoulders. As soon as we are planted in the sand, Lily runs off to jump in the ocean. When she returns, her hair is wet and tangled, and she looks giddy, like a little kid.

"Are you really going to complete the entire bucket list in one day?" asks Elizabeth. She is lathering herself with tanning oil. It gleams on her skin.

"Doesn't that cause skin cancer?" asks Lily. She's covering her face with a baseball cap. Compared to my sister and dad, we look like marble statues. Elizabeth ignores her.

I pull out a copy of Lottie's list to show her:

1. Watch the sunrise at Siasconset Beach.
2. Drive to Great Point Lighthouse.
3. Get onstage at the Chicken Box.
4. Win pickleball tournament.
5. Go whale watching.
6. Visit the Loines Observatory.
7. Have a beach picnic.
8. Name the cottage.
9. Crash a wedding.
10. Do something brave.

"We already finished number one, number two, number six, number seven, and number nine earlier in the summer. Number four didn't exactly work out, but I still consider it a valid attempt. So, all we have left is number three, number five, number eight."

"What about number ten?" asks Lily.

I lift an eyebrow. "I think we've done enough brave things this summer."

She looks doubtful but shrugs, returning to inspect the ocean.

"But as you told me this morning, Lottie didn't even care about this bucket list, right? She wrote it on a lark, basically," Elizabeth says.

We both turn to watch as our dad takes Mrs. Clay out of her carrier and cradles her like a baby in the shade, giving her water from a porcelain bowl he packed. The old me would wonder if he likes that cat more than he does us. But the new is trying to be more generous. I am trying to give people the benefit of the doubt going forward.

When Lily said that I ditched both her and Lottie for being imperfect during our fight the other night, it struck a chord. I don't want to be that kind of person.

"Yes," I admit to Elizabeth's point about the list. "But I still think it's worthwhile. Maybe Lottie didn't need it, but she still wrote it. It's still her words."

I wonder if I'll feel a sense of accomplishment when this day is over, after we've completed all of the items on the list. I can't help but think that it's the celebration of life Lottie would have wanted. She would have hated her funeral and the dark, depressing dresses we wore. She loved color, she loved life, she loved us, and she loved this island.

"Maybe it doesn't matter what Lottie would think," I say aloud. "Maybe it's more important that we do this for ourselves."

Elizabeth nods. "Well, it does sound fun, regardless. I'm sure you'll have a good time."

I look at her in surprise. "You're not coming?"

She looks equally baffled. "I'm invited?"

"Of course," I say. "She was your aunt, too. Besides, we want you there."

Elizabeth looks like she's going to cry again, but quickly, she lowers her shades. "Fine," she says, keeping the emotion away by squishing her lips in a short, puckered line. "I'll come then if it means so much to you."

I smile to myself. At least we're making some progress.

"Lil, what do you think about names for the cottage? Let's brainstorm," I say.

Lily looks at me, a strangely panicked expression on her face. "Oh, I don't know. Let's save that for last."

"Really? We might be here for ages, might as well debate some ideas now."

What I don't say is that I'm growing more and more doubtful that the whales will make an appearance at all. What are the odds, anyway? I've seen some before on tours, but it's certainly not every day.

"Um," Lily says. "Later, okay?"

I decide to let it drop. To our left, a volleyball match has begun, and we all fall into a silence as we watch the white ball bounce from one side of the net to the other.

"When's your boat home, again?" I ask Elizabeth.

She's spread out on a pink towel, baking in the sun. "Tomorrow afternoon."

"Do you think you'll come back again this summer?"

She sits up to look at me. "Seriously, what has gotten into you lately? You want us to come back?"

A girl in a red one-piece hits the volleyball out of bounds, and it lands a few feet away from our chairs. Lily stands to throw it back at them.

"Why not?" I say. "Life is too short."

Elizabeth raises an eyebrow and then lowers herself back down. "Maybe," is all she says, but there's a curve to her mouth.

The sun is beating down, but the breeze keeps the heat from being overpowering. I lean back into my chair, letting the sound of the waves soothe me. Sure, the fundraiser wasn't the evening I had planned, but the sun still came out. It always does.

Now that I'm free of William, I keep thinking of what to say to Tommy. Maybe it's time for number ten, after all.

As we soak in the sun, I think: If Lottie is anywhere, if heaven is real, I bet she's right here, on one of the many beaches she loved, sitting back with a good book. Charlie by her side.

The thought lulls me, and I'm on the edge of sleep when Lily's scream startles me awake.

"MOM!" she shouts. "Look over there."

She's pointing toward the horizon, but all I can see is the reflection of the sun on the sea and the white foam of waves breaking. "What?"

"I saw a tail. I swear," says Lily, standing up now and pointing to the distance.

I follow her line of sight. The volleyball match has paused, too, a few of the players looking out at the water. Then, in the distance, I see something myself: a flash of black and white. It's only visible for a second, but I can hear the other beachgoers begin to yell and point. The shape emerges again, the unmistakable outline of a black tail rising and then slapping the water. Wordlessly, all four of us walk closer to the water to see.

"I think there's more than one," whispers Elizabeth.

For a long pause, nothing happens. People begin to walk back to their chairs, losing interest. Then, the smooth body of the whale breaches the water once more, jumping in the air. When it twists, we can see its entire torso, a long patch of white.

"My God," says my dad. "Is that . . . ?"

"I think it's an orca," I say in wonderment.

"Is that even possible in these waters?" asks Elizabeth.

Usually, the only whales we see are right whales, humpback whales, or sperm whales. They all have large black or gray bodies and textured skin. They look nothing like the smooth creatures we're seeing now with their sharp color contrast.

"IT'S AN ORCA!" one of the volleyball players confirms.

We wait for it to jump back out, and when it finally does, we can see there are two of them, and then, three: a pod. It's like they're performing tricks for us, saying hello. The wild beasts jump and twist and flip in the air, making impressive leaps and then splashing back down into the sea. They look fake. It doesn't seem possible. My brain can't comprehend the image.

Everyone is clapping, trying to pull out their phones quick enough to capture the sight. But the four of us stand side by side, marveling. In the crowd, I hear someone explain that there have been sightings of orcas in New England waters before, but it's rare.

"Apparently," the girl in the red one-piece says, "there's been one consistent sighting of a sole male, nicknamed Old Thom, who swims with a pod of dolphins. His dorsal fin is slightly bent, which makes him easy to recognize. He keeps circling the area, like he's looking for something or someone."

We all nod along to the explanation, but this many killer whales swimming together? It seems impossible.

The truth is that the sighting is probably due to climate change, and the waters warming, or some other awful scientific explanation, but standing there on the shore, next to my family, watching the orcas splash and leap, it seems nothing short of a miracle.

When we tire of the beach and the whales have all returned to wherever whales go when they're not performing miracles, we drive home to shower and change. I drop my dad and sister back off at Josie's guesthouse.

As my sister is getting out of the car, I say, "Can you ask Josie if she's willing to come tonight, too?"

"Sure," says Elizabeth.

"Should I come, too?" asks my dad, and the way he says it breaks my heart a little.

"Of course," I say, trying to picture my father in his formal bathing suit at the dive bar. "Of course you should come."

Back home, the waves of exhaustion start to hit. It's an ambitious day: a pickleball tournament, beach day, and now a night out.

Lily looks nervous in the passenger seat, her green eyes darker than usual. "Are you ready to come inside?"

I can't understand the reason for her skittishness. Maybe she's just overly tired, too. Truthfully, from the fundraiser to this afternoon, it's been a rather emotionally and physically draining weekend.

"Sure," I say. "Let's go."

We leave the car. It's still a perfect summer day, and the light of the garden looks orange in the coming twilight. The smell of flowers and warm earth is overwhelming.

Lily looks back at me and runs a hand quickly through my hair. "That's better," she says, taking a deep breath. "One last meddle. I promise."

I'm starting to think she's really lost it this time when she opens the door to the cottage and ushers me inside. There, sitting at our old coffee table, is Tommy. Surrounding him are what looks like at least a hundred roses all in various sizes of glass jars. They dot the entire kitchen space, bringing the garden inside. On the table are two carved pieces of wood. I realize what they are immediately. One has "Lottie's Way" carved onto it.

"Too much?" he says, his voice both gruff and sheepish. "Lily helped me."

There's so much to say. There are questions I have. I want to ask him about the other night. I want to apologize for thinking he was with Josie. I want to tell him that I'm sorry I ever let Lottie and my dad convince me to break off the engagement. I want to say I'm sorry for letting William in at all. I want to tell him how much I've thought about him over the last three decades. But I can't seem to get any of it out. Every thought competes for space until I am standing there, mouth open, hands trembling.

The time to talk has passed. Now it is time to be brave.

I cross the room in a few long strides and grab his face. "Not too much at all," I say, and when he kisses me back, it is new, and familiar, and everything I've been waiting for.

Four hours later, we park the car at Stop & Shop.

"Remember the ice cream incident?" Lily says to me as we cross the street to the bar.

"I think you mean the detergent scandal?" I joke.

"What on earth are the two of you talking about?" asks Tommy. He wraps his hand around mine and smiles, and I think: Yes, this is it. This is how it should feel.

"Don't worry about it," says Lily.

Inside, a band has just taken the stage and a sparse crowd dances, strobe lights reflecting onto the wooden beams.

Lily says something in the ear of one of the bouncers. I watch their exchange as the bouncer's face moves from scowl to laughter in a matter of seconds. Only Lily has the power to talk her way into something like this. She comes over and grabs my hand.

"It's now or never. They said we could go up for one song."

"Are we really doing this?"

"We have to," says Lily. "For Lottie."

She takes my hand and drags me up to the stage. The lead singer mumbles into the microphone: "Apparently, we have some special guests joining for this next song."

Looking out at the dense crowd, my stomach turns. But then, I spot Elizabeth, and our dad next to her, looking totally out of place. Across from my dad, smiling, is Tommy. He shoots me a thumbs-up, the music starts to play, and Lily takes me by the arm. Soon enough, I forget about the crowd entirely, and we dance together like we did the first night of the summer: free, unencumbered. We dance for Lottie.

On the last verse, I look at my daughter, who is smiling and spinning. I have to yell to be heard over the music. "You know my speech that was interrupted at the gala?"

"Of course," Lily says, guilt deepening her voice. "How could I forget?"

"The speech I was giving was about you, Lily-pad. I was saying that my greatest honor is being your mom, watching you grow into yourself. You are my greatest joy."

I grab her hand and hold it for a moment, squeezing tight. Lily looks like she's about to cry, but instead she just smiles. For a moment, staring out at the crowd with the dark lights and moving bodies, it looks like the rhythm of the ocean. My heart is calm. It is all still water.

Chapter Thirty-Seven

Lily

August 5, 2023
One Year Later

The wedding is, predictably, filled with flowers.

Flowers cover the aisle, the garden of the church, the hair of the bride, and the laps of the guests. There is little decoration beyond flowers. It is simple, elegant, understated: exactly like the bride herself.

I walk down the aisle, the edge of my long dress dragging into the petals on the ground. In my hand is a bouquet hand-picked from Lottie's garden. It's almost like she's here with us.

We are at the Siasconset Union Chapel church. Built in 1883, the exterior looks like something out of a storybook, with its long, stained-glass windows, peaked roof, white barn doors, and rows of hydrangea bushes. Inside, it is light and airy. The pews are white wood with colorful, embroidered prayer cushions. It is the very same church Lottie was married in almost fifty years ago.

Guests smile as I walk past, but I keep my eyes trained on the altar in front.

Much has changed in the last year or so.

Rose has opened up her own private practice and called it "Growing Season." Tommy etched the name into the quarterboard. It hangs above her office downtown.

I helped develop the logo and branding. The office is in the upstairs space above a gallery downtown. It already has a months-long waiting list. My mom, so eager to help everyone, is debating whether to take on new clinicians to help with the load. I've also started seeing a new therapist of my own in New York to help with the panic attacks. I moved back a few months ago.

There's a term in art called *underpainting*, which refers to the first base layer of paint you apply to the canvas. You can use it to play with dimensionality. I've started to think of my life like an underpainting: one layer built atop another, a work in progress.

A month ago, I hosted my first art gallery. I took Theo's advice, stopped waiting for some external approval or permission to start. I created social media profiles of my work and sold a few prints directly to the small audience I garnered. Slowly, it gained traction. I went around New York City and posted flyers of my favorite pieces with a QR code attached that linked to my website. I put clickbait taglines on them like "Scan to find out who Banksy really is" or "Help me make my rent."

In the meantime, I've worked two part-time jobs, like Theo had before: bartending and teaching painting lessons at a community center in Brooklyn. The gallery was my first real show and I held it downtown on the island, directly below Rose's office. The paintings were all of Lottie, Rose, Jade, even one of Elizabeth, and other women in my life, some strangers: large, elaborate oil paintings celebrating them doing simple activities.

I sold every painting, except one I kept for myself, the image of Lottie bending in the garden. I donated the proceeds to the fundraiser we ruined, supporting mental health initiatives on the island.

Now, in front of me, in the left pews, is Emily with her girlfriend, Maya. The three of us have become close friends. I told her what I once thought about Theo and her having something last summer.

"Are you crazy?" she laughed. "That's the most ridiculous thing I've ever heard."

I felt stupid then for how utterly out of control I let my imagination go, creating a whole narrative out of nothing. Maya fixes a stray hair on Emily's head now, tucking it into place behind her ears. They had been long-distance that entire summer, and I was too blinded by my own insecurity to see it.

Two rows ahead of them are my grandfather and aunt. Elizabeth looks stiff and a little lost. She wears a powder-blue dress with a matching blazer. Her hair is impeccably coiffed in an elaborate updo. We've also been reconnecting this last year, and I've found it a pleasant shock how well we get along. She's different from Rose, uptight in all the areas where Rose is relaxed, but she is strong in her own way. When she sees me, her lips spread into a thin pink smile.

Two people down is Theo. He looks tanner, older after his travels. His hair is cropped and his suit is a blue that matches his eyes, the color of the Hudson. For once, his suit isn't too big on him, but his smile still is. He grins that large, toothy smile I love with the two front teeth slightly longer than the rest. I return it, almost dropping my bouquet.

My dad, James, is on the other side. His hair gelled and his expression curiously polite. We've been slowly reconnecting, too. It's slow going but it's better than nothing. Josie is beside him; Tommy's sister, Rachel, next; and to her left, my friend Jade, her hair now streaked purple instead of pink. After we made up, she and Mark stayed a few days with us the last week of summer, once Thomas had left for his new house. When we told her about the saga with Lottie, she agreed to take a look at the manuscript. She loved it so much that she ended up sharing it with her boss. Now we're discussing publication options.

At the altar, I take my spot and watch as my mom comes next. A hush falls over the room.

She looks beautiful in a white linen wedding gown. Her veil has colored flowers stitched into the gossamer. Tommy, beside me, is beaming. His daughters stand in a row, lined up expectantly. They were protective of their father at first, but over time, they have grown steadily more welcoming. I hope someday we'll be good friends.

I know when my mom gets to the front, when she marries Tommy, it will be an end to something—a shift in our dynamic—and a beginning of something else. But I'm also starting to realize that not all change is bad. Some of it can be great, actually.

The reception is held just a few streets away at the Siasconset Casino. String lights hang from the arched, wood-paneled ceiling. On the stage is a band, and the tables are covered in white cloths and wildflowers. What seems like the entire town has shown up. In Rose's hair is a blue brooch designed by Josie. I watch from my seat as Tommy twirls her on the dance floor and everyone claps.

"Hi, stranger," says Theo. He takes the empty seat next to me. "Long time, no see."

"It's been like a month, right? Hardly a long time."

After last summer, we decided to just stay friends for the time being. He sent me pictures of his travels, and I sent him updates on my portrait project. Theo is starting a graduate program in Boston in a few weeks. It's easier this way. Besides, all I care about is that I get to keep him in my life in some fashion.

"True, but you'll be seeing a lot more of me very soon," he says.

I tear my eyes away from the dance floor to look at him straight on. "What do you mean?"

"Well, I didn't want to tell you until everything was squared away, but I got accepted into New York University's teaching program this summer off the wait list."

"What?" I reach for his arm. "That's amazing, Theo. Really."

"So, all I'm saying is that there will be plenty of chances for us to hang out." He smiles.

I look at his endearing freckles, a face I adore. Is it romantic love or just friendship? I'm still not sure, but I do love him, however ridiculous that may seem. Finally, we will be in the same place for an uninterrupted amount of time, and there will be plenty of opportunities to figure it out.

"Remember that story I told you about how deer came to Nantucket?" I ask him.

"What?" he says, laughing at the turn in conversation. "Yes, why?"

"I think what I like about that story so much is that the town was so fixated on the deer's loneliness that they made this grand, romantic gesture, which ended up failing spectacularly. But I still appreciate it. I appreciate the effort, and optimism, and hope."

Maybe romance shouldn't matter in the face of larger, more systemic societal issues. Maybe art doesn't either. But, as Lottie said in her letter, nevertheless it does. In the midst of so much despair, love is what we do best. Art is the best part of us.

Theo's face looks confused, but there's a hint of his big smile threatening to break through the surface. In his hand is his place card. He twists it around. "You know," he says. "I forgot to mention that you got my name wrong on the invitation."

I grab it from his hands and check again. I spent weeks putting the guest list together, handcrafting every place card. The ink is gold, and each one has hand-drawn roses on it.

"What? No, I didn't." I check it again: Theo Cohen. It looks perfect.

"Yeah, well, technically I go by Theo, but my real first name is Harold." He squints at me, teasing. "Harold Cohen: HC. We have a lot to still learn about each other, I guess."

I think back to the psychic's prediction a year ago. "You will have two great loves," she'd said. "One greater than the other, but both have a first name that starts with the letter *H*."

When everything with Henry didn't work out, I assumed she was wrong. Now I wonder if I just wasn't hearing the full prediction. After all, it's impossible to realize the moral of the story when you're smack in the middle of living it.

"Wow," is all I can say. "I guess you're right."

"Lily!" Rose calls, approaching us and grabbing me by the hand. Her left hand feels the same as always: soft, too cold, but now there is a ring around the fourth finger. "It's Lottie's favorite song! We have to dance."

I oblige, following her to the dance floor. The two of us take turns spinning each other again, like we did at the Chicken Box. My heart feels so full it could split open. I'm so happy for her. I'm so, so grateful for her.

"Hey, Mom," I say as we turn. "Do you remember that psychic at last year's greenhouse fundraiser?"

"What psychic?"

"The psychic in the corner by the perennials?"

"I have no idea what you're talking about," says Rose, and then with concern: "Are you okay, honey?"

"You're messing with me."

"I'm really not," she says, but then she winks, which only confuses me more.

Did I imagine the whole thing, or is Rose joking now? My mom was in and out of the kitchen all night, running around the place, first in a hectic buzz and then later, in fury. It's likely she could have simply not noticed the psychic.

Last summer, maybe this would have made me anxious. Maybe the room would shake, the vertigo reappearing. But now, it's at bay. When the song is over, my mom pulls me into a long hug. It's strange to think that from now on, it will no longer be just the two of us.

"Everything is about to change, huh?" I say.

Rose squeezes my shoulder. "Yes," she admits.

"What are we going to do?"

"We're going to loosen up." Rose smiles. "Hey! I have an idea."

It's nearing midnight, and guests have begun to trickle out. Now only a handful of people are dotted around the dining room.

"What's that?" I ask, but it's only a formality. I'm already game for whatever she proposes.

"Let's go to the beach."

Moments later, we are running, laughing the whole way there, holding our heels in our hands as we sprint down, past the empty Sconset Market, the rotary with its flag rippling in the wind, the clock house, and the white bridge that springs from it like an arm. When we reach the sand, we ditch our shoes entirely and race each other, hitching our dresses up to our knees. The men follow, Theo tripping slightly and then regaining his balance by the lifeguard stand.

My lungs burn as I struggle to keep up, and then we are in the ocean, and the shock of the cold feels like waking up after a long sleep. I splash Rose, who ducks and tosses a handful of water back at me.

Everyone is laughing and the moon is a huge pearl in the sky, and the future stretches out before us, long and unknown.

Acknowledgments

Whenever we ordered takeout growing up, my mom and I used fake aliases. I can't remember exactly why or how the ritual started. All I know is that it brought joy to an otherwise mundane activity: my mom's specialty. Oftentimes, this added joy was essential due to the heartache and grief that awaited us at home, a topic I discuss at length in my first book.

So, we invented Lily and Rose Gardner. And under these aliases, we became different people. Lily and Rose Gardner, with their flower-themed, lovely names, were lighter versions of ourselves: happier. Eventually, the nicknames became a private joke.

Once I published my memoir, I knew I wanted to try my hand at fiction but I was surprised by who came waltzing in: Lily and Rose Gardner, a mother-daughter story. They popped back into my brain, fully formed, and demanded to be heard.

My goal was to tell a lighter story about love after loss and the joy of having a spectacular mother—a subject I'm somewhat of an expert on. While the character names started from this inspiration,

Lily and Rose soon took on a life of their own. They became their own people, as real to me as friends.

Here's the inspiration I took from my own life: mothers as best friends, late nights at the Chicken Box, walking the bluff, the fear of putting your artistic creation into the world, first love and heartbreak, the healing power of therapy and salt air, karaoke at the Rose & Crown, the Nantucket mall, nostalgia and mudslides at Gazebo.

Here's what's fiction: everything else.

Thank you to Carrie Feron for seeing the potential in this vision and constantly pushing the book to be better. Your fingerprints are on every page, and the novel is drastically improved for your insight, care, and talent. Your name should be everywhere in this book because it is as much yours as it is mine. It should be capitalized, italicized, underlined, emphasized in every way: *CARRIE FERON*. You are a literary wizard and a genius.

Thank you to my agent, Eve Attermann, for sticking with me from nonfiction to fiction. I often think back to the first time we met, when I was visiting your office as a naive, terrified (but also thrilled) twenty-two-year-old. It's remarkable how far we've come together. Six years! Two genres. Thank you for your patience and your belief.

My sincerest gratitude to everyone at Gallery who makes publishing possible: Jen Bergstrom (publisher), Jen Long (deputy publisher), Eliza Hanson (associate publisher), Ali Chesnick (editorial assistant), Caroline Pallotta (managing editor), Christine Masters (production editor), and Jaime Putorti (interior designer). Without each of you, this book would not be here.

Thank you to my love, Liam Moran, for listening to my every anxiety and self-doubt and giving me sage advice each step of the way. There's so much rejection and heartbreak in this industry, and I am incredibly lucky to have someone by my side who keeps it all in perspective.

To my dear friends Abby McFadyen and Caroline Kopfler, who are the protagonists of all my favorite Nantucket stories: Thanks for making me fun. There's no one I'd rather climb through bar windows and dance onstage at the Chicken Box with.

Thank you to Nantucket Island, for giving us a place to recover. Nantucket has been synonymous with summer for me since I was an infant. It's where my family was always happiest; where I first swam in the ocean and learned how to drive and even had my first date. But when I graduated high school in 2015, my mom moved to the island full-time and it truly became home. Through her, I have been fortunate to share in this warm and eccentric community, thirty miles out to sea.

I believe writing might actually contain magic. I wrote myself a happy ending in the pages of my memoir and in the process was able to move on. Similarly, by the time I finished this novel, my mom was in love and engaged to a wonderful man. So, to Michael Cataldo, thank you for giving my mom the happy life she deserves.

Thank you to my grandparents Everett and Nancy Hultgren, for the daily good-night texts and for loving us "to pieces," always. Your love makes me brave.

Most of all, thank you to my mom, Kerryann, for, well, everything. You are my very best friend and favorite person. I won the lottery when I was born your daughter. Thank you for reading all of my poems, short stories, and song lyrics when I was growing up and for holding back laughter, even when they were very, very laughable. (Except for those songs . . . honestly, I still think those were good.) These days, I bet Lily and Rose Gardner wish they were us.

And for my sister, Kaitlyn Lantz Leddy—while this book is certainly different from my first, you are still in everything I write and everything I do. Thanks for believing I could do it.

About the Author

Kyleigh Leddy is the author of the memoir *The Perfect Other: A Memoir of My Sister*, which is based on her *New York Times* Modern Love essay. Her writing has appeared in *The New York Times*, *New York Magazine*, and *Parents*, among others. In 2023, she was named on the Forbes 30 Under 30 Media list. She holds a BA from Boston College and an MSW from Columbia University. Kyleigh is a practicing therapist in New York City and teaches creative writing at Gotham Writers Workshop.